AF355010

WHISPERS OF THE NORDIC DRAUGR

A Steamy, Mythological Romantasy

Caroline Helenasdotter

Förlaget Annasdotter

Förlaget

Annasdotter

Copyright © 2024 Caroline Helenasdotter

All rights reserved

The characters and events portrayed in this book are fictitious. Any similarity to real persons, living or dead, is coincidental and not intended by the author.

No part of this book may be reproduced, or stored in a retrieval system, or transmitted in any form or by any means, electronic, mechanical, photocopying, recording, or otherwise, without express written permission of the publisher.

ISBN-978-91-527-8562-1

Cover design by: Anna Helena Annika Karlsson

*Dedicated to everyone who feels like they
belong in another realm or universe.*

"I used to think I was the strangest person in the world but then I thought there are so many people in the world, there must be someone just like me who feels bizarre and flawed in the same ways I do. I would imagine her, and imagine that she must be out there thinking of me, too. Well, I hope that if you are out there and read this and know that, yes, it's true I'm here, and I'm just as strange as you."

REBECCA MARTIN

CONTENTS

PROLOGUE

As the ethereal flakes of snow delicately descended upon his embattled form, Ulrik drew in a breath filled with despair, accepting the inexorable pull of his approaching demise. His limbs were fatigued; his essence was weary. Crimson blood drops trickled from his battered countenance, staining the pristine ocean of snow with the ominous hue of death's cold and eternal grip. He stood alone, without hope, hemmed in by adversaries, amidst the remnants of fallen comrades. Each one claimed by the merciless hands of their assailants until only he remained. The enemy surged forth with unrestrained ferocity, their onslaught relentless, reducing warriors to nothing but lifeless forms upon the frozen ground until only their last bastion remained. A formidable general persisted. His gaze bore into Ulrik with a maelstrom of ferocity and malice. His eyes stained with a sinister admiration that reverberated through the marrow of his bones, cutting deep within his core.

The air hung heavy, filled with the foreboding of a lone warrior's requiem. It was a day painted with grotesque beauty. A fine day to die. The general's lips curled into a sardonic grin, his eyes ablaze with a savage fervour tempered by a twisted hint of respect. Ulrik understood the peculiar kinship that could arise between adversaries in the crucible of war. Among the chaos and carnage of the battlefield, where shadows danced with death, one could glimpse the reflection of their own soul in the eyes of their foe, a mirror of atrocities committed, a reminder that survival came at any cost. There existed no room for notions of kings and country; only the primal instinct to safeguard the life standing beside you.

Though Ulrik stood alone, without allies, the general's satisfaction remained, his grin unyielding even in the face of imminent defeat. His laughter, a chilling lament that haunted Ulrik's very core, etched dread, and fear upon his soul. As darkness cloaked the general's countenance, infusing his features with a monstrous evil, Ulrik sensed the unmistakable presence of a fiendish entity. This was no mere mortal adversary. He had beheld monsters both human and demonic upon the battlefield, yet none possessed the supernatural aura that now surrounded the general in a smog of dread. The line between man and demon blurred in the trial of conflict, where savageries intertwined with the unholy actions of diabolical creatures.

With grim resolve, Ulrik braced himself for the ultimate confrontation, his thoughts fleeting to a distant home where love was bound to his heart in an everlasting hymn. But within the invading darkness, she was just an illusion, a beacon lost among the looming shadows of death.

This warrior fought alone, a solitary penumbra within the vast expanse of time, bearing the weight of countless battles etched into the foundation of his being. If fate decreed this to be his final confrontation, then he would unleash every ounce of his strength, drawing upon the reservoir of his bloodstained past. Before Ulrik stood a beastly opponent, a foe he knew he might not vanquish, yet he resolved to wage war with the very essence of his existence. Should death claim his very life this day, he would meet it with defiance until his very last breath escaped him. Defeat was not a notion he entertained. Even though he acknowledged the inevitability of his mortality, surrender to the enemy was inconceivable. Wars waged; battles fought had left indelible scars upon his soul. Combat had wrenched his heart from his body, yet his warrior spirit endured, undaunted by the terrors of unknown monsters. The creature before him awoke primal fear within his core, yet Ulrik pressed forward, undeterred. Evil assumed myriad guises, and to him, fear was nothing but another hurdle to surmount in the relentless pursuit of survival.

Drawing upon the last traces of his waning strength, Ulrik reached for his rifle, only to find himself swiftly overpowered by the infernal general. His futile attempt at resistance was met with merciless force. His blood boiled in anger when death closely watched over him. As the hellish vice-like grip constricted around his throat, Ulrik felt his life-force slip away, consumed by the wide abyss of oblivion. Thoughts of his childhood love swiftly passed before his eyes, offering him a last chance of redemption. If only faith had been different. As life ebbed away, Ulrik's only regret reverberated within his mind, omnipresent in its refusal to be silenced. He would never again have the chance to see the woman he loved, she who remained unaware of his true feelings. And now, it was too late. In the depths of his soul, a secret ember of hope flickered, yearning for the day when he might return home. Yet now, that cherished dream lay shattered, scattered like fragments of glass before his disillusioned gaze. Through the fog of approaching unconsciousness, he heard the general's dire voice, a prelude of the fate that awaited him in the liminal space between the realms of the living and the damned.

"You would make a lovely companion," the general whispered, his words a cold echo in the void as Ulrik teetered on the edge of oblivion, ensnared in the clutches of a monster whose depravity knew no boundaries.

CHAPTER 1

The forest lay dormant, tranquil beneath the midday sun, rendering the world both distant and tangible. Dreams intertwined with reality, creating an endless loop of hope and despair. Katarina stood amidst the warm summer sunlight, drifting between wake and slumber, a borderline between the waking world and land of the sandman. It felt eerily familiar, yet distinctly foreign. Was this a mere illusion, or had she traversed into another realm, lost between worlds? She experienced a peculiar sense of presence and detachment at the same time. Though unfamiliar, this part of the forest resonated with Katarina, reminiscent of the one near her home. Her spirit felt drawn to this forest, as if it were her destined place. The birdsong carried a soothing melody that seemed to calm the weary soul, while the gentle breeze enveloped the skin with its refreshing touch. The smell of flowers danced through her senses, imbuing her being with a feeling of joy and gratitude.

Suddenly, the ground began to violently shake beneath her feet, accompanied by a sinister rumble that reverberated through her very soul. Katarina lifted her gaze to behold an ancient creature emerging from the depths of the forest, resembling a spectacular creature from mythological folklore. It moved with a graceful yet formidable presence, captivating the attention of all who witnessed its greatness. The colossal beast exuded both elegance and dread, evoking both fear and awe within the heart.

As it slithered closer, Katarina beheld the mighty creature summoned from the darkest corners of myth and legend. The creature's captivating scales gleamed like molten gold under the intensifying rays of the sun. Its giant mouth appeared large enough to consume her entire body. In its eyes, Katarina glimpsed the reflection of time and space, echoing through her consciousness—an eternity waiting to be experienced. Standing in the presence of a Lindwyrm filled her heart with both trepidation and awe, it was a magical creature capable of bestowing either destruction or fortune upon all who entered the forest. The Lindwyrm began to speak with a voice that echoed within Katarina's head like angry thunder across the clear blue sky.

"I can hear you, your thoughts echoing within me." The Lindwyrm lowered its head to face Katarina, its words quivering within her consciousness, leaving an unforgettable impact. A sense of familiarity descended upon her heart, enveloping her senses with a whispered memory. It was as if Katarina had met this enigmatic creature before, in the ethereal realms of her dreams. She could feel its presence pulsating within the depths of her soul.

"What is it that you hear?" Katarina asked, her confusion evident, still unsure whether this encounter was a dream or an illusion. The Lindwyrm's beauty enthralled and mesmerised her senses. It slithered around Katarina, moving smoothly over the ground, leaving a trail of blooming flowers in its graceful path, birthing life wherever it went. "I have not been calling out for you." Katarina said, captivated by the creature standing before her.

"But you have!" The Lindwyrm insisted, its words filled with mystery and ancient knowledge, wisdom drawn from the annals of time.

"Why do I feel so connected to all the hidden creatures?" Katarina asked eagerly, seeking answers. Her heart vibrated at the same frequency as the magical, hidden beings.

"Their presences dwell within your heart, their spirits intertwining with yours," the Lindwyrm answered cryptically. Its head swayed gently to the caress of the approaching wind.

"Why are you here? Why have you come to me in this dream?" Katarina asked, admiring the magnificent creature standing before her.

"You have summoned me," the Lindwyrm replied, its voice both dark and serene. "You must seek me out, follow your path, and uncover the truth."

"What truth?" Katarina inquired, uncertain of the meaning.

"Why you can hear me, why I can manifest in your dreams," the Lindwyrm's words faded away as it slithered away back into the forest, leaving a trail of sprouting daisies in its wake.

Slowly, her dream faded away, guiding her from the astral world. The sharp claws of the endless autumn night pulled Katarina back into her cold realm. She was awake, laying in her bed. She felt the cold sting of reality feasting at her core. What horrors or fortunes awaited her? Katarina lay back, attempting to drift back into the realm of dreams. It was still too early to begin the day.

CHAPTER 2

The cool air descended upon the tranquil valley. Its magic enveloped the land in a sense of peace and bittersweet longing. The sun had yet to grace the forest with its presence. A humid chill permeated the air as the days grew shorter and the seasons prepared to transition. The woodland appeared serene in the growing, bright morning light, with birds just awakening and exchanging their final melodies before autumn's full arrival.

Katarina felt the fresh air enliven her. She cherished the gradual approach of winter each passing day. In September, the leaves had just begun their transformation, soon the landscape would explode in shades of yellow, red, and orange. Katarina held a special affection for autumn, viewing it as a time of change, renewal, and opportunity, contrary to the common disdain it received. She felt drawn to its darkness, sensing its essence pulse within her veins.

The temperature had swiftly shifted, with summer feeling like a distant memory as the cold weather sneaked closer. Katarina revelled in the beauty of the awakening forest around her. Its hidden mysteries resonated within her soul. She had always felt drawn to nature, ever since she was a child. Despite the forest's potential dangers, Katarina sensed a deep connection within her heart.

As a housemaid on a manor, Katarina's day began early, well before dawn, yet she found it easier to rise in autumn's darkness. The season infused her with newfound energy, even on days of strenuous labour. Hard work didn't bother her; in fact, it seemed to invigorate her, infusing her life with a greater sense of purpose. In times of uncertainty, one could only press onward, and Katarina was used to a tough life where she had to do the best with what was given to her.

The estate was located near the forest, just an hour from the nearest village, surrounded by several other large farms. Katarina herself came from a modest, self-sustaining farm a few hours away. Despite their modest means, her family often struggled due to her father Lars' inclination for squandering their savings on alcohol, perpetuating their financial difficulties.

Katarina's mother, Lina, embodied a gentle and nurturing spirit, her heart radiating pure kindness as she selflessly tended to the needs of others. Throughout Katarina's childhood, Lina provided never faulting care, offering comfort and protection whenever her daughter needed. Katarina cherished the memories of her mother's tender presence, finding solace and security in her embrace and devotion. Despite the family's struggles, Katarina's early years were filled with happiness, largely because of Lina's steadfast guidance and unconditional love. Lina kept her husband Lars on track, coaxing him away from trouble and holding the family together through adversity, never uttering a word of complaint. Her face was always graced with a genuine smile, reflecting her enduring love.

Tragically, Katarina's two brothers passed away in infancy. Their parting left Lina consumed by grief. Katarina vividly recalled the anguish in her mother's eyes when her younger brother succumbed at just four months old. Witnessing her mother's despair left an indelible mark on Katarina, a tragic reminder of life's fragility and unfairness. Lars' descent into alcoholism was spurred by the loss of his and Lina's firstborn, before Katarina's birth. Though he sought refuge in numbing his sorrows, the torment of anguish lingered beneath the surface, ready to erupt at any moment.

Despite her own pain and sorrow, Lina endeavoured to remain resilient for Katarina, and together they forged a life of happiness. Yet, a haunting absence lingered in Lina's eyes, following their tragic losses. Still, Katarina found joy in the memories of her compassionate mother, each recollection a loving melody that played upon her heartstrings.

When Katarina was 13 years old, her mother succumbed to illness. The news hit her like a sudden storm, sorrow piercing her soul, leaving her heart and spirit paralyzed, unable to comprehend the ruthless reality. Inconsolable, Katarina was engulfed by immense grief, feeling as if all hope had vanished into the void, leaving her breathless. The world fractured into shards of despair. She wept for days, unable to comprehend the harsh reality of losing her beloved mother.

As Lars' spirit drowned in alcoholism, Katarina found herself shouldering the burden of their household alone. A month later, Lars sent her away to work on another farm. Though her father's emotional distance had grown since Lina's passing, Katarina didn't protest. Each time she sought connection in his eyes, she found only emptiness staring back at her. Their bond was forever lost. It seemed as though Lars' essence had departed, leaving behind a hollow shell.

One day Lars vanished without a trace. People presumed him dead, and Katarina was poised to inherit the farm and land. However, Lars had accrued significant debts and was associated with unsavoury characters. To Katarina's dismay, the authorities confiscated the farm and land. Bereft of both parents and brothers, Katarina felt adrift and betrayed, wandering through life alone. Slowly, the memories of her mother began to fade, like leaves scattered by the wind, losing their colour.

Karl, the master of the farm where she was working, agreed to let her stay and work for him. Katarina did her best to survive on her own; she was a devoted and committed worker, and she never complained.

When Katarina was 18 years old, she received a marriage proposal. Katarina was very surprised; she never thought that she would get the opportunity to marry after losing the farm and her family. It was a good match, and Katarina was a loyal wife. She left her position as a maid and moved in at the farm of her husband. He was the youngest among three brothers and would not inherit a significant amount, but Katarina did not care. For a while, she was truly happy. Life on the farm was challenging, but Katarina was used to hard work. She gave birth to two children. Only her firstborn daughter, Edith, made it into adulthood. With Edith, Katarina once again experienced true joy and love, and Katarina felt that she was truly blessed with a good life. The days passed, and life went on.

Tragedy struck when Håkan, Katarina's husband, passed away on the same day their daughter turned 15. Life on the farm deteriorated further, and Katarina worried about her daughter's future. With poor harvests and dwindling livestock, the family faced dire circumstances. The future seemed dark.

Seeking guidance, Katarina turned to the church, where the priest proposed a suitor for Edith. Overjoyed at the prospect of assistance, Katarina saw it as an opportunity for Edith to live comfortably. She persuaded her daughter to enter into matrimony with the aim of ensuring financial stability and placing emphasis on leading a life of comfort and security. Her daughter reluctantly agreed, knowing that life often was hard and unfair.

Time passed rhythmically, like sand slipping through an hourglass; it had been seven years since Edith married and

Katarina began working on the farm. At first glance, not much appeared to have changed; routine and habit made time flow at a mundane pace. Katarina accepted her fate and felt content with her life and circumstances.

Karl, the master of the house, was not cruel; he could be quite stern, but he was fair and just. In Katarina's fifth year on the farm, the master passed away from illness. His son, Ulrik, assumed the role of master. Ulrik was a mysterious, peculiar man with an enigmatic presence and undeniable beauty. He bore the scars of war etched upon his soul like a somber testament to the horrors he had witnessed upon the battlefield. Once a shy and quiet boy, he had emerged from the war a changed man, distant and cold, with a darkness trapping his soul.

Karl had always kept Ulrik under control after returning from the war, sheltering him from the world. But with his father's passing, Ulrik had to step out of the shadows into the light he desperately wanted to avoid. During the five years since Ulrik's return, Katarina rarely saw him. He often mentioned his preference for the company of books over people. Katarina did her best to carve out a good life for herself on the manor. She worked tirelessly throughout the day, attempting to avoid Ulrik as much as possible. She didn't want to disturb the master or worsen the situation.

There were twenty other workers in the mansion under Ulrik's authority. They all cooperated and made efforts to maintain a peaceful environment, avoiding anything that might upset Ulrik. He had little tolerance for loud noises or disruptions, demanding that the area of the house where he resided always remain quiet and tranquil, without any surprises. He detested surprises.

Ulrik had three sisters, all married and living elsewhere. He himself never married, and Katarina understood why. He had enlisted in the army at a young age, and upon his return, it seemed as though all capacity for love and affection had been lost to him. The priest had suggested Ulrik as a potential suitor for Edith. Katarina refused. She had witnessed Ulrik's return from the war and knew he was not the same. The shy boy she once knew had vanished, leaving behind only a void. The memory of his innocence had faded, and Katarina could see that the light had extinguished from his eyes. It was as if his soul had departed, leaving behind a hollow heart. What was lost could never be reclaimed.

Katarina understood that many men returned from war devoid of their former selves, forever changed and lost in the abyss, longing for a salvation that would never arrive. She respected Ulrik and took great care not to upset or anger him. Yet, a part of her feared him, haunted by the memories reflected in his eyes, deeds that could never be undone, beyond the reach of forgiveness.
But Katarina needed to support herself and survive. She had nowhere else to turn.

Katarina was aware of Ulrik's watchful gaze on her, and whenever it fell upon her, she felt a cold chill run down her spine, disrupting her mind. As a young girl working on the manor, Katarina had known that Ulrik harboured feelings for her, and now those looks still lingered. She was aware of the dark shadows that dwelled within Ulrik's soul, and yet, he had never inflicted harm upon her or anyone else on the manor.

"Don't just stand there!" a voice pierced the silence, shattering the eerie stillness that lingered in the air. It was Elsie, another woman who worked on the farm with Katarina. "Stay away from the mist!" her words a dire warning that reverberated through the break of day. "You know that the mist spirits engage in their seductive play just before sunrise. If you're unlucky, they'll catch you, and you'll be lost in their world forever!" Elsie feared all väsen, the hidden creatures that shared this world with humans. Väsen, beings of ancient lore and legend, whispered tales of untold horrors lurking in the shadows of the forest, lakes and mountains, their presence a mystery and danger for those who dared to cross their path. They were magical creatures that moved between realms and dimensions. The priest used to say that väsen were the lost creatures that got thrown out of paradise, the same creatures that got left behind when God decided to drown the world and Noah built his ark. Katarina did not care much for the Christian religion. She recognised väsen to be ancient creatures, having an important part in this world.

Despite the undeniable sense of fear that penetrated the air, Katarina harboured a deep respect for väsen. It was a respect born of years spent in communion with the spirits that roamed the land. She had long advised Ulrik and his father to honour the tomte, the guardian spirit of the farmstead, with offerings. This gesture of goodwill would appease the unpredictable whims of the mystical creature.

Every farm and estate had at least one tomte, a small creature cloaked in mystery and magic, particularly fond of animals. They could help with the farm or wreak havoc depending on their mood. To incur the wrath of the tomte was to court disaster, for its powers were as vast as they were unpredictable. Therefore, it was best to be on the tomte's good side. Many people diligently set out offerings of porridge, milk, and other delights to please these mystical guardians, knowing that a contented tomte would attend to the welfare of the livestock and mend the fractures of the farmstead. Endowed with the gift of invisibility, tomtar were seldom seen; those fortunate enough to catch sight of them, described their stature to that of a big cat, bedecked in hues of red or grey with disproportionately enormous hats. Cruelty towards animals could incite the tomte's rage, compelling it to wield its magic in ways that would afflict a member of the human household with illness. On the final homestead where Katarina resided alongside her husband, the master dismissed the existence of such väsen as mere fables, tales fit only for the ears of children. Yet, it was foolish to discount their powers. From that moment forth, misfortune began to shadow the farmstead. Katarina, however, understood the stupidity of underestimating their powers. She alone persisted in leaving food and gifts for the tomte, observing each dawn as the offerings vanished without a trace.

"That would be exciting, wouldn't it?" Katarina laughed, looking at Elsie.

"Are you crazy!?" Elsie exclaimed, shocked. Her eyes closely monitored the forest.

"The mist spirits will drag you underground; you'll be in their kingdom forever, or they'll release you back, and you'll never be the same. Don't you remember Agatha's son? He disappeared into the woods and didn't return for a week. When he did, he said he'd been captured by the mist spirits, and he was never the same again. He became lost, always mumbling about their enchanting dance and mesmerizing beauty. They even seduced him! Can you imagine? The blasphemy! Engaging in such foul behaviour with väsen! Those who do are forever touched by the devil!"

"Oh yes, the horror!" Katarina said sarcastically, letting her mind wander off into a fairy tale.

"I'm serious!" Elsie stared at Katarina with angry eyes. "They will take your soul from you!"

"That's just something the priest scares children with so they won't get lost and die in the forest," Katarina said calmly, brushing away Elsie's concerns. She knew too well that fear led to misunderstanding. "Many people have encountered tomtar, trolls, dwarves, and giants, and they're fine!"

"But not the forest spirits and the mist spirits!" Elsie cautioned with a harsh tone.

"They are called skogsrå and älvor," Katarina rectified with diligent attention and precision.

"Nevertheless," Elsie looked around at the mist with caution. The dawn unveiled its chilling splendour, a haunting tapestry of ethereal beauty painted across the sky. Autumn's elegant hues commenced their majestic ascent. They cast their spell upon the world with a delicate grace that enchanted the soul. "One should be aware of the danger lurking nearby. Do not look at their dance, do not listen to their song, do not let them seduce you. It will end badly! Associating with väsen and demons never ends well!"

"The mist king is supposed to live in magnificent halls," Katarina let her mind wander, forgetting the responsibilities of her ordinary life. Her eyes soaked in the mysticism of the woodland realm.

"Stop it!" Elsie took Katarina's hand. "Come on, let's go back. The day is about to start, and we have a lot of work to do."

CHAPTER 3

The day had come to an end as Katarina returned home after an arduous day of labour. Despite her physical exhaustion, a sense of serene contentment filled her spirit. She found value in always continuing forward, doing her best to stay positive. As the sun began its descent, casting a warm orange glow across the sky, the melodious songs of birds filled the air. The scent of autumn filled the nose and lungs. Katarina found solace in the tranquil sight of the sun bidding farewell to the land. From a distance, the forest appeared enchantingly beautiful in the evening light. Katarina frequently gathered berries, mushrooms, herbs, fruits, and nuts within the forest. She even constructed traps to catch small animals. Her master harboured reservations about her prolonged absences, fearing the potential dangers residing within the forest. Many people got lost in the forest and never returned. Katarina knew very well that it was unwise to underestimate the forest spirits. She always tried to remain respectful and cautious when entering the forest.

When Katarina arrived home, Ulrik awaited her presence with weary and watchful eyes. Seated upon a chair, a book rested in his lap, his features concealed within the soft glow of the dim evening light. Ulrik wore a black coat, seamlessly blending with his enigmatic features. His raven black hair elegantly framed his countenance and his pale skin bore a resemblance to milk, its fairness almost ethereal. Despite enduring the ravages of war and its accompanying hardships, Ulrik retained a youthful appearance, a fact that struck Katarina as somewhat peculiar. Whereas many returning soldiers bore faces weathered and aged beyond their years, Ulrik's youth remained remarkably preserved. Though the scars of war had undoubtedly taken their toll on his spirit, his physical form seemed to have escaped unscathed, untouched by time itself.

"You're late," Ulrik remarked disapprovingly, gazing out into the abyss. The shadows almost seemed to fear his presence, avoiding his touch. As Katarina turned towards him, the flames in the fireplace leapt and danced with a fervent energy. Katarina mustered a gentle smile to scatter the tension. In the aura of his presence, a subtle disquietude whispered softly within her, a delicate tremor in the depths of her being.

"I was ensuring that the tomte received her food," Katarina replied calmly, the flames resonating with her words. Ulrik continued to regard her with a stern expression. "Remember how it went on my last farm?" Katarina pressed on. "It is important to maintain a good relationship with the guardian väsen."

"Yes, I suppose you're right," Ulrik pondered, his gaze lowering as he became lost in his thoughts. Ulrik was a strikingly handsome man with dark hair and piercing blue eyes. Sadly, his beauty was overshadowed by the torment evident in his gaze, carrying with it a weight of pain and haunting memories from a realm beyond. A tempest of conflicted emotions swirled within him, memories of deeds impossible to erase from the past, forever consuming his core. As Katarina accidentally dropped the book she was carrying, Ulrik flinched. His expression briefly contorted into one of cruelty as darkness seemed to envelop his being and claiming his soul.

"Please," Ulrik's voice rose in anger before he quickly composed himself. His hands betrayed a nervous movement. "Try to be more careful."

"Yes, of course," Katarina replied softly, careful not to worsen the situation. She always tried her best to keep a calm and peaceful environment within the household. Katarina possessed a kind heart, always striving to find ways to assist those close to her. Yet Ulrik remained an enigma, a puzzle she struggled to decode, unsure of the remedy she could offer to ease his burdens. "I apologize." She observed Ulrik closely, attempting to decipher his complex character. Despite knowing him to be a dangerous man, she couldn't help but feel a sense of sympathy towards him. The innocent boy she once knew, too shy to speak to her, seemed a distant memory. In his place remained a hollow man, devoid of warmth and life, his essence long since departed.

Katarina often contemplated whether he had been transformed into a draugr, a vicious and demonic creature known for its cruelty and monstrous nature. Such was the rumour circulating among the residents of the county. Devoid of soul, draugrs thrived on the suffering of innocents, bringing death, suffering, and pain wherever they roamed. These dark entities had the ability to transform humans into similar monstrosities through their bites. Identifying a draugr could be difficult, as many hid their true nature within a human facade, seldom revealing their sinister side. Yet, when they showed their demonic side, hearts froze in fear at the incomprehensible malevolence they exuded. Most draugrs inhabited graveyards, obsessively safeguarding the treasures of the deceased. These beings were putrid, decaying, with grotesquely deformed faces, yet possessed unearthly strength and speed. They thrived in darkness, rarely venturing into the light, preferring the night, and they were sensitive to silver and various herbs.

Ulrik, once a regular churchgoer in his youth, abandoned his beliefs upon his return home from war. Katarina pondered whether Ulrik's absence from church benefited the congregation or merely fuelled the rumours surrounding him. Speculation among the parishioners brewed imaginative tales of different demonic creatures. Ulrik himself claimed to have lost faith in God, dismissing church attendance as futile in a world deprived of divine intervention or salvation.

He had witnessed hell on earth, beseeching God for aid and redemption, yet his prayers remained unanswered, lost in a blurry noise. Ulrik saw no purpose in dedicating his time to worship a cruel and seemingly indifferent God. In his eyes, the world was a dark and horrible place. Humanity was left to rely on itself for survival.

Silver was strictly forbidden in Ulrik's home. Bringing that metal onto the mansion was grounds for immediate dismissal from employment. Ulrik explained that he wanted to maintain a welcoming environment for the various väsen residing the farm, many of whom were vulnerable to silver.

Rarely did Ulrik go outside during daylight hours. He asserted that the sun was for common folk, for peasants, while he, as the master, preferred to preserve his fair complexion untainted by the sun's harsh and unforgiving rays. He had endured his share of sun and heat during the war. Now he sought solace indoors, hiding away until sundown.

The farmhands harboured a silent fear that Ulrik might be a draugr. They suspected an unholy nature, yet they dared not voice their concerns for fear of upsetting their master. On one occasion, Wilhelm, another worker, extended an invitation to the priest for dinner. Though Ulrik begrudgingly welcomed the hypocritical clergyman into his home, he understood the necessity of accommodating the influential and powerful church, mindful not to needlessly accumulate enemies.

During the dinner, conversations revolved around Christian topics, with the priest emphasizing the virtues of being a devout believer, urging Ulrik to return to church. While Ulrik maintained his composure, Katarina sensed a simmering rage beneath the surface, a potent storm waiting to be released. As the priest departed, Katarina and Elsie approached him, with Elsie bravely questioning whether Ulrik might be a draugr. The priest chuckled, dismissing Ulrik's peculiarity as non-threatening and certainly not indicative of being a draugr. Yet, despite the priest's reassurances, the farm workers remained wary of Ulrik, sensing a cold detachment within him, perceiving a man who appeared to have lost his soul behind his azure eyes.

"Just be cautious out there," Ulrik warned with a dark and deep voice. His mind wandered off to a distant place, attempting to banish the haunting thoughts that plagued him. A stern expression settled upon his face as the inner battles raged within. "There are many väsen lurking around. Even a stallo has been spotted" He recounted a neighbour's recent sighting of a stallo, a robust creature often twice the size of a human. Typically, with only a single eye. Residing in the mountains or on the fjell, they occasionally ventured into the forests below. Known for their strength but lacking in intellect, stallo would resort to kidnapping and consuming children when provoked. Encounters with humans were usually uncommon. Most people were cautious enough to stay away from them.

"Stallo?" Katarina inquired; her curiosity piqued. "This far south?" she pressed eagerly for an answer. Väsen had forever held profound significance for Katarina, as if she could sense their very essence intertwined with her soul. From an early age, she felt a deep connection to their existence, comprehending their nature, and enraptured by their mystique. Since childhood, she had been irresistibly drawn to the realm of väsen, yearning to discover its mysteries and dive deeper into their world. In the depths of night, the realm of väsen enchanted her dreams. Within this ethereal dimension, a mixture of creatures conversed with her. Their voices echoed through the hallways of her subconscious. Yet amidst the beauty, some entities emerged with a haunting presence. The nightmares cast shadows that almost rendered the fabric of her being with their dread-inducing allure.

"Yes, I found it rather peculiar," Ulrik replied with a chill in his voice. "The trolls won't be pleased." His dark tone hung in the air as his gaze lingered on Katarina, a look that conveyed desire, something she had sensed from him before. Aware of her vulnerability as a maid, she knew that masters often took advantage of their housekeepers. Even though she was not a träl, or slave, her worth was diminished, and as a woman, her rights and voice were worth little compared to a man's. In the event of rape, society would likely turn a blind eye to avoid conflict, reluctant to challenge a master's authority.

Katarina observed the way Ulrik's eyes traced the contours of her body, watching her every movement. She took a deep breath, attempting to steady herself and ground her thoughts. Ulrik had never inflicted harm upon her, despite his cold, enigmatic demeanour. Initially fearful of his potential to do so, over the years she had spent on the farm, he had never laid a hand on her. Katarina found ease in the notion that as she aged, his interest might fade, leading him to seek a younger, more desirable wife. After all, he possessed both striking looks and wealth. However, the women of the village and the surrounding county regarded him with fear. They did not understand his nature and people feared what they did not understand. The villagers sensed the darkness seeping from his soul, an undeniable shadow following his every step. His gaze seemed to lay bare all the guilty deeds concealed within him.

"The trolls often venture into their own realm," Katarina remarked, glancing at Ulrik. "The forest teems with them." Trolls dwelled within moss, trees, and stones. They stood half the height of humans, with prominent noses, ears, and skin in shades of grey or green, often adorned with mushrooms, bark, flowers, and plants sprouting from their hair and bodies. Possessing long tails and adept in magic, trolls held a particular affinity for jewels and treasures. While they typically avoided human contact, they could pose a threat if provoked. Trolls possessed the ability to remain invisible to avoid a stallo or other creatures.

"If they happen upon our domain, I'll handle them. I will kill any trespassers," Ulrik asserted confidently. "You don't need a silver bullet to kill a stallo."

"I believe we can divert them away," Katarina persisted. "They're known for their gullibility and can be easily misled. There's no need for bloodshed," she added gently, her compassionate nature evident. Katarina believed the world to be violent enough already. Whenever possible, she sought a more peaceful solution.

"And how does one go about deceiving a stallo?" Ulrik inquired with a curious tilt of his head, his eyes alight with intrigue. There was something about her positive outlook on life that fascinated him. Ulrik recognized the world to be a very dark place, yet Katarina always appeared to be anchored in the light.

"Many tales tell of children outwitting stallo to save themselves," Katarina replied cheerfully, her fondness for fairy tales evident within her voice.

"We must safeguard the farm," Ulrik stated, his eyes appearing brown in the dimness. He had witnessed the strengths and abilities of many demons and supernatural beings. He was aware of the immense threat they posed. This home was one of the few remaining things in this world that grounded Ulrik, and he was prepared to fight fiercely to protect it.

"One can protect without resorting to violence," Katarina countered with serene composure, her response measured and resolute. "Cunning and wit are always preferable."

"Speaking like someone who's never witnessed war and its devastation," Ulrik retorted coldly, his words tinged with hidden pain.

"You're right, I haven't," Katarina responded with a tranquil demeanour. "I didn't mean to offend you or insult you," she added softly, aware of the villager's disdain for Ulrik. Despite the darkness within him, Katarina couldn't bring herself to hate him or participate in their unfair judgments. She knew that everyone had their own story, their own reason to act the way they did, and she did not want to judge anyone. Ulrik quickly composed himself after realizing his tone had become harsh. He didn't intend to raise his voice, and it pained him to see that Katarina appeared almost fearful of him. He would never harm her, but he understood why she avoided his company. Ulrik was aware of Katarina's connection to the realm of väsen and spirits. It was probable that she knew his true nature and wisely chose to keep her distance. Though he comprehended this truth rationally, a pang of wounded pride afflicted him as he came to terms with the notion that she could ever conceive of him as capable of causing her harm.

"Eat now and go to sleep. We have a busy day ahead," he commanded with unwavering firmness, his voice leaving no room for doubt. Katarina nodded politely and left the room. As darkness enveloped the night, she dined in silence, watching the flickering candlelight. Quietly, she retired to bed, awaiting the dawn of a new day.

CHAPTER 4

The night enveloped the room in its cold embrace, casting an unsettling aura that invaded Katarina's mind. Sleep eluded her, as strange dreams haunted her restless mind throughout the long, unforgiving hours. Her soul felt unsettled, adrift between realms, as it was beckoned by the calls of Lindwurms and other mythical creatures. Väsen intertwined themselves into her thoughts and dreams, whispering incomprehensible words.

Katarina's slumber was shallow and easily disrupted, akin to a trance where reality blurred with the astral plane. Fragmented worlds collapsed into darkness and despair, leaving her disoriented and adrift in the abyss. Although her body lay in her bed, Katarina felt her soul distant from the realm of dreams, suspended in an enigmatic space between sleeping and waking. She remained disconnected from both worlds, unable to fully succumb to sleep or awaken, trapped in a state of dissonance while her physical form remained present, lingering in this world. Ensnared within the labyrinth of her mind, she found herself ensconced in a prison of senses, each one bound in irons of its own making. The air was filled with the acrid scent of charred remnants. The misleading whispers of demons insidiously twisted through the chambers of her ears. Their lies were infected with deceit and manipulation. Within this cacophony, Katarina could almost discern the bitter taste of darkness lingering upon her parched tongue.

The room lay shrouded in darkness, suffused with the brisk scent of autumn. Though Katarina could open her eyes and regulate her breathing, her body remained immobile, devoid of her control, cut off from her consciousness. She found herself powerless, her mind refusing to heed her commands, relinquishing its mastery over her body.

A surge of panic seized Katarina as her heart raced uncontrollably, fear exploding through her veins like a relentless tide wave. This sensation was all too familiar, a recurring nightmare she had endured before, a terror from which she could not free herself. Tremors of apprehension spread through Katarina's body, enveloping her entire being, rendering her powerless against their grip of a monstrous entity.

It was the mare, ensnaring her body and poisoning her mind with its sinister enchantment. The air hung thick and dry, filled with the taste of imminent danger. Though Katarina longed to scream and flee, she found herself trapped in a fog of illusions, an unwilling servant to the monster's malevolent touch.

She began to breathe heavily, overwhelmed by panic and unable to wrestle back control of her body. Was this the end? Was she going to die tonight? A weight pressed heavily upon her chest, suffocating her life force. The mare, an evil demon known for inflicting nightmares and anxiety upon dreamers caught in the land beyond the wakening, snared her in its grip. Those who fell prey to its frequent visits often descended into madness. Slowly they lost their grip on reality, unable to break free from the clutches of sleep, trapped in a realm between the waking and the dreaming.

The mare sat on the victim's chest, weaving its dark magic into their dreams. The creature rendered them petrified and voiceless, yet painfully aware of their surroundings, drowning their soul in a pit of despair. With effortless fluidity, the mare assumed various demonic forms as it moved around in the room, all while maintaining its merciless dominion over its innocent prey. Once ensnared by the mare, victims found it nearly impossible to break free. It revelled in taunting and tormenting their souls, maintaining its suffocating grip and hellish manipulation.

Some claimed the mare appeared as a beautiful woman, but to Katarina, it was nothing but a dreadful, awful creature with piercing red eyes, elongated fangs, gnarled hands, contorted body, and pallid, decaying skin. The mare breathed heavily as it wrapped its hands around Katarina's neck, tightening its loathsome grasp, inching closer to the brink of death with each passing moment.

Katarina felt petrified, unable to move, desperate to escape the overwhelming dread that enveloped her mind and body. The walls seemed to crumble, while caving in, the promise of death prowled ominously nearby, patiently waiting for its next victim. Despite her futile attempts to break free, Katarina remained ensnared in the mare's violent grasp. She was trapped within its malevolent kingdom, a slave to its cruel game.

The mare emitted an unearthly sound as it drew closer to Katarina's face, its words haunting her to the core and extinguishing any flicker of hope that still hid within her bones. Its foul breaths grew nearer, the stench becoming unbearable. Despite Katarina's efforts to resist, the mare's grip only tightened further and further, drawing her nearer to the precipice of death. This was surely the end. Each breath felt like a burden, her chest weighed down with unbearable heaviness. Intense agony surged through her veins, choking any hope of rescue she might have harboured. As the room began to spin, Katarina felt herself overcome by dizziness. She made silent attempts to call out for help, yet her efforts proved futile as she found herself incapable of vocalizing her distress. Isolated and devoid of allies, she faced a profound sense of desolation. All hope was gone.

In the periphery of her vision, Katarina witnessed more demons emerging from the shadows, slowly pushing themselves out from the darkness. They floated swiftly across the floor, transforming into a swirling grey mist that engulfed her surroundings. Darkness encroached, extinguishing the faintest embers of hope that remained. The demons encircled her. Their touch sent shivers of revulsion and repulsions through her bloodstream as their grotesque limbs caressed her defenceless body. Despite her efforts to resist, she remained paralyzed, unable to control her body. Katarina fought back with every ounce of strength she could muster. The mere thought of these malevolent entities violating her body filled her mind with dread. This was not how she wished to depart from this world. Was this the fate that befell so many who perished in their sleep? Was her demise imminent? Would tonight be her last? Would they discover her lifeless body come morning? While many had survived encounters with the mare and lived to tell the tale, how many had succumbed to its lethal game in the dimension of sleep? The rapid pounding of Katarina's heart echoed in her ears as she teetered on the brink of unconsciousness, the grasp of death slowly tightening its grip on her life.

"Are you still in bed?" Elsie's voice jolted Katarina back to consciousness. She found herself drenched in sweat. Her gaze flashed around the room in panic. The first light of dawn had broken through the horizon, accompanied by the cheerful chirping of birds, yet the room remained devoid of any demonic presence. Katarina sat up in shock, her heart still racing, scanning her body for any signs of assault, but she could not find any marks, no evidence of any attack. It all seemed like a terrible dream, an inexplicable illusion, a vivid nightmare. "Are you listening to me?" Elsie persisted, her tone firm and instructing. "Today is not a day for sleeping in."

"I... I wasn't..." Katarina began, her heart still racing with panic. It had all been a dream, yet it had felt hauntingly real. She had traversed between realms, and now she had returned to her body and mind. But the memories of the mare lingered, haunting her thoughts, consuming her being.

"Get up, now! Before the master catches you!" Elsie urged; a worried expression etched on her face.

"The mare..." Katarina muttered dizzily, her voice faint and disoriented.

"What are you talking about?" Elsie questioned with a thoughtful demeanour, her inquiry poised and deliberate.

"The mare...it tried to strangle me," Katarina managed to gather her voice, her hand instinctively reaching for her neck as she attempted to ground herself.

"What?" Elsie's voice trembled with shock, fear evident in her eyes. "Not the mare!" she exclaimed; her eyes filled with dread. "Once they choose a victim, they never relent. They will haunt you for eternity."

"I thought they were going to kill me!" Katarina exclaimed as she rose from the bed, still trembling with shock. Her limbs still fully refused to obey her movements.

"Most of the time, they only torment your mind," Elsie responded, her tone imbued with genuine concern, conveying empathy and attentiveness. Elsie and Katarina had been friends for several years, providing mutual support and companionship through various trials and tribulations. Now, Elsie feared for the life and sanity of her dear friend. "Some are driven mad by their visits. They may come back tonight. Sometimes they choose to bide their time and wait for the opportune moment to return. People lose their sanity from the uncertainty of their reappearance, and they always come back."

"How can I rid myself of them?" Katarina inquired with an anxious tone, her voice betraying a sense of urgency and unease. She felt lost amidst all the uncertainties.

"There are various theories," Elsie replied. She was determined not to relinquish hope of rescuing her friend. "But most of the time, you cannot. Once they possess you, they refuse to let go. You must be resilient and learn to coexist with them. When they strike, strive to remain strong and grounded, resisting their attempts to claim your soul. Keep reminding yourself of who you are and where you belong. With that mindset, you will always find your way back."

Katarina tried to shape her lips into something resembling a smile. An ominous sensation chewed her from the inside, twisting her intestines. "Let's go, we have much work to do today," Katarina declared, as she and Elsie left the house to begin their day's labour. Despite her attempts to push them aside, Katarina couldn't shake off her worries about the mare's potential return and the insanity it might bring. The demon's presence still lingered in her mind, overpowering her existence.

CHAPTER 5

The night was dark and cold, its whispers settling within every heartbeat, casting long, apocalyptic shadows that stretched like skeletal fingers across the earth. Its twilight tinged with a bone-chilling magnetism that seeped into every cell of Katarina's body. The sound of nocturnal animals emanated from outside the window, while the scent of rain permeated the air.

She lay in her bed, afraid to fall asleep. Anxious thoughts kept her awake. Fretful thoughts coursed through her reflections, invading her mind with terror. A whirlwind of fear and confusion grew within. Katarina knew what they said about those possessed by the mare. They slowly went insane, forever lost to the empty void, living in madness. She couldn't understand why this was happening to her. What had she done to anger the demon? Why had the mare chosen her as its prey? The questions gnawed at her sanity, threatening to plunge her into the same abyss of madness that had claimed countless lives before her. It all felt unreal, like a haunting nightmare that refused to yield to the light of day, slowly strangling her from within.

During the day, Katarina had visited the priest, expressing her concerns about the impending danger she felt cutting at her core. She was afraid of what might happen next. Many people in the county had gone mad from encounters with the mare; it was all a bad omen. The priest had prayed for her, using holy water and incense to cleanse Katarina of the ruthless demon. During the priest's ritual, Katarina had felt no relief, no reprieve from the nightmare that stalked her every thought. She knew such efforts seldom did. Yet, hope was the only thing she could cling to when salvation seemed distant, nothing but a fading memory. Katarina's faith wavered like a flickering candle in an enraged storm. She had sought solace in the knowledge of the church, hoping to find answers to the relentless torment that plagued her nights. But the priest's words offered little comfort, his explanations as hollow as the echo of footsteps in an empty cathedral.

Katarina had queried the priest as to why the church's powers seemed impotent against the prevailing menace. She pondered why the radiance of God failed to repel the demon. Was the Christian God not strong enough to vanquish the enemies denounced by the church? The priest, visibly perturbed, offered the clichéd response that God works in mysterious ways, beyond the comprehension of mere mortals. Dissatisfied with this explanation, Katarina had observed the potency of various väsen, their magical powers, and the havoc wrought by demonic entities. Yet, she had never witnessed the intervention of the Christian God. The priest admonished her to maintain unwavering faith, cautioning against doubt. Questioning God could jeopardize her soul. Katarina struggled to reconcile the concept of an omnipotent God, as expounded by the priest, with the apparent apathy toward His subjects. In a world filled with suffering, disease, death, and malevolent forces, divine benevolence seemed distant. If God truly possessed the power the priest spoke of, then why did He permit such darkness and cruelty to roam the world? If He indeed represented the light, then why did He allow darkness to threaten her soul? If God truly held the power to banish such evils, then why did he allow the demons to flourish?

"Väsen are not creatures of the light," the priest's voice echoed through the dark chapel, his words carrying the weight of ancient warnings. His features were almost hidden within the shadows. "Most are wicked and evil!"

"I believe that väsen are just like us," she dared to question, her voice a whisper against the sombre backdrop of the church. Katarina adamantly rejected the notion that all beings of the supernatural realm were inherently malevolent. She had always felt a stronger connection to väsen than she had ever felt to God.

"What do you mean?" The priest's eyes narrowed, his expression one of stern disapproval. "You must not entertain such thoughts, my child," he admonished.

"Some are bad, and some are good; most have both darkness and light within them," Katarina explained. "Just like us, they embrace both what is good and what is bad."

"You must stay away from all väsen!" the priest warned. "Those who engage in activity with väsen will lose their soul and their chance to go to heaven!" he cautioned. "You are a god-obedient, hardworking, pure woman; do not say such things!"

"Then why has the mare chosen me?" she pressed; her tone tinged with a hint of defiance. Yes, she had been God-fearing all her life, not because she wanted to, but because she had no choice. The church held great power within society, and refusing to attend came at a high cost, especially for a woman.

"Calm down," the priest's voice echoed between the walls, but his words provided little comfort. "I am sure that the prayers and the holy water will aid you," he added, with hope in his voice. "Go back home and try to stay calm. Say your prayers at night, keep faith, and have your cross nearby. Have faith, and the divine light shall protect you." The priest's assurances felt hollow, a feeble attempt to silence the rising tide of fear that threatened to consume her soul. Katarina had never engaged in prayer; she remained uncertain of its efficacy. God never appeared to heed those who sought His guidance.

Hastily, Katarina returned home with an unsatisfied heart, in search of answers and scared of what might come to pass when night fell over the horizon. Anxiety and concern ached within her chest. Everyone in the household seemed to be asleep. Katarina lay awake, staring out into the darkness, unable to relax, afraid to let go of the land of wakefulness and enter the realm of sleep.

Suddenly, a dark figure appeared in the corner of the room, its haunting aura crackling, impossible to deny. Katarina felt unable to move, caught in obscurity, having lost the ability to move her limbs. Her heart began to race faster, beating to the rhythm of her fears. The creature stood in the shadows, watching her closely with its emerald-green eyes shining like poisonous stars in a crooked universe.

Katarina tried to scream, but she could not utter a single sound; something was covering her mouth, rendering her unable to communicate. Confusion echoed within her head—how was this possible? She had not fallen asleep yet, or had she? Nothing felt certain anymore; only fear remained, lingering, nibbling at every cell of her body.

Frozen in terror, Katarina watched as the creature slithered across the floor, focusing on its prey, its movements sinuous and predatory. With each passing moment, the air grew thick with dread, suffocating her in its grasp. The mare jumped into her bed, lifted Katarina's cover, and began to crawl along her body, touching her legs with its stone-cold, tree-like limbs. Its numbing touch against her skin sent shockwaves of fear coursing through her veins. Katarina's breath came in ragged gasps, her heart pounding like a drumbeat. It felt as though her heart might cease beating under the weight of panic galloping through her veins, devouring her entire being in an overwhelming pull.

What did the creature want with her? Its hands extended from the cover, stretching toward her neck. Its nails were dark, rusty, and menacingly sharp. Katarina's chest weighed heavily, making it almost impossible to breathe. Life began to ebb away from her body, never to return. She longed to scream, to flee and break free, but she found herself ensnared in the mare's ruthless spell.

Suddenly, Katarina woke up screaming, her heart almost jumping out of her chest. Panic and distress invaded her mind as she looked around the room. Only shadows remained, granting her freedom of movement. Her heart raced, panic spreading throughout her body. Swiftly the door swung open with a violent crash, revealing Ulrik's imposing figure silhouetted against the doorway. His gaze swept across the room, seeking traces of the events that had unfolded.

"What happened?" Ulrik's voice sliced through the air like a sharpened blade, cutting through the veil of silence that shrouded the room. His eyes, glinting with a cold fury, bore into Katarina's petrified form, demanding answers. "Why did you scream?"

"I didn't mean to wake you, master," Katarina stammered, her voice quivering with fear. Enveloped in the clutches of uncertainty, she found herself unanchored in a sea of anxiety and disorientation.

"I wasn't asleep," Ulrik murmured, his voice a low rumble that seemed to reverberate through the very walls. "What happened? Why did you scream like that in the middle of the night?" His expression softened, but the tension in the room remained, thick with an unspoken dread that infused the air. Katarina appeared petrified, frozen in fear. Ulrik hesitated to exacerbate her distress. Having witnessed the anguish of countless innocent souls in his lifetime, he harboured no desire to add to her burden. Though his heart yearned to offer aid and protection, uncertainty clouded his path, leaving him unsure of how to proceed.

Katarina's breath caught in her throat, her heart hammering against her chest like a caged beast desperate for release, her voice barely above a whisper. "It's the mare," she confessed, her words laced with terror. "The mare has come for me," Katarina reached out to the table, attempting to light a candle to illuminate the dark night. Her hand trembled, its colour paling as the capillaries contracted in response to the stressful situation.

"What?" Ulrik's countenance hardened. The desire to protect his home surged within him, its call refusing to be extinguished. Ulrik approached Katarina calmly and assisted her in lighting the candle. The flames initially flickered with a hint of agitation, but soon settled into a tranquil dance as Ulrik withdrew.

"Yes, it started yesterday when the mare first invaded my sleep. I sought help from the priest, but the prayers and incense didn't seem to help. The mare returned tonight. I was unable to move, and the creature climbed over my body, attempting to strangle me," Katarina explained, her words filled with fear and trepidation. Her tone conveyed a sense of helplessness in the face of a dire situation. Her words hung in the air, heavy with dread, echoing off the walls of the murky room. The horizon of tomorrow loomed ambiguous and undefined.

"The mare touched you?" Ulrik asked, his eyes darkening, his voice a low growl. The traumas of war still held his mind captive. He abhorred the suffering of the innocent and felt incensed when powerful individuals or creatures exploited those unable to defend themselves.

"What?" Katarina was uncertain about his statement. What did he mean? How was that relevant? "Yes, the mare moved its claws over my body under the covers before reaching towards my neck! I fear what it will do next! I fear for my life and my soul! Many have died in their sleep, and many more have gone insane under the grip of the mare!" Katarina felt extremely frightened, nearly on the brink of tears. An enraged expression began to spread across Ulrik's face. A fierce determination ignited in Ulrik's eyes; his features contorted with a burning resolve.

"Fear not," his voice cut through the silence as his eyes betrayed his anger. "The mare will not take your soul. Not as long as I am the master of this house."

"How can you be so sure?" Confusion clouded Katarina's expression, her eyes searching Ulrik's face for answers, her voice filled with uncertainty and hopelessness. She wanted to believe him, but what could he do to protect her against a demon?

"That creature will not claim your soul. Go back to sleep. I will take care of this. The mare will not bother you anymore, I promise you," he declared, his voice a low, ominous rumble. Before Katarina could respond, Ulrik hastily left the room.

Katarina sat on her bed, her mind a muddle of confusion and fear. What did he mean? Throughout the night, she remained awake, unable to surrender to the gentle embrace of sleep. With the break of dawn, Katarina rose from her bed, commencing her preparations for the day. Yet, the meaning behind Ulrik's statement continued to occupy her thoughts. How could he help? She recognized Ulrik's lack of fear towards väsen, unlike the priest and others in the county who harboured deep apprehension. But what could he do to help? Despite her uncertainty, Katarina felt gratitude that Ulrik had not dismissed her experience as mere nonsense. She tried to clear her mind and focus on the tasks of the day, but with each passing moment, the night drew closer, weighing heavily upon her heart.

CHAPTER 6

"You seem tired," Elsie remarked compassionately as she observed Katarina. Despite her efforts to smile, Katarina's energy betrayed the weight of her burdens.

"The mare visited me again last night," Katarina disclosed in a hushed tone, her words infected with concern. "It emerged from the shadows, attempting to suffocate me once more." Fear flickered in Elsie's eyes as she absorbed Katarina's words. The two of them had been friends for a very long time. When Katarina initially arrived at the estate as a teenager, Elsie took her under her wing. Over the years, their bond blossomed into a robust friendship, and Elsie was elated upon learning about Katarina's return to work with her. Elsie now harboured concern for the safety of her dear friend. Demons were intent on claiming her soul.

"Did the priest's prayer help?" Elsie inquired, attempting to inject a sense of optimism into the conversation. She wanted to maintain hope for the sake of her friend, but she was all too aware of the fate that awaited those chosen by the mare.

"No," Katarina responded with a hint of despair. "They were powerless. I was afraid to go back to sleep, I fear that tonight will be my last night."

"What did the priest say?" Elsie asked, her concern palpable in her words, unable to conceal her emotions.

"Not much," Katarina replied. "I will return to him tomorrow. But I have a sense that there isn't much he can do."

"Perhaps he could arrange for someone to perform an exorcism," Elsie suggested, her voice trailing off uncertainty.

"An exorcism?" Katarina repeated, her voice thick with disbelief. "Do you think I am possessed?"

"I cannot say," Elsie replied. "No one understands how or why the mare selects its victims. All we can do is our best to rid them of their demonic influence. Mares are common, yet there is no reliable method to eliminate them. Should we attempt to lure the mare into the forest?" Elsie proposed, considering potential solutions.

"We could," Katarina pondered the suggestion, her mind swirling with uncertainty. "Some try to relocate the mare to the forest by placing a branch with a 'markvast' in the victim's bed. The idea is that the mare would be drawn to the branch, allowing people to transport it to the forest, far from their home. Many have attempted this, though most have failed. It might be worth a try," Katarina suggested, trying to maintain a positive outlook despite her reservations. She understood that significant danger and obstacles lay ahead if she wished to survive and vanquish the mare. Uncertain of the path to victory, she remained courageous in her determination not to surrender. She had to keep on fighting. There was always hope, even in the darkest hours of the night.
"Yes, you have nothing to lose. Come, I know of a tree nearby," Elsie declared, rising from her seat, and gesturing for Katarina to follow, her footsteps echoing against the quiet backdrop of the evening. "The tree is just outside of the forest." Together, they walked away from the mansion towards the dark forest.

Elsie halted and hesitated for a moment, feeling the potential dangers of the forest poised to seize her soul. Beneath the cloak of the darkened night, the trees emerged as ethereal figures, their silhouettes hauntingly beautiful against the obsidian sky. The scent of pine and moss permeated the air, a fragrant mixture that seduced the senses. Meanwhile, the nocturnal chorus of animals and birds fleeing the ruling darkness, echoed through the stillness of the night. The sound painted a portrait of the forest alive with unseen mysteries.

"Do not worry," Katarina reassured, her voice a soothing balm against Elsie's mounting doubt. "Väsen do not come near the farm." Elsie harboured a profound fear of the creatures that inhabited the dark depths of the forest, avoiding it whenever possible.

"One can never be too cautious," Elsie remarked in a worried tone. "Some of them might." She glanced around with concern.

"Come on, let's hurry before darkness falls," Katarina urged, moving towards the tree. Cautiously, she broke off a branch adorned with markvastar. The sound echoed throughout the forest and resonated within her heart. "Let's return. It's nearly dinner time."

After dinner, the household prepared to go to sleep. Katarina tucked the branch between her bed covers. Her faith in its effectiveness was still wavering. Nevertheless, she clung to hope, determined not to yield to the mare's influence, willing to try almost anything for freedom. She may not be a warrior, but she would fight until the very end. Blowing out the candle, Katarina settled into bed. The night draped her in darkness, accompanied by the gentle patter of rain outside. Its fresh, moist scent permeated the room. The rhythmic sound of the rain was deeply soothing, and Katarina, still weary from the previous night, found herself struggling to stay awake. Despite her fear of surrendering to sleep's lullaby, she knew she had no alternative.

She couldn't remain awake indefinitely. Gradually, Katarina began to relax, focusing on maintaining calmness and faith in the plan's success. It had to work. With closed eyes, she breathed steadily. Before long, she drifted into sleep, surrendering her soul to another dimension.

Shrouded by the veil of night, the mare stealthily crept into Katarina's room through the keyhole. Its sinewy claws aided its descent down the door and across the floor, resembling a worm drenched in blood. Katarina jolted awake, panic coursing through her veins as she beheld the mare standing on the floor. Its bestial eyes fixed upon her with a malevolent look. With a silent scream echoing in the recesses of her mind, Katarina found herself paralyzed. Once again, she was ensnared in the mare's sinister web. She watched in silent horror as the creature prowled closer. Its eyes were ablaze with a feral hunger. Despite Katarina's attempts to rise from the bed, she found herself ensnared once more by the mare's enchantment, trapped in a state between wakefulness and slumber, lost in limbo, no longer the master of her own faith. The mare slithered onto the bed, its claws skittering across the covers. Its long hair was matted in blood and its visage obscured by a veil of tangled hair soaked in the ichor of its victims. Katarina felt a suffocating terror grip her. Unable to draw breath, she was swallowed by fear and panic. The mare exhaled heavily, its breath a tempest of foul odours that assailed the senses, suffusing the air with an unbearable stench.

Unexpectedly, the door burst open, and Ulrik strode in with a determined countenance, his gaze unwavering as it fixed upon the mare. The creature turned to face its new adversary, emitting a chilling sound as it leapt away from Katarina, now directing its attention toward Ulrik. Unsure if she was trapped in a nightmare or facing grim reality, Katarina grappled with the surreal horror unfolding before her. Ulrik remained steadfast, his eyes blazing with a feral intensity, as if on a mission to tear the mare apart limb by limb.

"Begone!" Ulrik warned with a dark voice, a thunderous decree that reverberated with an otherworldly authority, his gaze fixed on the mare. Anger exploded from his eyes. The creature responded with a hissing voice, burdened with quivers.

"This one does not belong to you! I claimed her first!" the mare spat, its words dripping with foul venom. Katarina felt her hairs stand on end as she listened to the demonic creature's voice, a dreadful, primal sound straight out of a horror tale. It was as though the creature's voice bore the weight of centuries of suffering, a proof of the darkness that dwelled within its twisted and evil form. Ulrik took a step forward, his eyes darkening and his skin turning grey. Shadows danced across his face, casting an aura of fear over his changed form. With each step forward, his presence seemed to swell, enveloping the room in an oppressive mantle of dread.

"Leave!" he commanded with decisive authority; the very air shivered with the intensity of his power. "This is not your domain. I am the ruler here." Ulrik's voice grew darker and colder, a stark reminder of the dominion he held over the realm of darkness. His voice compelled the mare to retreat a step, recognizing the strength of its enemy.

"She belongs to me," the mare persisted, its determination evident in every hissing word and animalistic gesture. "You have not claimed her, despite residing on this farm."

"She belongs to herself alone," Ulrik countered gallantly, his response infused with courage and chivalry. "Do you wish to challenge me?" he asked with confidence. "Dare you test the depths of my powers?" his voice lowered; a menacing undertone laced through his words as he addressed the mare.

"You do not adhere to the ancient agreement!" the mare warned, appalled, attempting to mask its insecurities. "The one who claims a human first is the one to whom the human belongs."

"You will not take her!" Ulrik declared, his voice coloured with burning loyalty. "I will not allow it! I will end your existence before I permit you to take her." His voice was a resolute vow to defend his one true love at any cost.

"There will be consequences," the mare's voice turned cold and icy, instilling fear in all who heard its words, slicing through the air like shards of frozen terror.

"Then let there be consequences," Ulrik stood firm, undeterred in the face of danger.

"Others will come; we will not let this transgression pass," the mare warned sternly. Its red drool dripped on the floor.

"I will await their arrival," Ulrik replied calmly. Stepping forward, he positioned himself just inches away from the mare. "Let them come, let them all come. It will make no difference; I will not yield," Ulrik asserted with a heroic voice.

"You are new," the mare observed quietly, its gaze keen and perceptive, taking in every detail with astute awareness. "I can sense it. You have not been a draugr for very long. You do not yet understand the rules. Walk away, allow me to have her, and we will not harm you," the mare scrutinized Ulrik.

"I do not fear you," Ulrik declared, meeting the mare's gaze head-on.

"Fool!" the mare exclaimed, its contemptuous tone dripping with disdain. "Many demons will come for you."

"I am prepared to face them all." Ulrik stood tall, resolute, prepared to sacrifice his life to protect Katarina. "You can bring as many as you like! I will confront them all!" His voice carried a battle cry-like intensity.

"I will return," the mare continued ominously. "This is not over yet." With those words, the mare disintegrated into a dark smog and vanished into thin air, leaving behind only the echo of the silent night. Ulrik remained standing next to Katarina's bed, turning his attention to her. She was still immobilized, ensnared in the demonic spell. Her breathing was shallow and fast.

"Do not worry," he reassured, his voice splitting the oppressive silence, a beacon of reassurance within the dark night. "It will soon be over. This will be nothing more than a dreadful nightmare, and you will awaken safe in your bed."

The next moment, as morning rapidly approached, and the rain subsided outside of her window, Katarina found herself awake. The aroma of freshly baked bread wafted delicately, gently caressing her senses and enveloping her in a warm feeling of nostalgia. She rose from her bed, her hands trembling, her mind clouded with uncertainty. It all felt distant, like a fading dream, a vivid illusion. Katarina couldn't recall anything specific from the night before, yet a peculiar sensation lingered within her core. Was the mare truly banished? Had their plan succeeded? Katarina dressed and decided to return the branch to the forest, leaving it on the cold ground. Despite her efforts to recollect what happened, the memories remained elusive, as if veiled from her consciousness. She felt a strange sense of unease settle over her, an inexplicable sensation that whispered of horrible secrets lost to the depths of forgotten dreams and nightmares. It all seemed surreal, ethereal, and inexplicable. Nevertheless, Katarina remained determined to uncover the truth. She just had to know what happened. Was memory loss a common occurrence after vanquishing a mare? As she glanced back at the mansion, she heard Elsie calling for her, breaking the silence of the serene morning.
"So, what happened?" Elsie inquired, her words tinged with excitement, eager to know what happened. A smile spread across her face. Her friend was still alive and appeared to be sane.

"I'm not sure," Katarina replied, her expression distant as she grappled with the elusive dust of memory slipping through her grasp. "I have a strange feeling." Her voice was subdued and detached.

"Strange how?" Elsie raised her eyebrows, her expression conveying surprise and curiosity.

"Something happened, but I'm uncertain what," Katarina stated, looking at Elsie.

"What do you plan to do?" Elsie followed Katarina's movements with her eyes.

"I must find a way to remember," Katarina declared. "Come on, we have a lot to do today." Together, they returned to the farm as the day began its reign.

CHAPTER 7

As night fell, casting its breath-taking magic over the land, Katarina found herself wrestling with uncertainty. Would the mare return? Would this be her last night? Would she be able to rest and sleep through the night? Fear continued to invade her mind like a ruthless enemy, dominating and twisting her thoughts. What awaited in the darkness? These questions swirled relentlessly, nourishing worry and anxiety that gnawed at her core. Exhausted from the day's events, Katarina lay down, attempting to steady her mind and relax. Before long, she succumbed to sleep.

In her dreams, Katarina stood in a vast summer field, adorned in a long, white dress. The warm breeze enveloped her, its gentle touch caressing her skin. As the sun began to descend, its golden rays painted the horizon with unearthly colours, casting a serene glow over the field. The air was filled with the seductive fragrance of flowers, teasing her senses with its inviting promise. The harmonious symphony of animal sounds and birdsong softly played in her ears. The essence of the mild summer hung in the air, calling forth a sense of tranquillity and peace.

Ulrik stood right before her. His hair flowed perfectly in sync with the gentle caress of the wind, swaying with each of its movements. His fair skin gleamed like diamonds reflecting the fading light of the sun, while his blue eyes sparkled like a lively ocean. Dressed in a long crimson coat, he seemed to dance in harmony with the wind's romantic whispers. His tall figure loomed over the fields, radiating an undeniable beauty that captivated the surroundings, drawing everything and everyone closer to his presence. Katarina detected a hint of melancholic sadness in his eyes, mixed with a loyal and sincere gaze. Surveying her surroundings, Katarina observed the magnitude of the field, stretching endlessly until meeting the distant forest and mountains.

"Where are we?" Katarina inquired gently, observing her surroundings. She found herself in a realm unknown, yet a sense of serenity enveloped her being. In her dream, Ulrik appeared transformed, radiating an aura of safety—a beacon of protection among the threat of the mare. For the first time, Katarina didn't feel the urge to retreat or avert her gaze; there was a soothing quality to his presence that beckoned her closer. A newfound curiosity ignited within her, kindling a desire to unravel the mysteries shrouding him.

"This is a field from my memory," Ulrik responded with a deep, steady voice filled with both strength and pain.

"Is this a dream?" Katarina pressed further as Ulrik took a step towards her, his presence unmistakable.

"Yes," he confirmed, his gaze proud as he stepped closer to her. "Here, the divine beauty dances across the fields."

"This place is beautiful," Katarina exclaimed. "But why are we here?". The breath-taking vista inundated her senses with a transcendent essence, leaving a hint of awe and wonder within her soul.

"This is my attempt to shield you from the mare," Ulrik explained, his voice carrying a protective undertone, indicative of his commitment to safeguarding those under his care.

"Within my creation, they cannot reach you."

"Shield me from what?" Katarina questioned, her brow furrowed with confusion as her gaze flickered between Ulrik and the ethereal landscape that surrounded them.

"The mare will return," Ulrik stated gravely, his eyes darkening with resolve. "Unfortunately, this is not over."

"Why? What does the mare want with me?" Katarina expressed, her voice trembling with fear, her pulse quickening at the thought of the vicious entity that haunted her dreams and turned them into nightmares.

"I do not know," Ulrik admitted solemnly, his expression grave, hinting at the seriousness of the matter at hand. "But I promise you, I will not let them harm you. I will do everything in my power to keep you safe. They will not have you," Ulrik swore with unwavering loyalty.

"The mare is a very dangerous creature, and you are just one man. Why would you risk your life for me?" Katarina observed the soulfulness in his eyes, already knowing the answer.

"I am not a man, not anymore," Ulrik's voice carried a weight of sorrow and lament, echoing through the quiet expanse of their dream landscape. "I would gladly risk my life to save yours. You saw me when I was a child; you were always kind to me, defending me, standing by my side. Now it is my turn to return the favour. I have witnessed much darkness and pain. If I were to perish, my ultimate act would be protecting someone precious to me—an act of kindness amidst all the dreadful deeds I have committed," haunting memories tainted his words. Within the darkness and torment that shrouded his past, fighting for Katarina would be a final act of redemption.

"What happened to you?" Katarina's voice quivered with a mixture of concern and intrigue as her eyes searched Ulrik's face for unknown answers.

"I was turned into a draugr during the war; turning a lost soul like mine was easy," Ulrik confessed as his expression turned ice cold. "I lost my soul a long time ago; the mare cannot harm me. Allow me to protect you. I would willingly jeopardize my life for the woman who always showed me kindness. There is nothing in this world I would not do for you. You were one of the few people who always cared for me while growing up. Do not weep for my soul; it is long gone," he uttered in a deep and mysterious voice.

"A draugr?" Katarina looked at Ulrik closely, studying him intensely. The coldness that had once reflected in his eyes seemed to have dissipated. As his gaze rested upon her, she sensed a genuine interest in safeguarding her well-being. Katarina recalled the shy boy with a polite manner and a kind heart, contrasting with the cold-hearted and indifferent man who returned home from the seemingly endless war. Though he had never been aggressive or malicious toward her, there had been a soulless expression in his eyes, something was taken from him during the countless battles. Now, that expression was gone, replaced by a determination to fight for what he believed in.

"What can you do?" Katarina inquired, her soul searching for reassurance within the hopelessness. "I have never heard of anyone getting rid of a mare, let alone several."

"They have not had the assistance of a draugr," Ulrik replied with a focused voice. Pain and strength radiated from his eyes, blending with devotion and fidelity.

"You have always had feelings for me," Katarina stated, gazing into his eyes.

"Yes, I will not deny that, but I have never harmed you, and I never will. I will never force you into anything against your will," his words echoed with an unrequited love. "I will remain by your side, protecting you from the demons if you allow me, and I will never do anything to cause you harm," Ulrik promised sincerely. "You have feared me since my return from the war, and I understand why; you are right to. A draugr is a dangerous creature. It was wise of you to stay away from me and avoid me, but you do not need to be afraid. I will prove my loyalty to you," he swore faithfully, loyalty shining in his eyes. Katarina knew she had no reason to fear Ulrik, but she remained uncertain, aware of the danger posed by a draugr. The wrath of the draugr cast a shadow over their conversation, a reminder of the dangers that lurked within him.

"You are still uncertain," Ulrik observed. "I understand. I'll still be here, protecting you." Suddenly, a loud blood-curdling scream pierced the air, its haunting echoes filled Katarina's heart with fear as she turned to face the horizon.

"What was that?" she asked as her heart raced with fear.

"It's the mare, attempting to breach my defences," Ulrik replied calmly, his voice becoming a steady anchor in the sea of turmoil. "Do not worry. You can rest here. I will safeguard you through the night." Though the screams were distant, they evoked fear within every fibre of Katarina's being.

Ulrik watched her with an admiring gaze. His eyes betrayed the truth within his attempt to conceal his emotions.

"Walk around here. You can stay during the day, and when dawn breaks, you will return to your body, having had a restful night's sleep," he assured her. Katarina gazed at the sky, its breath-taking colours painting the horizon with an alluring magic. She wandered the field, allowing herself to be enthralled by its haunting beauty.

In the blink of an eye, Katarina awoke in her bed. It was daytime, yet the strange feeling persisted. The sun shone brightly outside, accompanied by the lively barks of dogs, while the scent of autumn permeated the air. What really happened last night? The thoughts echoed within her head, leaving lingering questions.

CHAPTER 8

Katarina stood at the stove; the flames cast eerie shadows across the kitchen as she stirred the bubbling stew. Her hands moved slower than usual, as if they were reluctant to obey the smallest movement. Evening had descended, enveloping the skyline in darkness while the wind howled like a chorus of tormented souls. The lingering aroma of culinary delights graced the kitchen, a fragrant memory of flavours shared and savoured. The soft, ambient light pirouetted gracefully across the walls, casting delicate shadows that whispered secrets of the night.

"The strange feeling still lingers, doesn't it?" Elsie asked, casting a concerned glance at her friend.

"Yes," Katarina replied, tending to the stew.

"Well, you're still yourself, and you seem sane," Elsie attempted to sound positive, encouraging her friend. "Tomorrow, Hjördis and I will go to the village. Perhaps it would be a good idea for you to join us? We need to prepare for the feast on Saturday."

"If you need me, I will help you." Katarina responded with a smile.

"The priest will be attending the feast," Elsie continued, observing Katarina's reaction.

"I would expect nothing less; after all, he is the town priest," Katarina muttered, still focused on her cooking.

"Why must you mention the priest?" As he walked in, Ulrik's voice echoed through the room. His presence cast a sudden obscurity over the atmosphere, his footsteps unheard, masked by the encroaching night. Startled by their master's sudden presence, Elsie almost dropped her plate. She nervously glanced around, afraid to have upset the master of the house.

"Master," Elsie stammered, trying to compose herself. "You surprised me." Elsie attempted a polite smile. Ulrik inspected them both with watchful eyes.

"Dinner will be ready soon." With a wary glance, Elsie hastily left the room, leaving Katarina alone with Ulrik. Katarina remained, finishing up in the kitchen. As she met Ulrik's gaze, she noticed a subtle shift in the way he carried himself. The way he looked at her had changed. There was a newfound calmness in his eyes, a depth that seemed to pierce through the shadows that lingered in corners of the room. The sense of dread and foreboding was gone. An aura of protective resolve pierced through his gaze. The pain and hatred toward the world seemed to have subsided, replaced by an urge of protective strength and determination.

"How are you today?" Ulrik inquired, his voice hoarse. His dark hair cast shadows in the dimming light of the reigning night. Katarina hesitated. Ulrik rarely initiated conversation with her while she was working.

"I am fine, thank you," Katarina responded lightly. There was an ineffable grace in Ulrik's demeanour, a magnetic aura that eased her discomfort in his presence, drawing her closer with an unspoken invitation.

"No trouble sleeping?" Ulrik queried with a penetrating and unwavering gaze. Mystery echoed with his words.

"What?" Katarina asked, uncertain. She had no recollection of confiding in him about the mare. "No, I sleep just fine. Is there anything I can do for you, master?"

Her gaze lingered on Ulrik, probing the depths of his eyes for any hint of his intentions. In those dark orbs, she detected a complex amalgamation of emotions. Pain intertwined with an unyielding strength; a simmering violence tempered by unwavering loyalty. It was as if he harboured a fierce willpower, forged in the crucible of suffering. Tenacious to reshape the world according to his will, dispelling all anger and hatred.

"You seem different, master," Katarina continued, still captivated by his presence, ensnared by his character.

"How so?" Ulrik's voice remained eerily composed as he maintained eye contact with Katarina.

"Before, I saw a man filled with contempt for the world; now, I see a man with a mission, a man with purpose," Katarina paused, afraid she had overstepped her boundaries. Ulrik remained fixated on her, casting a spell of both discomfort and inexplicable security, causing her to feel both uneasy and secure.

"How observant of you," Ulrik replied, his mood unchanged.

"Well, I should continue working," Katarina forced a smile as she sidestepped Ulrik, unsure of how to handle the situation. As she passed him, her hand accidentally brushed against his. A wave of energy surged through Katarina, causing her to freeze momentarily and leaving her breathless.
Suddenly, she remembered everything. Her mind was flooded with memories of the harrowing encounters with the mare, each nightmarish detail etched into her consciousness. When she turned towards Ulrik, she offered him a respectful smile, careful not to reveal that she recalled the events of the previous nights. Ulrik maintained his gaze on her, his emotions veiled

behind his stern facade, betraying no hint of emotions.

Quickly, Katarina moved into the adjacent room. Upon reaching the table, she had to sit down, panting heavily. It was all too much to process. The feelings overwhelmed her. Panic claimed her mind. The mare was still present. The demon still lingered around the farm, intent on claiming her soul. However, now it had become a battle between a mare and a draugr. And Ulrik, yes, Ulrik was her sworn protector. He was determined to defeat the mare and free her soul from its repulsive grip, relentless in its pursuit of her soul. The feelings came over her like a tsunami. She felt lost in hopelessness, grappling with the unsettling questions that plagued her mind. She had hoped the mare was gone, but there was an ongoing struggle, growing more intense by the moment.

Why did the mare desire her soul? What drove the demon's inexorable pursuit? And could Ulrik succeed in safeguarding her? Katarina had harboured suspicions that he had been transformed into a draugr during the war, she wasn't surprised to discover the truth. Strangely, fear did not invade her mind. She knew well the peril posed by draugrs, yet within the depths of her being, she couldn't muster fear toward Ulrik. An enigmatic sense of security had woven its way into her consciousness, defying rational explanation. Katarina possessed a remarkably open mind, shunning judgment and refusing to diminish her regard for Ulrik simply because of his nature as a draugr. He had extended a gesture of aid in a manner befitting a hero, and she couldn't help but be swept away by a flutter of flattery.

Ulrik was her best hope for survival. Who else could assist her? Katarina decided to consult the priest on Saturday, seeking guidance on banishing the demon. As Ulrik departed the kitchen and entered the adjoining room, Katarina watched him, moved by his resolute dedication to shield her. She had long sensed Ulrik's affection for her, and now he stood ready to defend her safety against a demonic enemy.

"Stop sitting there contemplating!" Elsie's words snapped Karin back to reality. "There are still many tasks to complete before dinner," she added, inspecting Katarina with searching eyes. Katarina approached Elsie.

"Yes, of course. I'll help you," she replied.

CHAPTER 9

Bathed in the luminous glow of the moon, the bright light spilled over the land, casting enchanting shadows across the landscape. In the distance, the haunting melody of wolves echoed through the night. Their mournful cries spread a vow of longing and mystery.
Ulrik's brooding presence loomed over the kitchen table as Elsie and Katarina diligently attended to the after-dinner cleanup. His gaze was distant, lost in the labyrinthine corridors of his own complicated thoughts. An enigmatic aura enveloped him like a mask of shadows.

"You can go. I can manage here," Katarina said, addressing Elsie.

"Are you sure?" Elsie asked, while casting a concerned glance at Katarina.

"Yes, there isn't much left. It won't take me long to finish up," Katarina offered reassurance to Elsie, encouraging her to proceed and have dinner. She briefly observed Ulrik, who appeared lost in his own thoughts.

As the night approached and darkness swallowed the surroundings, the room was illuminated by candlelight. October was on the horizon, with autumn's cold and merciless winds already making their presence known. Summer had been spent preparing for the inevitable arrival of autumn and winter. The harsh, unforgiving winters could mean the difference between survival and ruin for the household. The eerie howling winds outside served as a warning of the bitter night ahead, a harsh reminder that those who were ill-prepared would face grave consequences.

Katarina pondered how to initiate a conversation. She felt hesitant in the presence of Ulrik. With insecurity gnawing at her insides, Katarina grappled with the uncomfortable silence that pervaded the room. The weight of unspoken words flowed rhythmically in the air. Ulrik continued to stare into space, seemingly lost in his own world, his gaze fixed upon some unseen horizon. In the suffocating stillness of the night, the boundaries between reality and nightmare blurred, casting a curtain of uncertainty over the promised nightfall.

"I remember," she said, her gaze fixed on Ulrik, her words infused with gratitude.

"You remember what?" Ulrik inquired, his voice echoed with an unnerving calmness, devoid of any traceable emotion.

"Everything," Katarina replied, stumbling over her words like a startled deer. Ulrik remained motionless, his gaze fixed on the darkness beyond the candlelight. Suddenly, with a fluid grace that disguised his towering stature, he rose from his chair. Striding towards Katarina with purposeful steps, Ulrik came to a halt right in front of her. His presence seemed to command time itself, catching Katarina off guard. She knew he was a dangerous man, yet she couldn't bring herself to fear him anymore. Instead, a curious blend of apprehension and fascination coursed through her veins. After years of working for Ulrik, if he had intended harm, he could have inflicted it easily. An intense longing emanated from his eyes, his desire to protect her rooted in their childhood acquaintance. Over time, his feelings had evolved into something deeper, and Katarina could sense the passion coursing through his veins.

"Tell me, what do you mean by 'everything'?" Ulrik's voice was a low, rumbling growl. His scent and energy made her nervous.

"The mare is trying to claim my soul, and you are trying to protect me from its foul grip," Katarina almost whispered the words, her voice hoarse. She met Ulrik's gaze, his eyes delving into the depths of her soul. Katarina could clearly see the reflection of a man willing to slay all demons and devils to rescue her from harm. He was a man haunted by the phantoms of his past yet fuelled by an unquenchable flame that burned within the hollows of his tormented soul. A man who would not bend or yield, invigorated by a fire that would consume all who dared to threaten those he held dear.

"You should not be able to remember that." Ulrik said in a low voice, his words slithered through the air like a serpent's hiss.

"I do remember," Katarina continued, her lips caressing the words. Each syllable was filled with an eerie certainty. He had given her hope in a dangerous situation.

"Are you not afraid?" Ulrik asked, curiosity etched in the darkness dancing across his face.

"The mare is a very dangerous creature," Katarina began, her blond hair catching the light from the flickering candles. "I do fear for my life and the state of my soul."

"I mean, are you not afraid of me?" Ulrik asked, lingering on his words as he took a step closer, standing just centimetres from Katarina. She could feel his presence, every ounce of his character leaning in towards her. Everything that was dangerous about him, and everything that was good about him, echoed within her soul. There was something truly perilous about him, the abilities of a demon combined with the past of a vicious monster. But there was also something safe about him, the memory of an innocent boy with hopeful dreams and a kind heart, blended with the ideals and morals of a noble man. Cruel and gruesome experiences had extinguished the light in his once hopeful eyes. Was Ulrik capable of killing her and every villager with his powers? Without a doubt. Had he committed heinous crimes during the war? Undoubtedly. He wore the suffering of his victims like a mask of shame. Ulrik was no longer human. He was a draugr, a demonic creature swallowed by darkness. It would be foolish not to fear him. And yet, Katarina felt no fear when looking into his eyes. Not anymore. She was confident that he would not wield his abilities to cause her harm or injury. The fear she once felt had transformed into a calm assurance. Now it seemed like Ulrik held the key to her salvation. Despite the darkness that cloaked him, she sensed a kindred spirit, a beacon of light among the endless darkness.

"No," Katarina uttered, surprising Ulrik, who found contentment within her words.

"Why not? You know my true nature; you know that I am a draugr. What is a draugr?" Ulrik's inquiry lingered in the air.

"A demon," Katarina replied in a low voice, each syllable heavy with the weight of forbidden knowledge. "A demon with powers capable of transforming into a vicious monster that devours humans. A monster with the strength, speed, and abilities of twenty men. A demon weakened by the sun, dwelling in the dark, often feeding on humans and capable of turning whomever it desires into one of its own. A creature of the night that prowls the shadows in search of prey " Katarina whispered, her response was scarcely more than a breath.

"And still, you do not fear me?" Ulrik paused, his question swayed in the air, a fragile thread poised on the precipice of oblivion.

"You said that you wanted to protect me, you said that you would fight for me," Katarina said honestly. "I trust that you will not harm me, even though you easily could."

"No, I will not harm you," Ulrik affirmed, sitting down on a chair, running his hand through his dark hair.

"Is it true that you do not age? Is it true that you are frozen in time?" Katarina asked, observing his movements.

"It is true that we are frozen in time but being a draugr is a curse!" Ulrik looked at the candle, the light dancing across his face. "To become what I am, one must lose one's soul. Only those with dark pasts, whose souls are already tainted by the blood of the many, can be turned into a draugr. But I suspect that my soul was already gone long before turning into this creature."

"I am sorry all of this happened to you," Katarina said compassionately. "You were such a nice and kind-hearted boy. Since you are willing to help me and sacrifice your life to keep the mare from me, then there is still good within you." Ulrik smiled upon hearing Katarina's words.

"Thank you." Ulrik's words, though tinged with sadness, carried a note of gratitude that echoed through the room like a whispered prayer. "For seeing the man beneath the monster, for offering me a glimpse of redemption among the dark shadows. But that boy is long gone. I can only repent by giving my utmost effort to save you." Ulrik looked at Katarina with faithful eyes, his longing echoed within his words.

"Is there any way to vanquish the mare? Nothing seems to help. You are my last hope. I do not know what more I can do. It all seems very uncertain." Katarina's voice faltered, still fearful of the dreadful creature.

"All demons can be vanquished," Ulrik replied, trying to grant her hope. "I do not know how; I have only been a draugr for a couple of years. The mare that is haunting you is indeed very old, it has been alive for centuries," Ulrik pondered with a concerned look, his voice carrying the weight of determination.

"I tried moving it to the forest with a markvast, but it was all in vain." Katarina's words were tinted with desperation, they soared in the air like a mournful dirge.

"No, I must kill it to stop it from coming back. This is my domain; this is my home. I am the demon dwelling here, and I will kill them all for trespassing!" Ulrik's voice was dripping with a possessive rage, he quickly calmed himself again. "Do not worry, I will find a way. I will not let them touch you; I will not harm you. You are safe with me," he said, looking at Katarina with a determined and steadfast look.

"Is it true what the mare said? Did she claim me, and now I belong to her?" Katarina tried to hide the fear in her voice as she spoke. "I do not know the law of demons. I do not know what to expect and what I should do. I am afraid that I will make the situation worse."

"This is my home; the mare should never have entered in the first place," Ulrik's voice carried a quiet resolve that brooked no dissent.

"Are there written rules between demons?" Katarina asked, her question cut through the tension like a knife through flesh. "The mare seemed sure of her cause. It seemed like she was willing to go to great lengths to claim my sanity."

"No, there are no written rules," Ulrik's response was immediate, his tone tainted with bitterness. "There are some unwritten. Demons should never invade each other's space, and demons should not take each other's humans. In this fight, no one is right, and no one is wrong. Other demons will not take sides in this battle. I will do everything in my power to solve this. Let me worry about the mare." Ulrik said with a secure voice.

"But the mare said that there would be others, that she would bring more like her," Katarina sounded confused, infected with fear.

"That might be true," Ulrik's voice, though calm, carried a note of grim foreboding. "Although the mare hunts alone, they can summon others to aid them. They can attack together; she will bring her sisters next time."

"And what about a draugr? Is there anyone that can help you?" Katarina seemed concerned.

"There is," Ulrik admitted, his gaze fixed upon the flickering candlelight, "but they will not. Since we both are breaking the agreement between demons, I must fight alone. I will find a way, I promise that no harm will come to you. I will protect you, come what may. The mare's claws may be sharp, her hunger insatiable, but I will not allow her to lay a finger upon you." Ulrik reassured Katarina with a faithful heart. "The mare can only harm you in your sleep, I will be watching over you every night," his eyes filled with loyalty and love.

"I am glad that you are here and that you are willing to help me. I am grateful that you are willing to sacrifice so much for my safety. Can the mare harm you?" Katarina asked worriedly. She harboured gratitude for Ulrik's assistance, yet she couldn't bear the thought of him being harmed or injured while defending her.

"Do not worry, the mare will not hurt you anymore. I will make sure of that," Ulrik swore loyally, his voice carrying a note of solemn reassurance.

"I was not worried for my sake," Katarina looked at Ulrik. His eyes had an intense look.

"Do not weep for me," he instructed, the burdens laying heavily upon his spirit. "My soul has already left my body. My fate was sealed long ago, my life ended the day I entered the war. I am already gone; I am already lost," there was a painful melancholic tone in his voice. Katarina could feel Ulrik's pain radiating from his eyes into her soul. She could taste the bittersweet sense from his memories.

"You are not lost," Katarina approached Ulrik, hopefulness echoing within her words, wrapping comfort around him "There is always hope; nothing is truly lost. There is always a way, even if it seems impossible." Ulrik lifted his gaze and met her inspirational words. Katarina perceived a resilient spirit within him, weary from numerous battles waged. A man compelled to confront the excruciating agony and the weight of loss unaided.

"It is getting late," Ulrik continued, uncomfortable by the situation, his words marking the end of their conversation. "Finish your work here and go to bed. I will be watching over you."

Ulrik rose from his seat and silently departed the room, overwhelmed by the intense positive energy. Katarina followed in his wake, the weight of his presence lingering like a ghost in the stillness of the night. The shadows seemed to fear his presence.

The candles stopped flickering when Ulrik left the room; the light remained with a serene energy. Outside, the autumn wind increased its intense howling. Darkness lay as a heavy mantle over the farm, and the orange leaves danced with the rhythm of the night. The smell from the cooked dinner still lingered in the room. Katarina finished cleaning, still uncertain about what the night ahead would bring.

CHAPTER 10

The night draped itself over the enchanting landscape. A veil of darkness cloaked the world in a supernatural stillness. The rain, a relentless torrent that battered against the windowpanes, had finally ceased, leaving behind a persistent sense of discomfort.

Katarina sat on her bed, the only source of light emanating from a single candle that flickered and danced with each passing breath of wind. The shadows stretched tall on the wall, imbuing the air with a sense of mystery.

The atmosphere was dry, and Katarina's throat felt parched. Outside, the night enfolded the land, asserting its dominance. Despite the darkness, the room carried a pleasant, sweet scent.

Ulrik entered, clad in a long, black coat that billowed behind him like the wings of a mythical raven, his dark hair flowing effortlessly with his graceful movements. He exuded strength and self-confidence, his presence both commanding and graceful. His blue eyes appeared almost grey in the dim light. As he crossed the threshold, the candle flickered, displeased with his presence. There was something undeniably ominous about his presence, a sense of power and danger that mastered the air like a storm cloud on the horizon. Katarina could not tear her gaze away from him, captivated by the dark allure of his presence.

"Why does the candle flicker when you enter the room?" Katarina asked, her gaze fixed on Ulrik's ethereal presence. His complexion was as pale as moonlight, almost resembling porcelain. His beauty was undeniable, and Katarina found herself admiring his celestial allure. She saw him in a new light, recognizing a loyal man who would stand by her side through the night and shield her from harm.

"It loathes me," Ulrik replied calmly, his eyes fixed on the flickering light. "The light senses my darkness and seeks to extinguish it. The only thing that can end the life of a draugr is fire, fire reminds us that we are not invincible," he added dramatically.

"What will happen tonight?" Katarina's voice quivered as she dared to ask the question that had been haunting her thoughts. "I do fear the mare. It holds immense power over me. When it is near, I cannot move, I am no longer in control. I lose myself in its presence."

"The mare will return tonight, and this time I suspect it'll bring reinforcements." Ulrik's voice was grave, his eyes dark with foreboding. The weight of his words permeated the air with a stifling aura, suffocating Katarina with a sense of an impending peril. "But do not fear, I am here with you" His voice, a soothing melody, sought to pacify her tumultuous soul.

"Why do you suspect that she will return?" Katarina's voice betrayed her worry as her heart pounded rapidly within her chest.

"Because the mare attempted to claim you before when I was near, and she failed. She knows I am much stronger than her, and she knows this is my domain. She cannot win without assistance from her kin," Ulrik explained, his eyes filled with focus, ready for another battle.

"Have you battled other demons before?" Katarina asked, uncertain if she truly wanted to know the answer. "Do you have any idea how to defeat her?"

"I've seen many things in battle, I fought numerous monsters and demons, not all of whom were human. In war, it's often difficult to recognise who is the hero and who is the villain. Most are merely monsters." Ulrik responded, his voice burdened with sadness and pain. Beneath the surface lay memories that could neither be healed nor ignored. "I will fight with everything I am to vanquish her. I have never surrendered in a battle before, and I will not begin now. How is your daughter? Have you heard anything from her?" Ulrik inquired, trying to calm Katarina's mind.

"She is happy, and she is having a good life," Katarina said, her lips curved in a gentle arc of warmth and affection. For a moment, she seemed to forget the troubles haunting her mind. "I received a letter a couple of days ago. She just gave birth to her third child. It pains me that she lives so far away in a foreign country, but I know that she has everything that she needs. Knowing that she is happy and has a safe life brings me joy." Katarina's words flowed with the essence of love.

"I am glad to hear that." Ulrik responded calmly.

"I cannot imagine what you've been through," Katarina said sympathetically, her mind returning to the present.

"Do not feel bad for me, my mission now is to protect you. My story is not unique." Ulrik continued with a solemn expression, his voice hollow, devoid of emotion. "Humans fear hell, but I have walked through hell. Whatever awaits me in the afterlife cannot be worse than the hell I've experienced. I've already dined with the devil and felt his minions feast at my core!" Ulrik concluded, his voice echoing with emptiness.

"When were you turned?" Katarina inquired; her voice filled with a desire to understand the enigma that surrounded Ulrik. "I only know that you have changed when you returned home. There is so much about you I do not know."

"It was a year before I returned home," Ulrik's voice was low, haunted by the weight of his vivid memories. "We were surrounded, outnumbered, my brothers fell one by one. Death watched over us like a shadow, but I was not afraid. I was ready to unleash my fury upon our enemies. I was ready to embrace death with open arms and leave behind the pain of life." A cold indifference crept into Ulrik's eyes, a darkness that mirrored the horrors of war.

"I fought with everything I had, fueled by anger and rage, until only the enemy general remained. I was determined to show the enemies the strength of our people. There was something in the general's brutal gaze, something otherworldly. As he approached me, his form twisted and contorted into something monstrous, something dreadful beyond this world." A cold-hearted indifference gleamed in Ulrik's eyes as he recounted the memory. "Slowly, he approached me with a smile on his lips. His skin darkened, his eyes turned purple, and his form transformed into that of a creature from a gruesome fairy tale. I knew what he was; I recognized the stories from my past. But the draugr did not devour me, nor did he feast on my flesh. Instead, he made me his companion, he saw my tainted soul, whose path had been painted with blood and pain. He relished the chaos and violence within me, and I did not care. Together we continued, hiding within the chaos of war, where a monster can feast on flesh and blood unnoticed. Destruction and chaos were all around us, surrounding us. Together, we eliminated anyone who dared to threaten us or stood in our way. War is a breeding ground for monsters, a playground for the damned." Ulrik confessed, his words stained with shame and regret as his soul grappled with the gravity of his past mistakes.

"Why did you return? What happened to him, your fellow demon?" Katarina asked, her curiosity piqued. The flickering candlelight seemed to dance more wildly as she uttered the word "demon."

"We simply parted ways," Ulrik replied. "I left to forge my own path. Returning home, I sought peace for the remainder of my days. I do not know where he is or if our paths will ever cross again. It does not matter, a draugr lives a solitary existence. Most of us spend our time in our demonic form. It is rare for a draugr to masquerade in a human guise. He was different, always choosing to hide in plain sight. I suspect he still does. As for myself, I do the same, despite the suspicions that may linger among the people in this county. The priest, supposed guardian of light and peace, turns a blind eye to my true nature." A glimmer of defiance flashed in Ulrik's eyes, a silent challenge to the world that judged him. "I care not for their judgments, for I am beyond the realm of mortal condemnation."

"Can you die?" Katarina inquired; the candlelight cast ghostly shadows across her face. "It seems like väsen are particularly difficult to kill. A lot of times, it requires special items or artifacts to extinguish their lives."

"Yes, a lot of väsen can be really difficult to kill. And me, I am already dead," Ulrik affirmed, his words infecting the air, an irrefutable reminder of his cursed existence. "Only the dead can become a draugr. We roam, bringing death, misery, and destruction. A draugr seldom remains in one place for long, at least not above ground. We may rest for centuries in tombs."

"But you have lived here for years, you are different from that description." Katarina observed, her eyes searching Ulrik's haunted gaze.

"Yes, I do reside here. I have witnessed enough bloodshed and death. Though I cannot perish, I am not invincible. Only fire can consume me. The sun weakens us, it leaves us vulnerable, which is why we shun the daylight," Ulrik clarified.

"Are vampires real?" Katarina queried, her curiosity extending to other supernatural beings she had heard of. She had heard the whispers, the tales of other creatures that prowled the night, thirsty for the lifeblood of mortals. "I remember the stories you sisters told me when they were younger, about the eternal demons who drank blood. But they were somewhat different from draugrs."

"Yes, they are real," Ulrik's reply was a sombre echo, his voice steeped in ancient knowledge. "Although they are more fragile than a draugr. The sun will kill them, silver will weaken them, and a stake through their heart will vanquish them. They drink human blood to remain strong. A draugr feeds on humans when or if they choose, but we do not weaken without human flesh. We could eat ordinary food if we wished. You see me eating your food every night. A vampire appears to grow stronger with age, but a draugr's strength remains constant. The church can use blessings and prayers to bind vampires, but there is nothing a priest, nun, or monk could do to stop me. No artifact, symbol, or object can halt me. To vanquish a draugr, one must catch them and burn them. However, vampires and draugrs tend to avoid each other, making confrontation unnecessary." Ulrik's eyes gleamed with a cold intensity as he spoke, his gaze pierced through the darkness like fragments of ice.

"You are an extraordinary creature," Katarina breathed, her voice infused with a mixture of fear and admiration. She knew she should be repulsed, but the allure of darkness was compelling.

"That is one way of looking at it," Though the shadows still clung to his features, Ulrik's lips curled into a smile. "I possess many powers," his voice a low rumble that seemed to reverberate through the room. "But my strength is a curse, a reminder of the darkness that dwells within me."

"Yet you choose to remain here, to resist the urges that haunt you," Katarina observed, her voice filled with wonder. She was surprised at how much his dark side spoke to her, pulling her towards his arms.

"I never thirsted for blood, I only lost myself in the chaos of war, consumed by the violence and the madness, caught up in the gruesome nature of war," Ulrik said, haunted by his memories.

"Have you taken any innocent lives?" Katarina built up the courage to ask, afraid of the answer. She dreaded the truth that lurked in the shadows of Ulrik's past. Ulrik's gaze turned inward, his eyes flickering with the memories of a thousand battles fought and lost. Katarina could reconcile that he had taken lives for survival and vengeance, but the notion of extinguishing the lives of the innocent struck a profoundly discordant chord within her. Ulrik paused, examining the approaching disappointment in her eyes.

"Who is innocent?" he mused, his voice a low rumble that seemed to emanate from the very depths of the abyss. "The war is filled with peasant boys who cry out for their mother. They did not choose to go to war, they had no choice but to take up arms. They do not know how to kill or defend themselves. In war, no one and everyone is innocent. There is no clear line, everything mixes in a blissful shade of grey. But I am guessing that you want to know if I killed or tortured any women or children, and the answer is no, I did not. But I killed and slaughtered any man or boy I met on the battlefield, anyone who threatened my existence. Did I harm and kill people who were forced to take up arms during battle? Yes, all the time. I could have let them live, but I did not. Evil men use excuses to justify their violent behaviour in war. I know that I am a monster; I am a draugr, and I accept it. So should you. I am a demon; I am not good. I know that you want to believe that I am, and I am grateful that you, after everything that happened, still believe that there is goodness within me." Ulrik's words touched Katarina's ears as the candle flickered wildly.

"You are here with me," Katarina's voice was barely audible above the thrum of her own heartbeat. "A cruel man would not care if I died." Katarina looked at Ulrik. There was something seductive about his tormented soul, her mind was a whirlpool of conflicting emotions.

"I will watch over you for the rest of your remaining life," Ulrik said, looking at Katarina with faithful eyes, his voice echoed in the dimly lit room, "Try to go to sleep, you are safe here. I need no sleep; I do not get tired. A draugr can choose to rest, but we do not need sleep to remain strong," he uttered valiantly. Katarina nodded; her limbs felt heavy with exhaustion. With Ulrik by her side, she felt a strange sense of calm descend upon her, like the stillness before a storm. Despite the horrors that lurked beyond the threshold of her consciousness, she knew that she was safe in his presence. As Ulrik approached the candle, a chill swept through the room, extinguishing the flame with a final hiss.

CHAPTER 11

Under the reign of darkness, Ulrik remained a faithful warrior, his form melded seamlessly with the shadows that danced along the walls. Despite the darkness that overpowered the room, Ulrik's senses heightened in the night's obscurity. Silence permeated the space, only Katarina's rhythmic breathing caressed his ears. The wind had quelled its fury, leaving a tranquil atmosphere in its wake. With several hours remaining until dawn, Ulrik maintained his watchful eye over Katarina as she slumbered peacefully in her bed. Swathed in layers of blankets, she appeared as an elegant figure cocooned in the protective haven of her bed. Ulrik's gaze lingered upon her form, his heart overflowing with a mixture of adoration and longing.

Watching over Katarina brought a sense of tranquillity to Ulrik. She was the sole object of his affection, the only woman he had ever loved. For as long as he could remember, Katarina had been a beacon of light in his tumultuous existence. The memory of her mild spirit offered solace in the darkest hours. Katarina remained a flickering flame of hope among the chaos and carnage that threatened to engulf his soul within the cruelties of war. Her image had remained etched in his mind like a guiding star, even within the havoc of war. In the stillness of night, when the stench of blood and death hung heavy in the air, he clung to the memory of her, a fragile thread linking him to a world that seemed a lifetime away.

Now, with her slumbering form before him, Ulrik found himself consumed by a sense of purpose unlike any he had known before. From his earliest days, he had held her in high regard, inspired by her kindness from her teenage years. Despite their age gap, Ulrik was bewitched by her presence, entranced by the purity that radiated from her very being.

Upon his return home, learning of Katarina's employment search, he had implored his father to rehire her. Now, he had the opportunity to safeguard the love of his life, to transcend the role of a battle-scarred veteran ensnared by his own traumas.

In his youth, Ulrik harboured dreams of Katarina becoming his wife. Her goodness and beauty captivated him, and he admired her diligent work ethic and unwavering moral compass. Even as he ventured off to war, Ulrik held onto the hope of one day reuniting with Katarina, but such fantasies were nothing but fleeting illusions in the night, drowned out by the relentless march of time and the weight of his own sins. In the end, all that remained were the shattered fragments of a dream that had never truly been his to claim. The war ravaged Ulrik's soul, leaving him a mere shadow upon his return. Though he never outwardly expressed it, he found comfort in Katarina's continued presence on the farm, offering him glimpses of a past filled with hope.

Deep down, Ulrik knew Katarina could never reciprocate his feelings, he feared that she would never love him in return. Perhaps if he had returned from war less broken, if he hadn't been transformed into a draugr, he might have mustered the courage to propose to her. But such notions were but fleeting dreams, overshadowed by the harsh realities of his existence. As a draugr, he was cursed to traverse the murky depths of the underworld, his soul tethered to the mortal realm by bonds forged in blood and sorrow.

The world was far from the idyllic illusion, and happiness eluded Ulrik's grasp. As a draugr, peril lurked at every turn, and the mare's relentless pursuit of Katarina likely stemmed from him. While attacks by mares on humans were not uncommon occurrences, the intensity of this situation hinted at deeper motives. The mere thought of the mare laying hands on Katarina ignited a primal fury within him, a seething tempest of rage and vengeance.

Ulrik's mind spiralled into madness, consumed by thoughts of retribution. The demon must answer for her transgressions. He envisioned himself rending the mare asunder, tearing limb from limb until her wretched form lay broken and lifeless at his feet, watching her life force ebb away. He would rip off the demon's ugly head and watch life slowly drain the creature's body. But such fantasies were mere illusions, he did not know how to vanquish this unholy abomination.

Suddenly, the shadows on the wall began to stir, chanting in a creepy hymn that filled the room with a scent of smouldering ash. From beneath the door crept the mare, contorting her form to slither into the room. Her body changed and shifted, morphing into a monstrous visage that bore no resemblance to anything of this world. Her eyes burned in orange as she emitted a menacing growl upon sighting Ulrik seated nearby. As darkness coiled around him like a serpent, the room itself seemed to pulse with malevolent energy.

"This is my domain," Ulrik declared calmly, exuding confidence. His voice sliced through the air like a sharpened blade, cold and resolute. "Leave now, and never return," he added, his gaze piercing the mare with fierce determination, poised to obliterate his enemy to safeguard his beloved.

"She is mine!" the mare growled, her voice was dripping with venomous hostility, every syllable filled with lethal intent.

"You cannot have her!" Ulrik's response thundered,

reverberating off the walls of the room with the force of a vengeful God. Beneath the door, three more mares slithered into the room, transforming into a menacing pack of demon dogs. Their eyes gleamed with feral hunger, their saliva coated the floor, and their foul odour overwhelmed the senses.

"We have come to claim what is ours," the mare declared, her voice haunting in the darkness.

"She is not yours to take!" Ulrik asserted firmly, his will unyielding in the face of malevolent forces.

"He promised that we could have her!" the mare spat angrily, tossing her head back and forth in frustration.

"What do you mean?" Ulrik inquired, though a part of him already anticipated the answer.

"By Vasilij," the mare revealed. Ulrik paused, his heart sank as realization dawned, his worst fears confirmed in the shadowed depths of the night.

"Why would he promise you that?" Ulrik pressed, a desperate plea for answers in a world steeped in darkness and betrayal.

"He said that if we found the draugr Ulrik, then we could claim the woman he loves, that she would belong to us. He gave her to us! We had an agreement," the mare screamed, her claws scraping against the floor. Ulrik's insides turned cold. So, the time had come. Vasilij was looking for him, dispatching other demons to do his bidding.

Vasilij, the architect of his damnation, had always despised Ulrik's desire for a chance at redemption. He preferred to keep his creation by his side, painting the world in pain, blood, and suffering. The draugr master reveled in the chaos, agony, and torment of the world.

But Ulrik had defied him, forsaking his demonic heritage to seek peace in his homeland. Now, Vasilij's dark presence had found him, reaching out from the shadows to reclaim his wayward disciple. He was planning to use Ulrik's affection for Katarina against him. By eliminating her, Vasilij hoped to make Ulrik more amenable to re-joining his crusades of death. With the aid of the mare, Vasilij's plan was now set in motion. Ulrik's maker was coming for him and there was nothing he could do to stop it.

"She is not his to promise," Ulrik asserted, a defiant declaration. He strove to maintain his composure.

"Then we must take her with violence!" the mare threatened, bracing for an attack, preparing to unleash its unholy fury.

"Do you really think that you can stop me?" Ulrik challenged, facing the mare without fear.

With a growl, the mare lunged forward, accompanied by her accomplices. Ulrik swiftly rose to his feet. Adrenaline coursing through his veins like liquid fire as he braced himself for the onslaught. He moved with demonic speed to position himself in front of the bed, determined to protect Katarina. While the mares were slower, their vicious nature rendered them formidable adversaries, and Ulrik had no idea how to kill them. The mares attacked in synchronized harmony, their claws scraping against the ground as they advanced, their movements a twisted ballet of savagery. Each step brought them closer to their prey. The scent of burnt ash grew stronger in the room, their orange eyes blazing like scornful suns in the dark of night, their long fur resembling an ocean of darkness.

The first mare aimed for Ulrik's throat while two others targeted his arms. The fourth went for his thigh, her jaws gaping wide like the maw of some infernal beast. Their gnashing fangs sought to tear his flesh. Ulrik maneuvered smoothly, fending off the intruders with precision, evading their savage incursion. His movements became a macabre dance among the infernal chaos. Ulrik struck back, each blow met with a dreadful symphony of screams echoing off the walls. Yet, with each assault, the mares grew more ferocious and frenzied. Their primal instincts drove them to ever greater heights of blood lust, their brown fangs dripped with drool, their strength escalating with every attack. Ulrik fought valiantly to defend himself and to shield Katarina. She remained oblivious to the chaos unfolding beside her as she slept soundly in her bed.

The brown-flecked fangs of the mares gleamed with viscous saliva, their sinewy forms writhing in a grotesque parody of combat. Despite Ulrik's efforts, one mare managed to sink her teeth into his arm, while another seized the opportunity to strike again, biting him in his stomach. The remaining two mares continued their assault, their teeth sinking into his calf and thigh. Agony surged through Ulrik's body as the beasts tore into his flesh, causing him to bleed profusely, his purple blood staining the floor. In a moment of revulsion, the mares recoiled and screamed, hurling themselves backwards in disgust.

"The taste! The taste! The awful taste!" she complained. Ulrik broke the neck of one mare and ripped the heart out of another. He dispatched the mares, stepping back cautiously, preparing to defend himself again. The wounded mares growled and screamed, while their unharmed kin came to their rescue. One mare picked up the mare with the broken neck, and the other retrieved the heart and torn apart body of her fallen comrade.

"This is not the end, draugr!" the mare growled, revealing her decaying teeth. Their canine forms turned into a blend of hound and man before swiftly retreating into the shadows on the wall. Ulrik remained still, breathing heavily as blood poured from his wounds. The blood cascaded down his body in relentless torrents, each droplet a frigid reminder of the world's cruel indifference. It soaked through his clothes, penetrating to the very marrow of his bones, as if seeking to extinguish the flickering flame of his existence.

Ulrik settled back into the chair, knowing his injuries would soon heal, and so would the harm he inflicted upon the mares; they would only be temporarily thwarted. They were caught in a never-ending cycle of violence and suffering, locked in an eternal struggle against an implacable foe. He could engage in an endless battle with the mares each night for eternity. Unable to use fire and with no knowledge of how to vanquish them, every night could become a skirmish of mutual harm. However, more pressing matters demanded his attention. Vasilij was searching for him.

When Ulrik had parted ways with Vasilij, he seized the opportunity to vanish and escape his maker's grasp. Vasilij had descended into delirium, consumed by his own cruelty. His maker's madness knew no bounds, the insatiable thirst for power drove him to ever greater depths of depravity. Vasilij's tyranny reigned supreme, his cruelty unleashed upon countless unsuspecting souls.

Ulrik was weary of death and violence, yearning only to return home and live in peace, far from the world. Yet, Vasilij insisted that a draugr must wander, never settling, traveling from grave to grave, death to death. Most draugrs roamed, taking refuge in graveyards, resting in tombs during the day, sometimes plundering from the deceased. They emanated the stench of death and decay, shunning human contact, hunting at night, and moving between graveyards. A draugr could sleep for decades in a tomb, silently guarding treasures, or other valuables. Once, Vasilij and Ulrik encountered a draugr who had inhabited a tomb for four centuries. It was common for draugrs to become fixated on the contents of a grave, some never departed and, transformed into restless spirits eternally protecting their burial place.

Vasilij differed from other draugrs. He refrained from sleeping in tombs, knowing it would taint his body with stench and decay, rendering him a grotesque creature. And Vasilij worshiped beauty. He revelled in manipulating humans, using the living for shelter during the day. His hunger for power, for dominion over life and death, was insatiable.

At night, Vasilij ruthlessly slaughtered anyone he disliked. Impressed by Ulrik's courage, rage, and viciousness, Vasilij was reluctant to lose his companion. He yearned to reclaim his protégé, to resume their grim march of death. Ulrik preferred the tranquillity of his life in the mansion. Vasilij considered such a life a waste, believing that adhering to mortal norms was beneath them. Ulrik knew Vasilij would not easily relent. His maker always obtained his desires and sought to bend the world to his will. Vasilij would stop at nothing to bring Ulrik back.

Ulrik understood he had no choice but to comply with Vasilij once more or confront him in battle and defeat him. Could he extinguish the life of such a formidable creature as Vasilij? Could he truly stand against the ancient might of his ruthless maker?

Vasilij was born among the flames of war, his legacy drenched in centuries of bloodshed. For five hundred years, he had existed as a draugr, his human life marked by renown as a warrior. He too, had been transformed within the chaos of battle. His maker lay in eternal rest among the unmarked graves of soldiers who had perished in Vasilij's homeland, forever preserving their enigmatic tales and treasures.

Vasilij used to assert that a draugr's duty was to watch over graves or slay humans—there was no middle ground, no alternative path. Now, he would endeavour to force Ulrik onto the same course. Ulrik must steel himself; there was no telling whether Vasilij would appear tomorrow or in years. And when he did, he would have the mares and other demons at his side.

Ulrik sank back into the chair, knowing there was at least an hour before Katarina awoke to begin her day. He must remain resolute, finding a solution to the approaching threat. As the wounds of battle slowly mended, Ulrik steeled himself for the storm that awaited, knowing that when Vasilij returned, he would bring with him an army of darkness. Silently, he pondered, while the night's howls echoed in the background.

CHAPTER 12

Katarina awoke with a sense of tranquillity enveloping her, a profound peace settled within. The night had granted her respite, free from the clutches of haunting nightmares, undisturbed by any inner turmoil. She felt rejuvenated. No nightmares had plagued her dreams, and her body felt invigorated. Outside, darkness still prevailed. Autumn maintained its firm grasp on the land as the leaves gracefully descended from the trees to the ground. Their vibrant hues of yellow, orange, and red adorned the treetops, creating an enchanting myriad of life. The chill of impending winter had begun to permeate the air, a prelude to the harsh season ahead. Glancing around the room, Katarina observed Ulrik seated in a chair beside the bed with a contemplative expression across his face. His eyes reflected untold secrets as they held a sombre intensity. Katarina offered him a grateful smile, which faltered as she noticed that Ulrik was cloaked in what appeared to be dried blood. Her relief soon turned to dread as she noticed the purple stains that marred his once pristine form.

"Is that blood?" she asked, her voice filled with concern, as she rose from the bed and approached Ulrik to inspect his wounds, her worry evident in her actions.

"You don't have to worry," Ulrik replied reassuringly. "I heal quickly, and I cannot bleed to death," he added, his voice adopting a calming tone, seeking to reassure those present and alleviate any tensions or anxieties.

"What happened?" Katarina's eyes widened in horror as she surveyed the wounds that tainted Ulrik's flesh, the evidence of a gruesome battle etched upon his skin. "Let me help you," she said, her heart filled with compassion, as she reached out towards Ulrik, her touch hesitant yet filled with genuine compassion. Initially, he withdrew, uncertain of her intentions. Sensing his discomfort, Katarina paused, not wanting to intrude. Slowly, she touched his neck, revealing gruesome scars from the mare's fangs. As Katarina's hand gently brushed against his neck, tracing the jagged scars left by the mare's fangs, a sense of calm washed over Ulrik.

"It will heal in a couple of hours," Ulrik reassured, aiming to alleviate Katarina's concerns, his voice a mere whisper against the backdrop of darkness. As she traced his inflicted scars, she found Ulrik's skin soft and smooth, making it difficult to believe he was anything but human. Despite the horrors that plagued his existence, there was an undeniable humanity to him, a reminder of the man he once was. Meeting her gaze, Ulrik appreciated her gentle and caring touch, a silent expression of gratitude. Though he remained composed, controlling his emotions and actions, he allowed himself to find solace in her tender touch. For him, it was worth enduring the pain, suffering, and battles of the world just to experience her gentle caress. His heart had always belonged to her, and he vowed to remain by her side until the end of her days.

In the depths of Ulrik's gaze, Katarina glimpsed a love that transcended time and tragedy, a silent oath to stand by her side until the end of days. "Do you self-heal?" Katarina inquired, her hands gently gliding down his face touching his hair.

"Yes, and so does the mare. They will return, perhaps not tonight, but in the days to come," Ulrik responded, his thoughts drifting away, his gaze fixed on some unseen horizon beyond the confines of the room.

"They did this to you," Katarina stated, her concern evident as she remained close to Ulrik. Despite the circumstances, she found safety in his presence, though it troubled her deeply that he had been injured while protecting her. Yet, she couldn't help but admire his unwavering devotion and willingness to sacrifice for her safety.

"There were four of them this time, just as I had anticipated. I must prepare myself for yet another, greater battle," Ulrik explained, his mind momentarily transported to a distant place as his eyes struggled to conceal his emotions.

"Will the mare bring more companions?" Katarina asked, her mind struggling to grasp the magnitude of the danger that surrounded them.

"No, but other creatures and demons will come," Ulrik replied tersely, fully aware of the approaching dangers.

"Why?" Katarina's confusion was palpable. "Why are they after me?" she asked as a lock of her blond hair fell across her face.

"They are not after you, they go after you because of me," Ulrik's words were a solemn admission of guilt, his heart heavy with the burden of responsibility. "I am sorry that you have been drawn into this. It is my fault that you are in danger. If I believed it would help, I would send you away, but the mare already knows your scent. They would pursue you; they would find you," he lamented, sorrow evident in his voice. "Your best chance is with me, and I will not abandon you."

"I trust you," Katarina replied, gazing at Ulrik. His eyes radiated strength and resilience, a reflection of all the battles he had fought, trials he had endured, and all challenges he had overcome. Tenderly, she reached for Ulrik's hand, but he pulled away abruptly and rose from the chair, his gaze clouded with a sense of mystery.

"I must prepare for the night ahead," he said, his words faltering as he glanced at Katarina, his silhouette a stark contrast against the shadows that danced along the walls. "We need to find a way to defeat the mare." With that, Ulrik hastily left the room, not looking back. Katarina watched his departure, feeling a twinge of confusion. Despite Ulrik's evident affection for her, he had fled like a startled deer. She had seen the depths of his affection for her, yet there was an unspoken distance between them, a barrier that he seemed unwilling to breach. Despite his bravery in battle, Ulrik remained haunted by his own inner turmoil, unable to confront the emotions that threatened to consume him.

With each passing moment, Katarina felt herself drawn closer to Ulrik, captivated by the enigmatic allure of his courage and sacrifice. There was something compelling about his bravery and his willingness to fight for her. In the darkness of the night, among the impending threat of demonic forces, she found herself inexorably bound to him, their fates intertwined in a hazardous dance of survival and salvation.

Katarina carried on with her day, the weight of imminent danger nestled within her heart, casting a shadow over even the simplest of tasks. She joined Elsie and the other members of the household as they worked diligently to tend to the farm and estate. Though she worked assiduously, her mind was consumed by thoughts of Ulrik and the malevolent mare that lurked in the shadows. Determined to find a way to defeat the mare, she struggled with where to begin.

In the quiet of the evening, Katarina made her way to the farm to make an offering to the tomte. Entering the stables, she carefully placed the stew she had prepared for the creature. The barn lay bathed in a soft, sublime glow. Mysterious shadows danced among the golden hue. The scent of hay wafted gently, a sweet embrace that lingered in the air. Stillness filled the heart. The cautious rustle of animals moving about filled the ears.

Suddenly, a peculiar sound from the hay caught her attention. A small figure emerged, adorned with an oversized hat. The entity, clad in grey with a prominent nose and long brown hair, stood no taller than half a meter, peered up at Katarina with a gaze that bore into her soul. Though no larger than a small dog, the creature exuded an aura of ancient wisdom and otherworldly power.

Caught off guard by the unexpected encounter, Katarina took a hesitant step backward. Her heart pounded in her chest. She had heard tales of the tomte, the elusive guardian of the land who seldom revealed itself to mortals. It was said that the tomte possessed the ability to move unseen among the shadows, its presence known only to the animals and creatures of the night.

"There is trouble on this farm," the tomte spoke with a surprisingly deep voice for its small stature.

"Trouble?" Katarina questioned, still taken aback by the unexpected conversation.

"Yes, trouble!" the tomte reiterated with a hiss. "I have sensed the presence of the mare, along with other lurking demons," it continued with disdain. "It's bad enough that a draugr claims ownership of this place, though I do respect him. He maintains order and does not harm the animals or other creatures residing here," the tomte added. "You wish to rid the farm of the mare, do you not?" it inquired, its lips caressing the words with a hint of vengeance.

"Yes," Katarina replied, beginning to see the potential in this unexpected alliance. "But I have no idea how. I've attempted to lure her into the forest with a branch."

"That will not suffice," the tomte stated harshly, its tone tinged with impatience. "Do you think a mere branch will capture and banish her forever? You must stab her with a dagger crafted from an ash tree," it warned. "Aim for the head! Only a weapon forged from the ash tree will be effective if you want to vanquish her for good," the tomte insisted, its expression grave.

"Very well, then we shall fashion a dagger," Katarina agreed, smiling politely at the tomte. She gathered her resolve and tried to stay focused within this unusual situation. "Thank you for your help; I am truly grateful ". Katarina understood that it was best to show respect to the ancient guardians that shared her home.

"It must be you who slays the mare," the tomte continued sternly. "The mare has come for you. No mortal, nor undead, nor even the divine can rid you of this curse. Only you hold the key to your salvation. Only you possess the power to end her existence," it emphasized. Katarina stood silently, contemplating the tomte's words.

"The mare is a powerful creature," Katarina admitted, her voice trembling with fear. "She paralyzes me with her abilities. When she draws near, I am rendered defenceless. How can I defend myself against such a creature?"

"You don't have to face her alone; you only need to destroy her alone," the tomte replied, her gaze mysterious. Within the tomte's eyes shimmered the light of an ancient being, weary of the endless battles of the world. "I have observed you," the tomte continued. "You have always shown kindness to me and the animals. You diligently care for everything in this household. I do not wish for your soul and sanity to be claimed by the mare. I have dwelled here for many generations, witnessing the passage of time, and you have always prioritized the well-being of the guardian väsen. For that, I am grateful, and that is why I am aiding you."

"Thank you," Katarina's heart swelled with gratitude at the tomte's words, genuine appreciation coursing through her veins like a balm to her fractured spirit. "Thank you for tending to the animals and for safeguarding our home. We deeply appreciate your presence, and we hope you will remain here for generations to come."

"Be cautious," the tomte advised. "There are numerous creatures lurking in the darkness, demons and other väsen. All of them pose great danger." The tomte's visage softened, a fleeting glimpse of empathy flickering in its ancient eyes. Katarina nodded in acknowledgment of the tomte's warning.

"I will be careful. Have a pleasant evening," Katarina uttered softly before departing the barn, her words swallowed by the encroaching night that covered the land. Darkness draped its heavy presence over the world, nearly engulfing everything in obscurity. Katarina knew that enormous ash trees stood just beside their home, near the edge of the forest. If she hurried, she could make it back before darkness completely swallowed the surroundings.

The forest loomed ominously, already immersed in pitch blackness. Strange sounds emanated from its perilous depths, whispers of nature, echoes of ancient creatures, and the stealthy movements of nocturnal animals on the prowl. The delicate fragrance of moss and old trees enveloped the senses, painting the air with the verdant essence of the forest. Pausing for a moment, Katarina sensed the forest's inherent danger, especially at night. But the prospect of obtaining a sizable ash branch, potentially resolving everything by tomorrow, compelled her to take the risk.

With determination, Katarina continued advancing toward the forest. In the distance, the majestic silhouettes of ancient ash trees stood like guardians on the edge of the forest. Their mighty branches reached out like claws grasping for the heavens.

Her eyes quickly adjusted to the absence of light and her senses heightened in anticipation. Rhythmically, her heart raced in sync with the adrenaline coursing through her veins. The scent of moss and decaying leaves filled her nostrils as she cautiously navigated the forest's edge in search of the familiar ash tree. Every rustle and crackle seemed to echo around her, the forest alive with unseen movements. Damp air enveloped her, seeping into her skin. Finally, Katarina reached the forest glade, where the ashes' hues pierced the darkness, offering a glimmer of hope in the night. Hastening to the nearest tree, Katarina located a sturdy branch within her reach and snapped it off. The sharp sound reverberated in her ears as she took a deep breath, preparing herself to return home. Suddenly, a creature materialized before her. Katarina's heart skipped a beat, terror gripped her core in a suffocating grip, fear infected her essence as she struggled to breathe.

The creature drew closer, its looming shadow overwhelmed her senses. In an instant, everything plunged into darkness, and Katarina lost consciousness, consumed by the relentless touch of the unknown.

CHAPTER 13

Seated at the worn wooden table, Ulrik prepared to partake in the evening meal. The day had dragged on endlessly. Despite his efforts scouring through his books, he found no solutions. Lost in the labyrinthine depths of ancient tomes and arcane texts. Ulrik sought in vain for a ray of hope among the consuming shadows. The puzzles he tried to solve remained elusive, their whispered truths slipped through his fingers.

Ulrik understood there was little he could do to prepare himself for the impending battle against Vasilij. While Ulrik had been resting for the past half decade, Vasilij had traversed the blood-soaked landscapes of Europe, murdering and torturing, leaving death and destruction in his wake. His maker possessed both viciousness and cunning; darkness followed him wherever he went.

In a few days, the priest would join his household for dinner. Though the priest's outward support offered a semblance of protection, Ulrik could not shake the feeling that his true nature had been revealed before the eyes of the church. There seemed to be more to the priest than met the eye, he held secrets darker than the shadows that danced upon the moss-covered gravestones.

Ulrik hadn't stepped foot in the church since returning home, citing the loss of his faith during battle as an excuse. In truth, Ulrik knew the guardian of the cemetery surrounding the church—a particularly powerful kyrkogrim that prowled the churchyard's perimeter. Once a living creature buried alive beneath the consecrated ground, its tortured spirit now roamed the cemetery as a powerful sentinel charged with the protection of the sacred domain. This guardian spirit would never allow him to cross the border onto holy ground. The beast had formed an unbreakable bound to the church and the graveyard.

Ulrik had heard stories of this kyrkogrim since childhood, a notorious creature that protected the dead, an ancient warden fending off the encroachment of malevolent entities, demons, and malicious spirits like himself. Once a humble rooster in life, the kyrkogrim had transcended mortality, its corporeal form twisted into a grotesque apparition of its former self. Its claws and beak were lethal enough to rend a human in two, and its monstrous size dwarfed that of an ordinary man. Each night, it would patrol its territory, attacking any who disturbed the peace within its domain.
 Within the confines of the churchyard, the kyrkogrim reigned supreme, its power eclipsing even that of the dreaded draugr. It would not hesitate to attack even a human to safeguard its domain, relentless in its defence of the consecrated ground.

Ulrik understood the kyrkogrim's capability to inflict serious harm upon him, leaving him vulnerable while he healed. The creature, fuelled by a primal instinct to safeguard its domain, would stop at nothing to destroy any intruders. The kyrkogrim, a creature born of ancient rites and forgotten curses, was a fearsome foe. It would be foolish not to fear its powers.

Conversely, the kyrkogrim recognized that a draugr could only be defeated by fire. If a draugr dared to enter a grave within the kyrkogrim's territory, the guardian spirit would incinerate the grave with the draugr trapped inside, preventing its escape. In the battle between the undead and the vigorous guardian, only one would emerge victorious. The priest routinely left several torches at the cemetery, anticipating the kyrkogrim's need to combat adversaries during the night. Should a draugr attempt to rest within these graves, Ulrik knew it would be their final night. Fire posed no threat to the kyrkogrim, it could neither vanquish nor harm the indomitable guardian.

Elsie entered the room with a look of distress etched upon her face, though she managed a polite smile and nod towards Ulrik. He observed her closely; it was evident that something was amiss. Her eyes betrayed the turmoil that churned beneath the surface. Her fingers nervously touched her clothing, betraying her unease.

"Where is Katarina?" Ulrik inquired with a curt tone. Elsie appeared troubled, though she tried to conceal her stress. Her gaze flickered anxiously.

"She will be with us in just a moment," Elsie replied, forcing a smile, her words strained and unconvincing. A bitter tang of anxiety hung thick in the air. Ulrik could discern her falsehood; he could practically smell it on Elsie. Her heightened adrenaline and cortisol levels, dilated pupils, and nervous gestures betrayed her attempt at composure.

"You're not telling the truth," Ulrik stated calmly, his voice carrying authoritative strength. "You don't have to be afraid," he reassured, though Elsie still appeared fearful. Her eyes wavered, her words stumbling from her dry mouth.

"She's gone. We don't know where she is. We've searched everywhere." Elsie's facade crumbled further, her mask slipping away to reveal the raw fear that niggled at her insides.

"What do you mean, gone?" Ulrik's tone grew darker, a deep concern gnawing at him. "How long has she been missing?" Ulrik's blood ran cold at the revelation, a sense of dread coiled in the pit of his stomach.

"She was supposed to meet Astrid an hour ago to prepare dinner, but she never arrived. Hans searched everywhere, but we found no trace of her," Elsie stammered, her worry soared in the air.

Ulrik rose from his chair, stepping outside without hesitation, a silent determination etched into the lines of his face. The evening enveloped him in darkness, punctuated by distant howls of wolves. His senses, honed by years of vigilance, swept the estate with an otherworldly precision. The night whispered secrets to him, but there was no trace of Vasilij's presence, no lingering scent to betray the presence of another draugr or demonic entity. The only thing Ulrik could sense, and smell was Katarina's mild scent.

With uncanny speed, Ulrik traversed the grounds, his eyes searching for any sign, any clue that might lead him to Katarina's whereabouts.

"She went to the forest," a voice intoned from behind him. The dark sound pierced the stillness like an arrow searching for its target. Ulrik turned to find the tomte regarding him with a mixture of disdain and begrudging respect. "Normally, I detest draugrs!" the tomte spat on the ground with disgust, her voice tinged with scorn. "But you, you do not move from grave to grave. You keep to yourself here, and you take care of the farm to my satisfaction. I have nothing against you, and I happen to like that human. She always brings me gifts, food, and offerings. She is kind to everyone," the tomte added with admiration. Her long hair touched the ground when she moved her head. The tomte's clear blue eyes were small and almond-shaped, all the mysteries of the world were carried within them.

"Why did she go to the forest?" Ulrik inquired, his voice betrayed a flicker of concern.

"I presume she was going to collect a branch from an ash tree to kill the mare. I hate those damned creatures!" the tomte growled angrily. "They often attack horses and disturb the peace at the stable. One less mare in the world is a good thing," she remarked, while touching her thick hair. "I saw a light moving around in the forest just after she left. And I did not see her return," a glimmer of sadness flew across the tomte's features while speaking the words.

"A light?" Ulrik repeated, his gaze piercing the veil of darkness while glancing toward the forest.

"I am afraid the lyktgubbe took her," the tomte lamented with a sad tone. "Most likely, she is lost now."

"A lyktgubbe?" Ulrik pondered. "This close to the edge of the forest?" He knew the nature of the lyktgubbe, a dark spirit that lured victims with its mesmerizing light, leading them astray until they were lost and defenceless against the creatures of the night and forest. Once alive, a lyktgubbe was now cursed to roam the lands seeking treasures it once held dear.

"The chances of finding her are slim," the tomte continued with a hopeless expression. "But I hope you do, draugr. And I hope she kills the mare."

"I will kill the mare!" Ulrik vowed passionately, determination burnt bright in his eyes.

"You cannot kill the mare," the tomte muttered, annoyed. Only the one possessed by the mare can kill it," the tomte warned.

"How can one kill a mare?" Ulrik pleaded, desperate to save his beloved.

"All väsen can be killed by a dagger made from the ash tree. The tree gives life, and it takes it away, it is connected to the life-force of all living beings. One must stab the creature in the head, not the heart. Many väsen do not have hearts," the tomte explained cryptically. Dark shadows fell delicately across her face.

"I understand," Ulrik nodded.

"Good luck! You're going to need it," the tomte vanished into the night with a whisper of wind, leaving behind a trail of uncertainties. Ulrik set off into the forest, his heart felt heavy with the weight of unpredictability, in search of Katarina.

CHAPTER 14

Katarina stirred from sleep, her body was sore and chilled to the bone, every muscle protested tumultuously against movement. The darkness of the forest surrounded her. A dull ache pulsed through her head, clouding her thoughts in a haze of confusion. Disorientation reigned in her mind. In the dimness, she could discern only a solitary light in the distance.

Beside the lantern sat a tall, slender man. His face bore a bluish hue, wrinkled, and distorted. Only one eye gleamed from the depths of its socket, the other lost to darkness, swallowed by the abyss of time. His grey, unkempt hair and antiquated attire suggested he belonged to another era; a relic of a world long forgotten. The boots that adorned his feet bore the marks of countless miles, hinted at a past as a soldier.

Katarina surmised he was a lyktgubbe, a spirit lost to battle long ago, now condemned to wander the forest in search of his lost possessions. Typically, lyktgubbar did not harm humans; they merely led them astray, ensuring they never found their way back home, forever lost and doomed in the woods. Yet somehow, she now found herself in his custody.

Though his appearance was ghastly, twisted by the ravages of time and decay, there was a haunting sadness in his gaze. A heartfelt sorrow seemed to reside in the depths of his soul.

The lyktgubbe regarded Katarina through the glow of his lantern. Moss sprouted from his eyebrows, and his lips were encrusted with dirt. Despite his lost demeanour, there was no hint of aggression or malice in his character. As his gaze pierced the darkness, the light from his lantern cast flickering shadows across his weathered face. His eye held a glimmer of longing, a silent plea lost in the void.

"Where am I?" Katarina inquired, her voice steady as she attempted to orient herself in the darkness, where savage shadows danced and flickered around them.

"This is where I died," the lyktgubbe began, casting his gaze around. A haunting melody of sorrow and regret echoed within his voice. His eyes wandered over the desolate landscape, where the twisted forms of ancient trees reached out grasping for the sky. Katarina sensed a profound sadness emanating from the depths of his being, a silent lament for a life lost to the passage of time. "I wanted to show you this place. All my comrades and brothers lie buried in unmarked graves in this forest, forgotten, erased by the hands of history, their memories swallowed by the unforgiving earth." He added, his tone respectful yet pained as he touched the ground.

"I am sorry that you died here. I am sorry for what happened to you and your fellow soldiers," Katarina expressed compassionately, extending sympathy towards the creature. Her heart ached with empathy for the tormented spirit before her, trapped in an eternal cycle of longing and despair.

"I have missed you," the lyktgubbe continued, his warmth and love evident as he looked at Katarina. The sounds of animals moving in the distance punctuated their conversation, a reminder of the lurking dangers in the forest.

"Who am I to you?" Katarina asked, attempting to refocus the conversation as the lyktgubbe seemed lost in his own illusions.

"Why, you are my wife, of course," the lyktgubbe replied, his voice a ghostly echo of love and longing. He attempted to smile, though his expression remained frozen in time. "How silly of you!" he remarked before his tone shifted to one of concern. His features distorted into a grotesque semblance of a smile. "Karin, why were you wandering alone in the forest? Do you not know the dangers that lurk here? Fortunately, I found you before the others. Who knows what could have happened? I dare not think of it. Having lost my comrades, I cannot bear to lose you." His voice carried a heart-breaking tone, wavered with emotion.

"I was going to take a branch from the ash tree," Katarina explained. "The mare has been haunting me." At the mention of the mare, a flicker of recognition passed over the lyktgubbe's features. "I need a dagger made from an ash tree to kill her," Katarina continued. The lyktgubbe listened intently to her words, then rose and approached the nearby trees. With great strength, he severed a branch from an ash tree, then returned to Katarina's side. From his coat, the lyktgubbe extracted a knife and began fashioning a dagger from the branch.

"I have failed you in so many ways," the lyktgubbe confessed with sadness in his voice. "There is nothing I can do to redeem myself, but I will help you with the mare. I am sorry, my love. I am sorry for everything."

"What are you looking for here?" Katarina inquired. "What treasures are you guarding? Why have you not found peace?"

"I am part of this place; I must guard these lands," the lyktgubbe intoned while looking up into the starlit sky. His voice was a solemn echo in the stillness of the forest. "I must ensure that no one defiles the secrets buried here. You must return to our home, Karin, and know that I am sorry, please know that I do regret it all," deep regret laced the lyktgubbe's voice.

"I forgive you, but there is nothing to forgive," Katarina responded warmly. "You can let go of your guilt towards me. I do not hold it against you," she assured him with a gentle voice.

"Thank you for helping me with the mare." A smile illuminated the lyktgubbe's face, cracking his dry skin when hearing Katarina's words.

"Oh, Karin, thank you," the lyktgubbe expressed with relief. A serene aura enveloped his body, softening his once cold and foreign presence. As he gazed into the darkness, happiness seemed to grace his features. His eye appeared less stern and tormented. "I am glad I have had you in my life. I am sorry that I never said that to you before," he whispered as his voice faded into the night.

"I always knew," Katarina replied calmly. She sought to grant his spirit peace, to aid him in crossing over and breaking free from the curse of eternal torment. Katarina believed that everyone deserved peace in the afterlife, regardless of the sins committed in this life. Some souls were just lost, in need of compassion. "You can let go; you can rest now. It is okay," she reassured him with a gentle and caring voice.

"No, not yet," the lyktgubbe persisted. "Go to sleep. I will watch over you during the night. My lantern will keep the mare away; she will not dare come near me!" There was strength in the lyktgubbe's voice. "Tomorrow, you can return to the farm," he added in a resolute tone. With each passing moment, the lyktgubbe seemed to grow more distant, his spirit preparing to depart this world and find peace in the realm beyond.

Katarina smiled and laid down. She had no choice but to stay; she did not know where she was, it would be unwise to wander off alone in the pitch-dark forest where väsen and animals hunted in the mysterious night. Uncertain if she could trust the lyktgubbe, she reasoned that she would be safer with him, given her lack of direction. Katarina attempted to rest, but the cacophony of the forest overwhelmed her senses in a numbing grip. She knew that more vicious creatures lurked in the deep, dark forest. Many of them were hostile to intruders in the night.

Throughout the night, the lyktgubbe remained seated, his gaze vigilantly fixed on the lantern, a beacon in the oppressive gloom. Nearby, Katarina heard animals and creatures moving in the dark, most wise enough to fear the lyktgubbe's presence. However, Katarina struggled to sleep, uncertain if the lyktgubbe would honour his promise or vanish, leaving her alone in the dark.

Morning eventually arrived, and as light permeated the forest, Katarina saw that the lyktgubbe had become one with the forest. He had transformed into a rotten tree, covered in bark and moss. Beside him, the lantern still burned with a lively strength. Katarina retrieved the lantern, and the dagger gifted by the lyktgubbe. It was autumn; the trees were ablaze with bright red, orange, and yellow hues, the ground glowed with their vibrant colours, its spirited tones shaded with a haunting beauty. The wind whisked the falling leaves in a melancholic dance, their rhythmic rustling brought a sense of peace to Katarina. Examining her surroundings, she attempted to ascertain her location in the boundless forest, where she seldom ventured far from her berry and mushroom trails.

In the sinister silence of the forest, a sudden disruption shattered the tranquillity. The sound clawed its way into Katarina's consciousness with a wild force. She swiftly turned around, only to find a Jötunn standing before her, a colossal figure cloaked in primal fury. Katarina's blood froze, and her heart skipped a beat out of fear as she beheld the towering giant, his form eclipsing the surrounding forest. The Jötunn stared at her with angry eyes. With every step, the earth trembled beneath his massive size. Long blond hair framed his face, and sapphire blue eyes glared menacingly. In his hands, he held a giant axe, its gleaming edge poised to rend flesh from bone. With a deafening roar, he unleashed a primal scream.

With fear coursing through her body, Katarina fled in panic, her senses heightened as she fought to save her life. She understood the toll for trespassing into Jötunn land, whether intentional or inadvertent: death. Brutal death. They hated humans and showed no mercy towards intruders. Though the Jötunn's strides were strong and mighty, his lumbering gait struggled to match Katarina's desperate pace. She ran as fast as she could, desperate to avoid certain death. Through tangled undergrowth and twisting branches, Katarina raced, her lungs burnt with exertion. She dared not glance back; the Jötunn haunted her every step. In the realm of the Jötunn, danger prowled at every turn, and those who trespassed upon their domain did so at the risk of their own lives.

Jötnar dwelled outside human society, preferring the company of their own kind. Some believed them to be related to the ancient Gods, inhabiting their own realm beyond the confines of the human world. While some possessed the ability to traverse between realms, others remained bound to the earthly plane. Aside from their imposing size, Jötnar bore a striking resemblance to humans.

Katarina ran with all her might, her destination uncertain, driven only by the need to escape and survive. Only one thought existed in her mind; Do not stop. Each step she took was a struggle, her heart was pounding mercilessly in her chest and her lungs were boiling in panic. The forest blurred into a chaotic frenzy of shadows and whispers as she raced onward. Encouraging herself to run faster with every stride, Katarina pressed on, oblivious to whether she was running toward or away from danger, her sole focus on evading capture.

Behind her, the Jötunn unleashed furious, monstrous sounds, the ground trembling beneath his powerful strides. His monstrous bellowing echoed through the forest. In her haste, Katarina's foot became ensnared in roots, causing her to stumble and fall onto the leaf-covered ground.

She turned around to face the Jötunn, who had raised his axe to strike. Katarina's pulse thundered in her ears as she braced herself for the impending blow, her breath was caught in the grip of terror. Death was near. The end had come.

In an instant, the sound of steel clashing against steel echoed through the air, shattering the stillness. Katarina looked up to see Ulrik standing before her, wielding his sword. With fluid movements, he deflected the Jötunn's attacks, catching the giant creature off guard. The Jötunn stumbled, momentarily losing his balance. The giant halted his assault, lowering his axe as he regarded Ulrik with astonishment, stunned by the unforeseen resistance. Katarina was still in shock. Her heart raced wildly within her chest as Ulrik stood protectively in front of her, sword raised, prepared to face the Jötunn should he attack again.

"You are trespassing! This is our land! We protect this part of the forest. Humans are not allowed here. All they bring is destruction. I have the authority to end your lives! It is an ancient agreement." The Jötunn warned. "What are you?" the Jötunn's gravelly voice rumbled through the air, heavy with a mixture of curiosity and suspicion. "You appear human, yet you possess strength greater than a Jötunn. You do not smell human, you must be some kind of väsen," the creature mused, searching for answers. His eyes gleamed with an otherworldly light.

"We will leave your territory," Ulrik stated confidently, his gaze remained steady, his expression calm but resolute. "We have no desire to intrude."

"I did not know," Katarina interjected, forcing herself to speak. "I did not realize this was Jötunn land. We apologize and will depart." She said remorsefully. The Jötunn continued to regard Ulrik intently, intrigued by his new opponent.

"Will you allow us to leave?" Ulrik inquired, meeting the Jötunn's gaze. "We do not wish to cause any trouble. We respect the ancient agreement and acknowledge the significance of the work of your people."

"We do not look kindly upon those who trespass our borders. All enemies must die. I must protect these lands and my kinsmen," the Jötunn replied, his displeasure evident in his tone. "I am hesitant to engage in combat with an unknown adversary, especially when you are willing to depart," he added, his words laced with caution. The wind brushed against the Jötunn's hair, as if in sync with his rhythm, lending the creature an almost mystical air. "You must be some kind of rå," the Jötunn concluded, likening Ulrik to the skogsrå and bergsrå.

"I am not," Ulrik affirmed, extending a hand to help Katarina rise from the forest floor. "Are you alright?" he inquired softly; his concern evident in the gentle touch of his hand upon her shoulder.

"We understand that you want to safeguard your land and your family. I did not mean to be disrespectful." Katarina addressed the Jötunn.

"If you leave now, and promise never to return, then I will let you go. But only for this time. I will murder you, should you return again." The Jötunn's eyes shone with strength. "Before you depart, please enlighten me as to your nature," the Jötunn requested, his gaze probing. "I am greatly intrigued."

"I am a draugr," Ulrik declared, meeting the Jötunn's gaze with unwavering certainty. "We will leave now and swear never to return. "

"A draugr resides in graveyards, not among humans. We do not have any agreements with your kind!" The Jötunn's brow furrowed in disbelief, his features contorting with a mixture of scepticism and suspicion. "You do not reek of decay."

"Nevertheless, I am a draugr, and I do live among humans," Ulrik asserted, the certainty in his words leaving no room for doubt.

"You are out in the daylight," the Jötunn continued, his voice as dark as the endless night. The wind and sun accentuate the strands of his hair.

"Daylight weakens me and my abilities; it does not kill me,"

Ulrik clarified, putting his arm around Katarina. "We will leave now. Thank you for allowing us to pass through." Ulrik nodded towards the Jötunn, who remained standing firm as Katarina and Ulrik departed. The lingering gaze of the Jötunn followed them, his curiosity unsated and his suspicions left unspoken as the intruders vanished into the shadows of the forest.

As they ventured forth, Ulrik maintained a vigilant watch over their surroundings. His senses were attuned to the subtle whispers of danger that lurked within the depths of the woodland realm. Katarina felt a surge of relief within Ulrik's protective presence, his crimson coat a vivid contrast against the backdrop of autumnal hues that painted the forest in shades of crimson and gold. His hair, woven from the deepest night, danced with the gilded rays of sunlight, each strand a masterpiece of shadow and radiance.

"How did you find me?" her words borne on a gentle breeze that stirred the leaves above them. Katarina felt the reassuring weight of Ulrik's arm around her waist, leaving her feeling safe and secure. Ulrik had saved her from certain death, coming to her rescue.

"I searched for you the entire night. We are far from home," Ulrik replied, keeping his eyes on the forest. "I looked for you all night and finally caught your scent. What happened?" he asked, concern evident in his voice.

"I met the lyktgubbe; he brought me here," Katarina explained.

"How did you get rid of him? How did you outsmart him?" Ulrik inquired. "Most cannot escape his deception."

"I helped him find peace," Katarina replied, looking at Ulrik, drawn to his chivalry. The dangers of the forest seemed distant when he was near. "After the night, the lyktgubbe was gone, and the Jötunn began to hunt me. I'm grateful you arrived when you did. I would have been dead if you had come later." Katarina put her arm on Ulrik's back. Feeling her touch, he paused for a second.

"We cannot linger here," Ulrik said as he picked up the pace. "We must leave their land." He uttered as he led them through the forest, away from Jötunn territory.

CHAPTER 15

Ulrik sat by the fire, his gaze ensnared by the mesmerizing war of flames, each flickering a fleeting tale whispered by the ancient spirits of fire and ember. The flames crackled and hissed, their untamed dance casting haunting shapes upon the walls, each twist and turn a menacing apparition reaching out with malevolent intent. Katarina observed him from afar, her gaze drawn inexorably to the enigmatic figure by the fire. Elsie's voice broke through the ominous silence.

"Are you okay?" she asked, her tone laced with concern as she approached Katarina.

"Yes, Ulrik saved me," Katarina replied, her voice barely above a whisper as she continued to study Ulrik's features, each line and contour etched with an air of enigmatic allure. This mystical man now consumed her thoughts.

"I'll go to bed now," Elsie continued. "We have a lot of preparations for tomorrow. Everyone else has already gone to sleep. The priest will arrive at six. I'll wake up earlier tomorrow. Will you be alright? You were gone the entire night. I was afraid some creature had taken you. I feared you might have died." Concern and fear for her beloved friend echoed in Elsie's words.

"I'm fine," Katarina reassured. A faint smile danced upon her lips, a feeble attempt to mask the unease that gnawed at her core.

"And how about you? Are you okay?" she reciprocated.

"I'm fine. I was just worried. I don't know what Ulrik is, but he's never harmed any of us, even though he exudes a powerful and unsettling energy that gives me the creeps," Elsie said, shivering as she spoke.

"I'll finish up here, then I'll go to bed," Katarina nodded towards Elsie. "Thank you for caring, thank you for telling Ulrik that I was missing," she expressed with gratitude.

"Just be careful," Elsie cautioned, her voice a light echo in the darkness as she departed, leaving Katarina alone with the enigmatic being who had emerged from the shadows to save her. Katarina continued to watch Ulrik, knowing he likely heard their conversation and felt her gaze upon him. Slowly, she approached him, moving with the grace of a fox in the forest. Ulrik remained seated, his gaze fixed on the flames, seeking answers in the unpredictable night.

"The flames behave differently whenever you're near them," Katarina remarked as she stopped next to Ulrik. He briefly glanced at her.

"They know my weakness. It angers them," Ulrik replied. "You should go to bed. It's been a long night and day for you," he continued. "Keep the dagger nearby. I'll wake you up when everything is ready and safe for you to kill the mare. We can get rid of it tonight," he added with a focused expression, his eyes ablaze with determination.

"I don't want to go to sleep, not yet," Katarina said softly, almost whispering. She felt a tremor of uncertainty coursing through her veins, unsure of how to navigate the labyrinth of emotions that swirled within her. "Thank you for saving me," she continued, her hand tentatively reaching out to touch Ulrik's arm, her fingers trembling with a mixture of fear and desire. But before she could make contact, Ulrik swiftly withdrew, his eyes betraying a flicker of apprehension that lingered beneath the surface of his stoic expression.

"You owe me nothing," Ulrik said firmly, keeping her from touching him. "You don't have to offer me your body to show gratitude. I will continue protecting you and ask for nothing in return," he spoke seriously and sincerely. "I would never take advantage of you or use my powers against you. I have no interest in being physically intimate with a woman who doesn't crave my touch," Ulrik affirmed as he met Katarina's searching eyes. "If you do not desire me, then I do not want you to touch me," he added, his voice tinged with a hint of sadness at the thought of being unwanted.

Yet Katarina's longing was intense, a hunger that burned within her like a flame flickering in the darkness. She felt a yearning deep within. There was something undeniably seductive about Ulrik's mysterious and strong character that awakened whispers deep within her.

"I want you," she said honestly. "Not because I owe you something, but because I yearn for you," she expressed with longing. Ulrik met her gaze, sensing her sincerity. "Your willingness to protect me makes me feel safe and seen," she whispered. As their eyes met, a silent exchange of longing and desire took hold. His gaze, a gentle caress upon her soul, traced the contours of her being, igniting a fire within Katarina's body.

With a breath stolen by anticipation, Ulrik leaned in, his lips a promise of unfathomable depths waiting to be explored. Each kiss echoed like a romantic sonnet upon her skin. In the intimate brush of his lips against hers, they waltzed among the stars, their souls intertwined in passion and devotion. Ulrik's fingertips embarked upon an erotic pilgrimage across the expanse of Katarina's longing body.

At the core of her pleasure, her voice soared, a sincere moaning that pierced the veil of silence. Each erotic moaning, a symphony of pleasure, echoed through the corridors of her soul, carrying with it the weight of untamed passion. In the depths of her pleasure, she surrendered to the wild tempest raging within, yielding to his seductive touch.

With the grace of a gentle breeze caressing the surface of a tranquil lake, his hands began their tender exploration across her body. Each movement, deliberate and unhurried, a homage to the boundless depths of passion waiting to be released.

Katarina's moaning voice rent the air, a primal cry that tore through the veil of silence like a thunderclap in the dead of night. As Ulrik kissed her neck, she surrendered to the pleasurable storm within. Her moaning echoed off the walls of her soul.

With the tender care of an artist admiring his masterpiece, he began removing her clothes. His fingers, gentle yet determined, caressed the smooth surface of her skin, tracing her curves with a reverence reserved for sacred artifacts.

As the layers fell away beneath his touch, revealing her soft flesh hidden within, he marvelled at the perfection of nature's design. As he beheld the naked beauty that laid bare before him, Ulrik couldn't help but feel a profound sense of gratitude for the simple pleasures that adorned life.

With the tenderness of a gentle breeze lifting a feather, Ulrik took Katarina into his arms, cradling her as though she were the most precious treasure in existence. With each step towards the bed, he moved as if carrying a fragile bloom, mindful of her every breath. His touch, a whisper upon her skin, conveyed a depth of adoration that words could never hope to capture. As she settled upon the soft mattress, he lingered for a moment, gazing upon her with an intensity that deeply manifested his devotion. With a gentle caress, he brushed a stray lock of hair from her forehead, tucking it behind her ear.

As his lips grazed the delicate contours of her neck, a cosmos of sensations unfolded beneath his touch. Each caress ignited a symphony of passion that danced along her senses. With each lingering kiss, he traced the pathways of her desires, leaving a trail of fire in his wake. Katarina found herself facing Ulrik. Her breath got caught in her throat, a gasp escaped her lips like a whisper of silk. In the depths of his gaze, she glimpsed a kaleidoscope of emotions, each flicker of his eyes a silent declaration of desire.

In the soft sighs that escaped Katarina's lips, Ulrik found stillness, a melody of pleasure that echoed through the depths of her being. And as he surrendered to the intoxicating allure of her essence, he lost himself in the maze of her embrace, consumed by the flames of passion that burned between them.

As Ulrik entered Katarina's body, a gasp escaped her parted lips. The mere presence of him within her body enveloped her in a torrent of emotions, a whirlwind of sensations that threatened to sweep her away in its wake. With each inhale, she drank in the essence of his being, the air saturated with his intoxicating aura.

Katarina's heart quickened its pace as they started to move their hips together at a synchronised speed. A tide wave of anticipation pulsated through her veins as she felt his strides within her. In the halo of his presence, she felt herself drawn into a puzzle of desire, each step forward, a plunge into the depths of her own longing. Every nerve in her body seemed to hum with a primal energy. She found herself drowning in the depths of his gaze.

With an abrupt yet graceful motion, Ulrik pivoted her around, his touch a powerful caress against her back. Katarina moaned out in pleasure, finding it hard to contain herself. She could feel every fibre of her body longing for him, longing for more. With a gentle yet firm hold, he guided her, their bodies swaying in synchrony to the rhythm of their unspoken yearning.

As they moved together, entwined in the passionate choreography of desire, Katarina surrendered to the intoxicating allure of Ulrik's touch. With each turn and twist, their bodies became vessels for the unspoken language of yearning. She felt herself losing all sense of self, consumed by the fiery inferno of their mutual longing.

With a whisper of intent, he allowed his hands to roam down between Katarina's legs, caressing her clitoris, each movement a silent declaration of his desire to explore every contour of her being and every part of her pleasure. She felt desire exploding within her body. Katarina surrendered to the exquisite pleasure of his touch. Her skin was burning with the electricity of their shared encounter. Ulrik's hands moved with a dynamic rhythm, seamlessly shifting between tempos while he took her from behind. His other hand caressed her nipples with a determined grip.

At times, they moved with an urgent haste, like a whirlwind of passion sweeping Katarina into a vortex of ecstasy. Each touch was a fervent declaration of longing, igniting sparks of fire that danced along the surface of her skin. She basked in the warmth of his presence, feeling the powerful rhythm of his breath against her neck while moving passionately within her. With each change in tempo, they surrendered to the ebb and flow of their passion, lost in the exquisite bond of their shared connection. Ulrik's hands navigated the sophisticated design of Katarina's being, adapting to the ever-shifting currents of their desire. She moaned out in pleasure, filling the air with her erotic longing. Katarina felt herself getting close to climax as Ulrik's hands moved intensely between her legs, stroking her clitoris. Katarina wanted more, desperately gasping for air. With each inhale, she surrendered to the intoxicating spell of their shared intimacy, allowing herself to be swept away by the currents of passion that enveloped them. And as his breath danced across her skin, she felt herself almost reaching an orgasm.

As Ulrik held Katarina's hips with a possessive grip, she felt a sense of liberation wash over her, as if the weight of the world had been lifted from her shoulders. With each movement of his hands, she experienced herself being guided towards the brink of ecstasy, her senses ablaze with the heady rush of their mutual longing.

With an exquisite medley of movement, Katarina allowed her legs to glide with ethereal grace. With each extension and contraction of her muscles, she felt herself being carried away in a hurricane of euphoria. Katarina revelled in the freedom of her own pleasure, surrendering to the melody of ecstasy that echoed through her horny body.

"I am close", she moaned. As the crescendo of their passion approached its zenith, she felt herself teetering on the precipice of release. With each heartbeat, Katarina felt the tide of pleasure rising within her, an ocean of sensation that threatened to overwhelm her senses with its relentless intensity. Every nerve in her body hummed with anticipation. Each pulse of desire propelled her closer to the brink of ecstasy.

As Katarina surrendered to the exquisite pleasure coursing through her veins, she felt herself being consumed by the flames of longing, her essence merging with Ulrik's in a fusion of passion and intimacy. With each passing moment, she felt herself being carried away in the allure of euphoria, lost in the timeless expanse of their shared ecstasy. With a final gasp of surrender to her orgasm, she let herself be carried away on the currents of pleasure. Her essence merged with his in a crescendo of passion that echoed through the depths of their souls.

CHAPTER 16

Ulrik maintained a steady, watchful eye over Katarina as she slept in front of the fireplace, bathed in the warm glow of the firelight. He admired her features, finding her eternally beautiful, regardless of the passing years. She was the light in his otherwise dark world, a beacon that illuminated the depths of his lost soul. Her beauty transcended the boundaries of time, etched into the depths of his immortal core. For her, he would vanquish any demon, overcome any obstacle, and wield all his powers to protect her until the very last day of her life. He would gladly traverse the depths of hell itself to ensure her safety.

As the night deepened, the shadows stretched across the walls, casting haunting images. Whispers echoed within the chamber, and the scent of ash and brimstone permeated the air, heralding the approach of evil. Ulrik remained still, anticipating the mare's attack with careful vigilance. One by one, the mares attempted to infiltrate the room: one squeezed through the gap under the door, another pressed its head through the keyhole, a third emerged from the floorboards, and the fourth emerged from a shadowy corner. The enemies maintained their dark, twisted forms, resembling deformed humans with elongated arms, moving on all fours with greyish skin akin to that of a lizard. Their eyes glowed like embers in the darkness, and their claws scraped against the floor as they advanced. Despite their grotesque appearance, Ulrik remained unfazed; to him, they were merely adversaries to be defeated. He had faced horrors far worse than these and emerged unscathed. As the mares encircled him, he remained calm and patient. They may have outnumbered him, surrounded him with their vile presence, but he would not falter, he would not yield.

"You have returned," Ulrik remarked, eyeing the largest mare standing before him.

"Give her to us!" the mare demanded in a deep, ominous voice, eager to claim what had been promised.

"No demon can control another demon," Ulrik asserted firmly, more resolute than ever to protect Katarina. "There must be a deeper motive for your presence here than a mere promise," he continued, trying to taunt the demon. The mare hesitated briefly.

"I will claim her soul and I will burn you!" she hissed, her mouth oozing tar.

"I've pondered this extensively; this must hold personal significance for you," Ulrik pressed on, meeting the mare's diabolical gaze with a steely resolve. "I believe you're in love with Vasilij." The mention of Vasilij caused the mare to pause momentarily. "But I know Vasilij," Ulrik continued, rising from his chair. His blue eyes sparkled like diamonds in the firelight, the flames dancing with a newfound intensity. "Vasilij is drawn to beauty; he would never love you. He's merely exploiting you!" Angered by Ulrik's words, the mare screamed in fury, tossing her head back and forth.

"I will kill you!" her screams reverberated through the chamber. The time for words had passed; now, only bloodshed awaited.

"That will not alter the truth. Move on, find another victim. Should you challenge me again, it will spell your demise. I will never allow you to have her. I will obliterate you," Ulrik declared, a darkness descending upon his eyes, turning them black as the flames gradually dimmed.

The mare growled in anger and launched an attack, her claws extended with murderous intent. Her sisters rallied to aid her. Ulrik fought with valour and tenacity. The flames, as if sensing the intensity of the moment, flickered wildly, casting ghostly shadows that twisted and contorted with Ulrik's movements. The mares assaulted from all angles, more ferocious and determined than before. They attacked with renewed fury; their movements synchronized in a deadly dance of destruction. This time, they were prepared and resolute to emerge victorious, regardless of the cost. Nothing would deter them. Each movement seemed to stoke the fire's fury, sending sparks flying into the air like angry spirits seeking vengeance.

Ulrik moved swiftly and with endurance, endeavouring to repel the intruders. He evaded their claws and teeth, but the mares, strong and coordinated, fought as one this time. Ulrik sensed their strength and power, permeating the surroundings like an indomitable virus. The mares were relentless, attacking from all directions with savage intent. But he refused to yield, pushing himself beyond the limits of mortal endurance as he battled against the demonic horde.

The mares sank their sharp teeth and devastating claws into Ulrik's flesh. Agony surged through his bloodstream as purple blood spilled onto the ground. Despite his efforts, Ulrik felt overpowered, exerting all his force to combat the intruders. He fought with instinct and experience, his spirit unbroken even as his body grew weary and battered, yet the mares outnumbered him, forming a formidable enemy. Their fiendish screams filled the air as they attacked relentlessly. The largest mare withdrew, allowing her sisters to continue their assault on Ulrik. Her face contorted into a gruesome, taunting smile.

"I will claim her, and there is nothing you can do!" she declared, turning toward Katarina. Ulrik battled the other three mares relentlessly as they bit and scratched him with their sharp claws. He exerted all his strength to fend them off and prevent the mare from reaching Katarina. The largest mare advanced slowly, confident of reaching her goal. A sinister grin spread across her face as she stood beside Katarina. Ulrik unleashed all his powers, but to no avail. The battle seemed lost. His blood stained the floor, the other mares pinned him down, continuing their assault. Ulrik fought with a courage forged in the depths of his core, a fierce determination burning in his eyes as he clashed against the demonic onslaught. He could feel their strength and power permeating the room, like a malevolent energy infecting the environment. It spread like a resilient virus, seeping into the earth beneath his feet and swirling through the shadows cast by the dancing flames. With a smirk of victory, the largest mare approached Katarina, fully aware of her impending triumph. Despite the odds, Ulrik persisted in his fight, determined to rescue Katarina from the clutches of the infernal mare. He refused to yield, unwilling to break his promise to protect her. As the mare revelled in her victory, preparing to claim her prize, a small shadow emerged from beneath the bed.

Katarina opened her eyes. Swiftly, she plunged the dagger into the mare's forehead, gripping it firmly with both hands, adrenaline coursing through her veins. In an instant, the mare froze, petrified, and dissipated into grey smoke before Katarina's eyes. The otherworldly creature didn't even have time to scream; it perished swiftly, unaware of its own defeat. The mare's sisters released Ulrik. Horror spread across their grotesque faces, their monstrous features contorted in dread and disbelief. They couldn't comprehend what had occurred. Their sister was dead. How could this be? What had happened?

Katarina breathed heavily as the fear gradually dissipated from her body. The mare was finally gone, she had ended the demon's life. Ulrik rose from the floor, blood dripping from all over his body onto the ground. The fire in the fireplace danced aggressively in response to his movements. The remaining mare began to scream in agony; their beloved sister was no more. Beside Katarina, the tomte appeared, a content smile visible across her face. She had been hiding in the room, remaining invisible to the mare, and when the demon approached, the tomte woke Katarina up, granting her the opportunity to vanquish the mare.

Katarina felt relieved; finally, the menace was gone, and she was free. The remaining mares, consumed by grief and rage, unleashed a deafening wail of anguish, mourning the loss of their fallen kin.

"Your sister is dead; now leave," Ulrik demanded, turning towards his enemies. The demonic entities shrieked in unison, their collective lament echoing off the walls in a mournful chorus of anguish and rage. "If you come back, we will vanquish every one of you. No other demon will join your battle knowing that a mare has already been vanquished in this fight, rightfully slain by the human tormented by the mare." The sisters growled and bared their fangs at Ulrik's words, slowly retreating into the safety of the fleeting shadows.

"We will return, and next time we will bring him!" The mares warned in unison, lingering like a sinister omen. Ulrik stood tall and strong, the echoes of their voices still haunting his mind. Meanwhile, Katarina exhaled a shaky breath, relief flooding her features as she realized the immediate threat had passed. She didn't care that the demons had threatened to return; she was grateful to be alive, and she had rid herself of the mare. Finally, she had killed the mare. The tomte looked at Katarina and nodded in approval.

"Thank you," Katarina murmured softly, her voice filled with genuine appreciation. "If it weren't for you, I couldn't have done this. You woke me up and helped us execute this plan. I will forever be grateful for your help." Relief washed over Katarina's face, joy beginning to reclaim her mind. The tomte returned her smile with a solemn nod. Her expression conveyed a sense of grim satisfaction at the demise of the foul creatures that had terrorized the land.

"I'm glad that beast is gone," the tomte said with a dark voice. "Those devils have been tormenting the horses and cows; I'm happy to be rid of them."

"Are you okay?" Ulrik asked gently, approaching Katarina, his touch tender and reassuring.

"Yes," Katarina answered. "I'll manage. I slept with the dagger, just like you instructed, and I prepared myself to attack her as soon as I woke up, knowing she would be just a few centimetres away. What did she mean when she said they will return, bringing him?" Katarina's brow furrowed with confusion, her mind racing to decipher the cryptic message hidden within the mare's ominous words.

"Yes, what did they mean?" the tomte asked suspiciously, dreading the answer.

"I will handle it," Ulrik said, avoiding a direct response.

"Who is coming here?" the tomte persisted, unsatisfied with the evasion.

"Ulrik?" Katarina interjected, wanting answers, her curiosity piqued as she sought clarity amidst the growing uncertainty.

"Vasilij, my creator," Ulrik replied with a bitter voice. "A vicious monster, determined to destroy the life I have here. He will do anything in his power to destroy my home and everyone living here." A fleeting sense of despair crept into Ulrik's tone, quickly overshadowed by a steely resolve. "But I will not let him. I will find a way to defeat him. I will not let him take you." Ulrik turned towards Katarina, gently touching her face.

"Another draugr unbound by the grave," the tomte said with a troubled voice. "That is surely a bad omen. You are going to need more help if you are going to defeat a couple of vengeful mares and a draugr."

"Why does he want to harm you and destroy your life?" Katarina asked.

"He wants me back," Ulrik confessed, a bitter edge underscoring his words. "We got separated, and I took my chance to leave him. I was fed up with the life he lived, always surrounded by death and despair. I wanted to return here. He could not tolerate that, and now he is coming to do everything in his power to have his will."

"You are going to need a better plan," the tomte said. "And I am not sure that I will be able to help you," she contemplated, overwhelmed by the information. "This has already gotten too far."

"Thank you for your help," Ulrik acknowledged, addressing the tomte. "You are a faithful guardian of this farm. I will think of something; I will be prepared. You have already done more than enough for this home."

The tomte nodded towards Ulrik. "Have a good night, draugr," the tomte's parting words lingered in the air. "I will go and watch over the animals." With that, she slipped away, leaving Katarina and Ulrik alone in the magical stillness of the night.

"Do not worry," Ulrik said with a calm voice. "There is nothing I would not do to safeguard you. There exists nothing in this world I would not sacrifice to have you unharmed. I will do what is necessary to defeat my maker."

"I will help you," Katarina vowed faithfully. "I might not be as strong or fast as you, but I will do my best, and I will stand by your side." Ulrik reached out, his touch tender as he caressed her face.

"You should go to sleep; it has been an eventful night. You must be tired; you were exceptionally brave," Ulrik looked at Katarina with pride in his eyes. She examined the wounds, noting with relief that they had already begun to mend.

"Your wounds," Katarina interjected, concern etching her features, "are you okay?" she inquired softly, her heart heavy with guilt. "Let me tend to them."

"They will heal," Ulrik assured, though a flicker of pain flashed across his face.

"Does it hurt?" she inquired softly.

"Yes," he replied. "These wounds hurt just as much as they would for a human."

"I am sorry," Katarina said.

"You have nothing to be sorry for," he leaned in, pressing a tender kiss upon her lips, "Your presence makes all the pain vanish. Within your company, I am complete."

Ulrik's gaze, imbued with the fervour of a thousand sunsets, caressed Katarina's body with a certainty born of boundless ardour. The flames of unfettered passion danced within his eyes. An unquenchable and wild flame mirrored the untamed spirit that thrummed within his very being. With each glance, he traced the delicate lines of her essence. Passionate anticipation hung heavy in the air like the heady fragrance of a blossoming rose, promising the sweet intoxication of a lover's embrace.

Ulrik, attuned to the silent symphony of desire that echoed between their souls, recognized the unspoken yearning mirrored in Katarina's every gesture. His own heart, a tempest of passion and longing, beat in harmonious rhythm with hers, whispering secrets of shared fervour across the silent expanse of their connection. Yet, in this delicate dance of seduction, she awaited his lead, a willing participant in the unfolding drama of their mutual desire.

In the quiet depths of his being, Ulrik bore the weight of his own conviction, a strength tempered by humility and grace. He possessed an intimate knowledge of self, an understanding as vast and boundless as the starlit heavens above. And in the cadence of his breath, Katarina found the echo of his intentions, a map to the uncharted territories of their passion.

Katarina stood unyielding in her own allure, a beacon of confidence among the swirling currents of their mutual attraction. Patiently, she waited. Her spirit was ablaze with the anticipation of his touch, yearning to be consumed by the fiery promise of his desire. With every fibre of her being, she longed to surrender to his seduction, to be claimed by the tempest of his love in every conceivable manner.

Within Ulrik's touch, Katarina yielded to his dominance, a willing supplicant to the mercies of his ardour. In his firm but gentle guidance, she found liberation, a freedom to explore the depths of her own passion without fear or restraint. He was the architect of her surrender, sculpting ecstasy from the raw clay of their shared desire with a deft and practiced hand.

As Ulrik drew near, his fingertips traced her form like a maestro conducting a symphony of desire. With unwavering resolve, he entwined his fingers in the silken strands of her hair, a gesture both commanding and tender, and lowered his lips to kiss her neck.

With a languid surrender, Katarina arched her neck gracefully, baring her skin to the caress of his kisses. She loudly moaned, caught up in her own ecstasy. Each brush of his lips against her form sent erotic shivers cascading down her trembling body, igniting a firestorm of longing within her very core. She felt desire taking over her body, enslaving her senses. His touch was a revelation, a divine melody that echoed in the chambers of her soul, stirring her senses to life with an intoxicating fervour. Katarina wanted more, she gasped for air as his hands claimed her body.

Ulrik's lips trailed a path of fire along the curve of her neck, feather-light and yet searing in their intensity. With each tender nibble and whispered caress, he stoked the flames of her desire, igniting a conflagration of desire. In his arms, she felt herself teetering on the edge of oblivion, lost in the dizzying whirlwind of his passion.

As Katarina's hands sought out the warmth of Ulrik's skin, she surrendered herself completely to the dance of seduction that unfolded between them. With each breath, she drank deeply from the cup of his desire. She allowed herself to be swept away in the magical pull of his seductive artistry. As Ulrik's hands touched Katarina's nipples, she moaned out in pleasure.

In the brush of his fingertips against her skin, Katarina discerned the silent language of desire, an unspoken declaration of his insatiable thirst to claim her as his own. With a primal longing, Ulrik set about the task of unveiling the secrets hidden beneath the layers of fabric that cloaked her body. His movements were deliberate and resolute, fuelled by an inferno of passion that reigned within his body.

In his touch, Katarina felt the searing heat of his desire, a wildfire that raged unchecked, consuming everything in its path with a hunger as ancient as time itself. With every layer peeled away, Ulrik embarked upon a journey of discovery, his hands tracing the contours of her body with a reverence akin to that of a pilgrim traversing sacred ground. He savoured each moment, each revelation, as if committing the map of her flesh to memory, an indelible imprint upon his core.

And as Katarina revelled in his touch, she surrendered herself completely to the magical sensation that unfolded between them. In his exploration, she found liberation, freedom to bask in the ecstasy of her own surrender, to lose herself in the sweet oblivion of their shared pleasure. Slowly, he took off her clothes and intensely studied her yearning body.

In a seamless choreography of desire, Katarina's movements synchronized with Ulrik's. With a strength born of primal instinct, he effortlessly lifted her, firmly holding her in his arms. Gently, yet with an undeniable authority, Ulrik laid her down upon the bed. With a tender command, he guided her, turning her face away from him.

His hands, roughened by the trials of life yet tender in their touch, traced a path along the curve of her spine, following the shape of her back. Each stroke was a whisper of longing, a silent plea for her to indulge herself to the rapture of their shared passion. Katarina moaned out in pleasure when feeling Ulrik's hands claiming her body.

She found herself lost in the depths of his touch; her senses overpowered with the intoxicating allure of his presence. With every caress, she felt herself drawn closer to him, as if being pulled by the irresistible tide of their desire. As Ulrik's hands traced a path of fire along her back, she relished in the sweet taste of longing. Katarina could barely contain herself when Ulrik kissed her back, his erotic touch igniting a fire within her body. He took a firm hold of her hands while exploring her body.

Enthralled by the intoxicating currents of the moment, she gave herself to his addictive pull. She allowed the tide of passion to sweep her away into the depths of his desire. In his strong and steady grip, she found both sanctuary and adventure, a willing captive to the magnetic force of his touch.

Ulrik's quest to unravel the mysteries of Katarina's being was driven by an insatiable thirst for intimacy. It was fuelled by a relentless determination to explore every part of her body.

As he moved his fingers along her skin, she trembled with anticipation, her every nerve alive with the electric pulse of their connection. Katarina gasped with excitement, every part of her body was screaming for more, calling out for him to take her. Ulrik started to kiss her collarbone, continuing down towards her breasts, his every movement burning with desire.

Katarina let herself be taken over by the ethereal flow of his touch, swept away by the sensations that unfolded before her, her body yielding effortlessly to the gentle guidance of his hands. There was a sublime intimacy in the way he held her, a mutual trust that transcended words and drifted freely between them like a river of light.

She basked in the radiance of his presence as he kissed her nipples, her spirit alight with the fires of passion and longing. Rhythmically Katarina started to move her body, her senses overwhelmed with the intoxicating allure of his touch.

As his tongue descended towards her thighs, her desire for him resonated in the air like an ancient melody. Katarina's moanings became sonata that enveloped them both in its divine embrace.

Ulrik, attuned to the subtle nuances of her essence, felt the magnetic pull of her desire drawing him ever closer. In the depths of her eyes, he glimpsed the fiery passion that smouldered within. She gasped and moaned, caught in the labyrinth of her thoughts.

Ulrik grabbed a firm hold of Katarina's hips and let his tongue meet her pulsating clitoris. Intense pleasure exploded within Katarina's body, when Ulrik's tongue playfully teased outside and inside of her body. With each twist and turn of his tongue,

Ulrik adjusted his tempo, fluid and adaptable, attuned to the ever-shifting clues of Katarina's body. Like a masterful dancer, his tongue moved with an effortless fluidity, navigating her clitoris with an uncanny intuition. Katarina gasped for air, filled with pleasure as he put his entire tongue inside of her. Swift as the coursing river, his tongue flowed with an agile grace, bending, and weaving to the contours of its environment with an instinctual finesse. Ulrik's tongue moved with the fluidity of a silken breeze, his pace a symphony of cadence and rhythm. In the next heartbeat, he quickened his stride. A tempest unleashed upon Katarina's body, his tongue a whirlwind of passion and fervour. Katarina twisted and turned, overwhelmed with ecstasy, her body screaming for more. With each breath, she revelled in the ebb and flow of his tongue's movements upon her clitoris. Her entire body was quivering with pleasure, ready to explode in an orgasm. Ulrik felt the subtle tremors of her energy as it shifted. With each lick, he drank deeply from the wellspring of her being, his senses alive to the symphony of her presence. Her taste was as if nectar from the heavens had descended upon his tongue. With each delicate sip, he savoured the sweetness of the moment, allowing its mesmerizing essence to envelop him in a cocoon of bliss.

Every fibre of Katarina's being thrummed with an exquisite ache when Ulrik's tongue played with her clitoris. A primal yearning pulsed in the chambers of her soul. From the depths of her essence to the very tips of her trembling fingers, she felt the electric rivers of desire coursing through her bloodstream. It ignited a fire that burned with an intensity unmatched by any earthly flame. She was ready to finish and embrace her orgasm. Every part of Katarina's body was screaming out for Ulrik to take her, to enter her body and fill her with his penis. Ulrik became acutely aware of the subtle shifts in her essence, each gasp and moaning a whisper of her approaching orgasm that stirred the very depths of his core. Enveloped by the entrancing allure of her approaching orgasm, Ulrik found himself ensnared in the delicate web of the moment's seductive enchantment.

In the depths of his being, he felt the tendrils of desire weaving their way through the corridors of his soul as Ulrik heard Katarina moan and move her body to the rhythm of his tongue. Like a sailor lost at sea, he found himself adrift in the boundless expanse of her sensation, carried away by the currents of passion that surged within him. Ulrik felt himself drawn deeper into Katarina's approaching climax, his senses ablaze with the heady fragrance of possibility. In the swirling maelstrom of erotic emotions, he committed himself completely to the magnetism of her pleasure, allowing its siren song to guide him through the labyrinth of desire.

In perfect synchrony with the rhythm of her being, Ulrik accelerated his movements, each motion of his tongue a graceful dance in harmony with the cadence of her yearning. Like two celestial bodies caught in the gravitational pull of mutual attraction, they orbited each other with increasing velocity. Their energies intertwined in an exquisite ballet of motion and desire.

With each lick, Ulrik matched Katarina's pace, his actions fluid and agile as he chased the elusive melody of their shared momentum. In the overture of their synchronicity, they moved as one. Their bodies were attuned to the subtle nuances of each other's motion, weaving together in a crescendo of passion and longing.

As their tempo quickened, so did the intensity of their connection. Katarina moaned and gasped, unable to control herself, overtaken by endless pleasure. With every breath, they pushed the boundaries of their physicality, transcending the limitations of time and space in a divine communion of movement and spirit.

Time seemed to stand still as Katarina surrendered to the captivating mixture of sensations that enveloped her when reaching climax. Ulrik could feel her pulsating orgasm as his tongue lingered on her clitoris. And as the last traces of sweetness remained upon his lips, Ulrik was left with a bittersweet ache, a longing for the ephemeral magic that danced upon the edges of memory.

CHAPTER 17

"Welcome," Ulrik nodded towards the priest as he entered, his demeanour calm yet tinged with an air of mystery. The priest offered a polite smile, though his eyes betrayed a lassitude far beyond his years. His footsteps were heavy, though his body seemed light. His hair was almost entirely grey, and his face was weathered with wrinkles. Despite his appearance suggesting hardships and endurance, a friendly aura lingered in his eyes, spreading across his face.

"It is my pleasure to be here," the priest responded courteously, his voice carrying a hint of reverence. Ulrik forced a smile in return. He could often sense evil in other creatures; in humans, it could be detected on their skin, the blood once spilled impossible to entirely wash off. But there was no recollection of forceful violence and suffering upon the priest's hands. He appeared to be a genuine and kind-hearted person.

"Please, sit down and join me," Ulrik gestured graciously, rising from his seat to greet the priest as the housekeeper guided him to the table.

"The housekeepers will not be dining with us?" the priest asked, a little confused. For an instance, an uncomfortable look spread across his face when he realized that he was going to spend the evening alone with Ulrik.

"As the master of the house, I normally dine alone," Ulrik replied, unbothered by the priest's insecurities.

"Beneath the grace of God, all creatures will be judged the same. I have seen servants and peasants closer to God than noblemen ever will be!" the priest raised his voice without sounding disrespectful, still keeping graceful manners." Your lineage holds no sway over your worth as a human being. If you do not mind, I do like everyone who works in this household, and I would very much like it if they could join us for supper," the priest insisted, speaking with warmth, passionately believing in his own words.

"You speak the truth," Ulrik said, recognizing the righteousness residing within the priest. "What you deem to be a good and bad person can be found in every social class." His gaze lingered on Elsie; a silent command conveyed in his eyes. "Elsie, please get the others," Ulrik asked in a relaxed tone. "We will all dine together." Upon hearing Ulrik's words, Elsie nodded and left the room. "So, tell me, father," Ulrik continued, still intrigued by the priest's naïve heart, "in your world, who is good and who is bad?" Ulrik asked curiously. As the question fell, the priest uncomfortably twisted his body.

"Only God can truly know that; only He can judge the content of our character." The priest began, his words imbued with the conviction of faith. "We have our guidelines that the Bible teaches us, we must be righteous and moral men," the priest spoke in a convincing tone, believing his own words. Faith echoed with emphasis within his heart.

"And what is a righteous man?" Ulrik asked, both intrigued by this philosophy and annoyed by naïve simplicity. His voice was edged with a hint of scepticism.

"A man who follows the Christian teachings, a man with a pure heart and a clear conscience," the priest continued preaching his beliefs, letting faith uplift his words. For the priest, the path to true righteousness lay in devotion to God.

"Oh father, I have seen psychopaths slaying and torturing with a clear conscience, raping and torturing women and children; they simply do not care. The absence of a guilty conscience does not make one a righteous man!" Ulrik said, almost upset, still haunted by his memories, wounds that would forever be doomed to stay open. "Almost every one of them called themselves Christian; some of them even quoted the Bible while committing crimes," Ulrik said with contempt. His countenance remained stoic.

"The nature of war is dreadful indeed," the priest replied, unsure how to respond to that comment. The priest knew very well of all the dreadful deeds one was forced to witness at war; many were not strong enough to resist and stand up to their own beliefs and fell under the pressure of another man's evil game. Ulrik's gaze seemed distant. He clenched his fingers, and his jawline seemed tense. Elsie entered the room with the rest of the household. With them, they brought plates, cutlery, and food for everyone to enjoy a well-cooked dinner.

"You are here," the priest seemed relieved. Although he held no contempt or dislike towards Ulrik; he was still uncomfortable in his presence, eager not to be alone with him.

"Father," Katarina smiled towards the priest, who burst out in a welcoming smile when laying eyes upon her.

"Please, join us," the priest seemed relieved, joy emanating from his eyes as he invited Katarina to join them. The housekeepers sat down at the table. Together, they enjoyed a pleasant dinner. Katarina conversed politely with the priest, who seemed to enjoy her company and happily shared stories and anecdotes. Ulrik sat quietly, observing every detail of the people present. When the hour grew late, the priest finally addressed Ulrik.

"If you do not mind, Ulrik, I would like to speak to you in private before leaving and returning home. After all, it is very dark outside. The night is about to arrive, and I have responsibilities in the morning," his voice determined yet gentle.

"Leave us," Ulrik said with a controlled voice, his words brooking no dissent. The housekeepers got up from their seats, ready to leave the room. "You can stay," Ulrik turned to Katarina, his eyes fixated upon her being. The priest had a hesitant look on his face.

"This is only meant for your ears," the priest seemed nervous, worried about the things that were yet to be uttered.

"Whatever you have to say, you can say when she is present," Ulrik said in an uncompromising tone. "I trust her, and I confide in her," Ulrik looked at Katarina with loyal eyes, admiring her spirit.

"I can leave if it makes you uncomfortable," Katarina turned towards the priest, not wanting to cause differences between them. Her eyes met the priest with a steely resolve that belied her gentle manner. The priest had always been kind to Katarina, displaying nothing but goodwill and benevolent intentions.

"No, if Ulrik insists, then so be it, I hope that you know what you are doing, Ulrik. I hope that she will be ready for this," the priest looked at Ulrik with serious eyes, warning him of the words yet to come.

"You do not have to worry, she knows," Ulrik said without letting go of Katarina with his gaze.

"She knows what?" The priest seemed confused, careful not to reveal information within his tone.

"The same thing you know but are yet to utter," Ulrik said, turning towards the priest with dark eyes. "The thing you know but pretend to have no knowledge about when faced with questions from other people. The truth that you dare not speak aloud, even in the sanctuary of your own thoughts." Ulrik's words bothered the priest. "I suspect that is why you have invited yourself over this evening; you will finally address the matter," Ulrik waited patiently for the priest to answer.

"Right," the priest mumbled. "Well, I need your help," the priest seemed worried, casting a gaze behind the shadows.

"With what?" Ulrik pressed, his curiosity piqued. Katarina listened with inquisitiveness, intrigued by the situation. Although the priest was a gentle soul, his confidence never seemed to waver. Yet now, he stumbled upon his words.

"I knew what you were the moment you came back from the war; it was quite obvious," the priest began with a dramatic voice, luring in his audience. The light from the candles started to dance wrathfully to the rhythm of the priest's words. "I was looking for ways to kill you, a draugr is never a good thing, they only bring death," fear tainted his tone. The priest paused, slowly studying Ulrik. "But you kept to yourself; you did not visit the cemetery; the kyrkogrim never saw you; you seldom left your home. You did not harm or hurt anyone. Yes, people feared you; they had the same suspicions as I did. They even asked me to investigate whether you were a draugr or not. I watched you for days, carefully following you, and you, you did nothing. So, I decided to let you be. After all, a draugr is a very powerful creature, and I was hoping for the kyrkogrim to kill you. To kill you myself would be almost impossible, and I kept telling people that you were not a draugr and that they should stay calm. I swore that I would find a way to get rid of you, should you ever harm anyone. But you kept to yourself, and I saw no reason to go after you. One day, I might be needing your assistance."

"How would you kill me?" Ulrik's voice dripped with disdain, each word laden with contempt. "Even if you wanted to get rid of me, you are just a man!"

"The church has many connections," the priest said secretly, hiding his sources. "But they are far away." The priest looked at Katarina to determine whether she was shocked.

"What is it that you would like to ask me?" Ulrik asked, starting to lose interest.

"There is a creature dwelling not far from here," the priest looked serious and concerned, casting a fast glance at the shadows outside the window. The night howled, and autumn forced itself upon everyone that dared to challenge its dominion.

"What kind of creature?" Katarina asked, her interest in the hidden ones and väsen shone through her words.

"A strandvaskare has taken over an abandoned house near the east hill," the priest said, his eyes filled with sorrow and compassion.

"That is not possible," Ulrik stated. "They only live near the sea; the lake near the forest is not big enough to appeal to its presence." He countered, scepticism evident in his voice.

"And that is what is so peculiar about the whole situation," the priest admitted, a furrow formed between his brows. "Why would such a creature dwell here? I need you to vanquish it or chase it off."

"A strandvaskare can exist within the smallest of lakes," Katarina interrupted. "It is merely a soul, lost in the waters, unable to move on. If it died there, then it sure can haunt the area. It will continue to do so until it finds peace."

"Why would I help you?" Ulrik asked, not convinced.

"To help our community," the priest said with a righteous voice. "It is the right thing to do, and one must always do what is right."

"I am not a part of your community," Ulrik said in a harsh tone.

"But you do have the strength and power to help us. People are afraid; we need your help," the priest continued speaking for his cause with determination.

"What has this community ever done for me?" Ulrik asked, annoyed, disdain revealed within his voice.

"Ulrik," Katarina said with a mild voice. "If there is a chance that you can help, then you should, please." Katarina pleaded. Ulrik's expression softened when hearing Katarina's words, though a flicker of annoyance still lingered in his eyes. He wanted to do everything in his power to make her happy, but he was not too keen on undertaking a battle that was not his.

"For you, I will," Ulrik said and looked at Katarina, his eyes spoke of affection, his words in a devoted tone. The priest looked confused.

"So, you will help us to get rid of the strandvaskare?" The priest asked again with a hopeful tone.

"Yes," Ulrik replied. "But after that, I want to be left alone, and if I ever come to you and need help with anything, then you must agree to help me."

"If it is within moral and ethical guidelines and if it does not go against the church's beliefs," the priest said faithfully, at the same time wondering whether it was truly wise striking a bargain with a draugr.

"Do not worry," Ulrik said, perceiving the priest's hesitation. "If I ever ask for help, it will be to vanquish another demon."

"Agreed," the priest nodded concordant. "Well, thank you for dinner," the priest turned towards Katarina, his smile uplifting the room. "And let me remind you that it is impure to covet a woman who is not yours. You should do the right thing and marry her, even demons should aspire to righteousness," the priest said before leaving the house in haste. Regardless of the consequences, the priest felt an irrepressible urge to always speak the truth. Ulrik seemed surprised by the priest's words; he was caught off guard by the priest's sudden outburst. Katarina turned towards Ulrik.

"It is late; come with me," she said and took Ulrik's hand, leading him away into their privacy.
Ulrik moved closer, enraptured by the ethereal allure of Katarina. His heart fluttered with an ineffable longing. He leaned in, his breath mingling with hers in a silent plea of desire. Their lips met in a wild union.

With a languid grace, Ulrik began the delicate unveiling of Katarina's clothes, each layer a hidden promise concealing the treasures nestled underneath. His fingers, guided by passion, danced over her yearning body, gently unravelling the mysteries shrouded beneath her clothes. With each layer peeled back, the air seemed to shiver with an intense sense of erotic wonder. As the final barrier yielded to his touch, unveiling her entire naked body, time stilled, and he beheld with awe the beauty before him.

With a fervour born of the deepest depths of his core, Ulrik embraced Katarina. His touch, a soulful caress upon her longing body, awakened echoes of ancient hymns, each note a sigh that spoke of lusting and ecstasy intertwined. As his fingers glided over her body, down in between her legs, a powerful ballet of passion and grace unfolded. Katarina moaned out in pleasure. She found herself ensnared in the labyrinthine depths of her erotic emotions. A tempest of desire and longing raged within her like a wild, untamed storm. Her spirit, like a fragile bird with wings of flame, fluttered against the confines of her being, yearning to break free and soar into the boundless expanse of the heavens. Every fibre of her being quivered with the intensity of her passion. When Ulrik started to caress her clitoris, Katarina surrendered to the primal call of her desire, casting aside the forceful veil of restraint that had bound her. She allowed herself to be consumed by the blazing touch of passion's timeless flame.

Katarina let herself be seduced by the enchantment of the moment. Ulrik rhythmically moved his hand between her legs, caressing her inside and outside. Her every movement was an opus of passion and surrender. Like a solitary leaf dancing upon the breath of the wind, she yielded to the currents of desire, her body a vessel of untamed emotion, carried away by his blissful touch, evoking a burning fire within. Each subtle shift and undulation deeply manifested the raw intensity of her longing, an affirmation of the boundless depths of her soul's yearning. As Ulrik changed between rhythms while paying close attention to her clitoris, Katarina's spirit alight with the fervour of passion's intense flame. She cast aside the veil of inhibition to bask in the radiant glow of pure, unadulterated ecstasy.

With a reverent, determined movement, Ulrik gently parted Katarina's legs and entered her body. Katarina gasped when she felt his penis pushing into her body. Her breath escaped her in a delicate sigh, a whispered hymn to the erotic wonder unfolding within her. Her gasp echoed through the silence. Every atom of her being trembled with the weight of sexual ecstasy. Katarina's body gave in to his strong touch, as Ulrik let his hands find their way over her back. Every fibre of her being screamed out for more.

In the molten embrace of their fervent tango, they became vessels of passion incarnated, their bodies entwined in a tempestuous choreography that spoke of a desirous inferno. With every ardent movement, they ignited the night with the blaze of their longing. Each fiery movement traced a tale of ardour and yearning.

Caught up in the moment, Katarina sensed the whisper of his breath upon her neck, bringing her immense pleasure. Sexual passion pulsated through her body, filling her every cell. It was as if the very essence of Ulrik, imbued with warmth and longing, danced delicately upon her neck. Each breath sent shivers of anticipation cascading down her spine.

As she closed her eyes, surrendering to the intoxicating sensation, she felt the weight of his presence enveloping her, wrapping her in a cocoon of intimacy that transcended the boundaries of mere physicality. In that shared breath, they forged a bond that stretched beyond the confines of this world, weaving their destinies together in the chambers of eternity.

Ulrik's movements were infused with an aura of strength and purpose. Each push inside of Katarina left her yearning for more, unable to resist his alluring spirit.

As Ulrik's gaze traversed the contours of her silhouette, he began a journey of exploration, tracing the uncharted territories of her essence. With each calculated movement, he unearthed hidden treasures buried beneath her surface, treasures that sparkled with the brilliance of her innermost thoughts and desires.

With each harmonious progression, a sexual crescendo of anticipation built within Katarina's body. She was getting close to climax. As union swelled, she found herself poised at the precipice of completion, her body and spirit alight with the fervour of imminent fulfilment. It was as if every movement struck a chord within her, awakening dormant desires, bringing her closer to her orgasm. Ignited flames of passion danced in the recesses of her being. Her cells screamed out for more, giving in to the approaching orgasm.

With every breath, Katarina approached the culmination of their shared journey, her senses heightened to a state of strengthened awareness as she prepared to embrace the bewitching climax. In the exquisite tension of the moment, she felt herself teetering on the edge of infinity, lost between the realms of ecstasy and transcendence.

Ulrik's breath became a tempest, quickening in pace. Katarina's entire body became possessed by the desire to climax. Beneath the caress of his gaze, her pulse became a wild symphony, its rhythm echoing the thunderous cadence of a thousand galloping stallions racing across the expanse of her soul. With each beat, it seemed to echo the primal call of passion, a call for an impending orgasm. Katarina welcomed the exquisite tumult that surged within her, her body quivering in anticipation. Ulrik became acutely attuned to her excitement. It was as if he could discern each delicate tremor that traversed the landscape of her body. With every glance, he glimpsed a universe of passion that flickered within her depths. She was getting near her climax. As Ulrik basked in the radiant glow of Katarina's approaching orgasm, he felt himself swept away on a tide of suspense. His own spirit was alight with the fervent intensity of her energy. It was as if her excitement became his own, in an exquisite melody of longing.

As Katarina neared the culmination of her orgasm, she moaned out in pleasure. The pulsating rhythm of passion coursed through every cell of her body as she was on the edge of climax. Ulrik found himself harmonizing effortlessly with the rhythmic cadence of Katarina's body. Hearing her moan out in pleasure awoke a wild yearning within his core. Ulrik melded with the ebb and flow of Katarina's rhythm. Every movement, every gesture, became an expression of their shared yearning.

In the seductive grip of desire's fervent dance, passion seized Katarina like a tempestuous storm, while her orgasm loomed nearby. Each sensation, a blend of fire and longing that coursed through her blood vessels like molten lava, igniting every fibre of her essence with an insatiable hunger.
As the flames of ardour licked at the edges of her consciousness, she forfeited willingly to their irresistible allure. Her body became a vessel through which the primal essence of passion found expression.

Katarina lost herself in the tumultuous currents of desire when she let her orgasm wash over her. Ulrik discerned the vibrant thrum of her orgasm. It was as though the air around them shimmered with the radiant glow of her orgasm, casting a spell that beckoned him closer to his climax. Ulrik capitulated to the enchanting pull of her exuberance, his spirit intertwining with hers in a sublime pas de deux when he reached his orgasm just seconds after Katarina.

CHAPTER 18

Katarina nestled in the safety of Ulrik's arm, her gaze locked with his, peering into the abyss of his troubled eyes. Within their depths, she glimpsed a spectrum of turmoil and contradiction, a tortured soul with myriad depths. His eyes held the weight of countless experiences, each one etched into the misery of his soul. Despite his suffering, he endeavoured to save her, embodying two opposites that united as one.

In his gaze, Katarina saw the duality of his existence, a soul teetering on the edge between darkness and light. Within him lay a profound capacity for both unspeakable violence and profound tenderness, a dichotomy that both intrigued and unnerved her. His essence hinted at depths of emotion and turmoil that few dared to fathom. It held the capacity for both immense destruction and extreme kindness, merging danger with romantic depth.

Beneath his stoic appearance, Ulrik bore the scars of a tumultuous past, each mark a reminder of the countless battles he had waged, both within himself and against the world. His scars lay concealed beneath a cold exterior; few glimpsed the true essence of his being. Behind his surface of survival, a shield forged against life's recklessness, his soul remained hardened by the harshness of existence.

Yet, among the shadows that haunted his being, there flickered a glimmer of something more. A romanticism that belied the darkness that encased him. His soul remained solidified by the brutality of existence.

As Katarina let her fingers travel over Ulrik's face, she felt the weight of his suffering, the burden of his past, and the desperation of his desire to protect her.

"Why do you not sleep?" Katarina asked, her concern evident. She reached out, her fingers barely touching Ulrik's soft hair, its texture akin to silk. "I thought draugrs slept every day," she continued, seeking understanding.

"Yes, it is true," Ulrik replied, touching Katarina's cheek with a promise of protection and devoted love. He would never stray from her side; his touch conveyed his faithful commitment. His words could crumble, but it wouldn't matter, his love for her was eternal. She was the sole owner of his heart, having claimed every part of him.

To Ulrik, time held little significance. He understood that Katarina would inevitably grow older and one day pass away, leaving him in this cold, unforgiving world. The mere thought of parting from her was almost unbearable, and he fiercely resisted the excruciating reality of death that lingered at his core. Yet, until that inevitable day when his heart would be wrenched from his chest, he vowed to remain steadfastly by her side. In his eyes, she would always remain beautiful and awe-inspiring. His devotion transcended any physical aspect that this world could comprehend.

"But you don't?" Katarina remarked, perceiving the depth of his love for her. She could sense his commitment even in his silence. His dedication was palpable in the spaces where truth and life intertwined, a silent pledge of devotion.

"No, there are other demons that haunt me at night," Ulrik

replied, his gaze drifting into the shadowed abyss of his memories, as if he were lost in another realm. A profound anguish gripped him, twisting his heart from within. "A draugr does not need to sleep. I manage just fine without it. But I have never encountered another draugr who does not rest. Most draugrs slumber for extended periods, sometimes for years on end, before moving on to the next place, always guarding their treasures, hiding from the world within their own isolated existence."

"Is it true that you wanted to return to me?" Katarina inquired gently, her yearning for his affection was evident in her voice. She found herself captivated by his presence. She experienced a profound sense of joy in his company. In the tales, a draugr was said to exude the scent of death and decay, yet Ulrik possessed a fragrance that danced through the senses, enticing from within. Katarina had unexpectedly fallen in love with him, a development she never anticipated. The once cold and indifferent man now enveloped her in his protective embrace, forever safeguarding her. Despite the darkness that followed him, she saw a glimmer of humanity within, a spark of tenderness that defied the horrors of his past.

"Yes," Ulrik affirmed sincerely. "The memory of you has always held a special place in my heart, and now I have you here in my arms. I will stay by your side for as long as you want me here. I swear that I will never harm or hurt you, and if you wish for me to leave, then I will oblige. I will never force you to do anything; it is your free will I seek. It is your unconditional love I crave. I have hoped for this moment for such a long time, this is all I have ever dreamt of," Ulrik's voice resonated with longing and eternal passion, his heart beating to the rhythm of love's everlasting cadence. "Just to touch you and to feel you near, to know that you want me and desire me," his voice whispered a promise that echoed through the corridors of eternity. "I have desired you for lifetimes, and I will desire you for as long as I shall live. It pains me that we must part in the afterlife, whatever it may be. I swear to protect you, to cherish you, until the end of days," both dread and pain echoed within his tone.

"What do you mean?" Katarina asked, her eyes searching Ulrik's for answers among the swirling shadows of their conversation.

"I am already dead. I died when Vasilij decided to take my life. One can only become a draugr if one dies. My soul is already condemned, and there is nothing I can do to redeem my mistakes and actions. If the priest is right and hell exists, then surely that is where my soul already resides," darkness danced upon his tongue as he spoke. "And you, my fair and sweet," Ulrik touched Katarina's face and smiled, "your heart is pure and full of goodness. I cannot recall a time when you were mean or unkind. Your soul will be heading in another direction. And for that, I am glad. I do not wish for you to suffer in the afterlife. I must pay the price for my actions; I accept my fate and embrace my punishment." Ulrik was ready to meet whatever danger would haunt him the day he left this realm.

"You already paid the price for your actions," Katarina said, unable to believe that there could be something as gruesome as hell, should there be an afterlife. "You suffer every day for the things you did. You could choose to live like Vasilij and continue killing, but you have left that life. If anyone truly repents, then they will be forgiven, according to what the Christians believe." Katarina had a hopeful tone in her voice, faith resting within her heart.

"What does that do to help those whose lives I have already taken?" there was hauntingly deep regret in Ulrik's voice, memories tainted by remorse. "Should I be forgiven just because I repent? How about the suffering I placed on others? Why should my plea for forgiveness and peace overpower their pleas for justice? I do not know if I believe that forgiveness and peace should apply to all just because you repent before you die. There are many who deserve to suffer for their deeds. We deserve to pay the price, and I am prepared to be held accountable for my actions," there was acceptance in his voice when the last words fell.

"I believe that everyone deserves peace in the end. I believe in forgiveness and letting go," Katarina smiled and touched Ulrik. She wanted to see the best in people, she wished everyone a peaceful passing.

"That is what sets you apart," Ulrik said, lost somewhere between despair and hope. His expression softened, though a shadow lingered in the depths of his gaze "I would kill all those monsters and make them suffer for their deeds, had I the power," emptiness appeared in his eyes. "But you," he turned to Katarina, admiring her spirit, "you would save everyone."

"So much anger," Katarina continued with a gentle heart. "We cannot let anger consume us; we must move on and find peace for our own sake. Do not cling to the past, remain in this moment. Peace can only be found in the present moment. I want to help you," she said faithfully. "I do not want you to suffer, in this life nor the next. Let me help you."

"You are the best part of me," Ulrik said, his eyes alight with a fervent devotion that transcended the bounds of mortality. "And I do not want to do anything to taint you and befoul your life. I do want to marry you," he said and looked at Katarina with a convinced look filled with love and respect, a promise that would echo in the timeless chambers of eternity. "I want you to be my wife. I do not want to have you as a lover; that is not right by you. Even if I am a draugr and our communion would not be approved by the church, I want to make that commitment with you. There is no one else I would want to spend my life with no matter how many days I have left."

"You are right, the church would probably not approve," Katarina said disappointed, a fleeting shadow that crossed her features.

"You do not care that I am a draugr," Ulrik said with a resolute voice.

"No, I care about who you are, not what you are," Katarina said, her heart moved by his proposal.

"I will make a proper proposal," Ulrik said, stopping Katarina from uttering another word. "I want to make everything right. Never should you falter in anything; I shall forever be by your side. As long as there is life within me, I will face any danger or obstacle to safeguard you. I am eternally yours, forever bound to you, in my past life, in this life, and in the next," he said and kissed her.

Ulrik took Katarina in his arms, a sanctuary of strength and tenderness. From the depths of his being, he held her close. For her, he was a shield against the world's uncertainties. His touch, a pledge of reassurance, whispered promises of protection and devotion.

With each gentle caress, Ulrik created a fortress of love in which she could surrender her fears. His embrace became a shelter among life's tumultuous seas. He protected Katarina's soul with a timeless warmth, melting away every doubt and insecurity.

In the silent language of surrender, his actions told eternal tales without uttering a word. Each touch was a sonnet of affection. As their spirits thrived in harmonious union, Katarina found happiness in Ulrik's embrace. Fears faded into whispers and love reigned supreme.

Tenderly, Ulrik assisted her in shedding the clothes that clung to her body, like autumn leaves relinquishing their hold to the gentle breath of the wind. With each garment gracefully unfurled, a delicate unveiling transpired, revealing not only the silhouette of her physical being but also the vulnerability and beauty residing within.

His touch, teeming with esteem, traced the shapes of her skin.

His touch became a silent ode to the exquisite artistry of her existence. Katarina's clothes yielded to the floor, surrendering to the gravity of their shared presence.

In his eyes, she glimpsed a reflection of her own soul's yearning, a longing to be seen and cherished in the raw authenticity of her being. Katarina stood naked before Ulrik, a vision spun from the threads of his dreams and desires. Every line of her form bespoke a story untold, written in the language of curves and contours that whispered secrets only Ulrik's heart could comprehend. Her presence, like a spell uttered by moonlight, held him captive in a trance of adoration. In the halo of her presence, time itself seemed to pause, and Ulrik found himself caught in the mist of their intertwined destinies.

With each breath, Katarina exhaled an affirmation of longing and possibility. Her breaths filled the air with the spellbinding fragrance of hope. As Ulrik beheld Katarina, his core stirred with a primal fascination, a hunger to explore the depths of her essence and lose himself in the puzzle of her complexities.

In the dance of their gazes, sparks ignited, illuminating the darkened chambers of their hearts with a dazzling intensity. The world outside faded into insignificance. They existed in the transcendent chrysalis of their shared gaze, where nothing else mattered save for the boundless expanse of their profound connection.

Ulrik leaned in, his lips a whisper upon the surface of Katarina's skin. Each kiss was a brushstroke painting an eternal masterpiece of desire and devotion. With every tender caress, he sought to unravel the mysteries that lay hidden within her. He traced the contours of her being with reverence and awe.

As their souls intertwined in the hallowed alchemy of their embrace, they became lost in the maze of sensation. Ulrik caressed the curves of Katarina's body and let his hand slide down between her legs, caressing her clitoris. His fingertips, like whispers upon the strings, coaxed forth a symphony of longing and yearning. Each stroke became a testament to the depths of his soul. Katarina moaned out in pleasure when feeling his hand inside and outside of her body. Her voice rang out like a silken melody. Her erotic call, a mixture of longing and desire, echoed across the room. It reached out to Ulrik with an ethereal allure that beckoned him closer.

As Ulrik moved his hands repeatedly over Katarina's clitoris, he felt the resonance of her moaning, a siren's song that called to him from the furthest reaches of his heart. With each erotic syllable, she painted a portrait of yearning and passion. As he listened, enraptured by the cadence of her moaning, he felt himself drawn relentlessly towards her.

Ulrik cradled Katarina's form as delicately as a poet holds a cherished verse. His touch traced the contours of her being with a reverence that bordered on worship. Katarina gasped out. Within her ignited a fire that burned with the intensity of a thousand suns, as Ulrik parted her legs and entered her body.

Katarina moaned out in excitement when feeling his penis inside of her, each motion a dance of passion choreographed by the universe itself. Their bodies, drawn together by the gravity of their desires, swayed in perfect harmony. Their rhythms intertwined like vines in an enchanted forest. With each synchronized movement, they surrendered themselves to the primal crescendo of their longing.

Katarina felt the frequency of passion swirling within her like a tempestuous sea, drawing her ever closer to the precipice of ecstasy. Each movement inside of her fuelled the flames of desire that burned within her, igniting a firestorm of longing that consumed her senses. With every movement Katarina's clitoris rubbed against Ulrik's pubic bone, sending shockwaves of pleasure coursing through her veins. Her approaching orgasm carried her on a journey of rapture that transcended the limitations of the physical world.

As Ulrik went deeper and harder, Katarina teetered on the edge of bliss, on the precipice of release, towards her climax. Katarina's form quivered with the intensity, as Ulrik turned her around and whispered "Not yet". Waves of ecstasy coursed through her veins as Ulrik entered her from behind. Her every nerve vibrated with an erotic, melodic resonance. As Ulrik put his hands on her hips, Katarina hailed the storm of sensation crashing upon the shores of her being. She felt the boundaries of her existence blur and dissolve, merging with the pulsating rhythm of their entwined desires as his penis moved deep within her. A cascade of sensation electrified her senses and left her gasping for breath as Ulrik moved his hand to caress her breasts. Each tremble, each convulsion, was an offering filled with pleasure. Once again Katarina quivered on the brink of orgasm as Ulrik let his hands move up and down her body while his penis claimed her inside.

Gently Ulrik guided Katarina, turning her with the grace of a maestro while whispering "not yet" in her ear. Katarina could barely contain herself. Every cell of her body screamed out in erotic ecstasy, longing for his penis to re-enter her. Her pulsating clitoris yearned for more.

Katarina seized the reins of their dance with the commanding grace of a goddess guiding mortals through the celestial realms as she placed herself on top of Ulrik. As Katarina took the lead and placed Ulrik's penis inside of her, she felt the pulse of their connection quiver beneath her fingertips.

With each movement and subtle shift of her weight, Katarina communicated with the silent language of trust and understanding, leading their sexual encounter with tender authority and confidence. She felt the power of their connection pulsing beneath her, as her pelvis rubbed against his body. Each movement spoke of determination and resolve.

Ulrik's hands found their place upon the curve of her hips, guiding Katarina's movements in unison with their shared pleasure. He traced the contours of her form, as if reading the braille of desire inscribed upon her skin. Katarina moaned out, taken over by passion, as her clitoris rubbed against Ulrik's body, his penis filling her inside. She surged forward with an intensity that mirrored the flames of passion licking at their souls. Her movements became a blur of motion, like the fleeting dance of a comet streaking across the night sky. With each swift motion, she propelled them deeper into the labyrinth of ecstasy. Every movement was a declaration of ardour, a fervent plea for an impending orgasm.

Katarina's pulse began to beat faster as she acknowledged the irresistible rush of sexual sensation. Ulrik felt her excitement, turned on by her gasping and approaching climax. Katarina's whole body was shaking, her pelvic muscles squeezing around Ulrik, provoking a loud moan out of him. Katarina felt Ulrik vibrating and pulsating inside of her. Her entire body trembled with the orgasm that took over, a scream of pleasure tore from her lips as she welcomed her climax and surrendered to the intense sensation.

Ulrik enfolded Katarina in his arms, pressing her against the wall with a passion that bordered on divine fervency. Their bodies melded together like two halves of a whole when he entered her body again. Katarina gasped when she once again felt Ulrik's penis inside of her. Ulrik moved with a purpose that resonated through the very essence of her being. Each stride within Katarina's body was imbued with a sense of resolve. When taking Katarina against the wall, he exuded a raw power that commanded the attention of the universe. His strong muscles safeguarded her with a poetic resolve. In the intensity of his motion, there was a primal urgency that stirred the depths of her soul. His determination was undeniable, a force that surged through the space between them. Their energies converged in a tempest of desire. As Ulrik reached his climax, he drew Katarina near, enfolding her exquisite form within his arms. In that intimate embrace, every contour of her body melded seamlessly with his. As Ulrik climaxed, Katarina felt herself inviting the magnetic pull of his presence, her senses alight with the enticing fragrance of his essence. Their bodies pressed together like pieces of a puzzle finding their perfect fit, as if they were meant to be intertwined for all eternity.

CHAPTER 19

In the heart of the winter forest, where the icy tendrils of snow clung to the barren branches like the limbs of the damned, Katarina found herself ensnared within a surreal tableau. The air was thick with an eerie stillness, broken only by the soft descent of snowflakes, each one a delicate promise of impending doom.

As Katarina reached out to touch the cold flakes, her fingertips met the frigid veil of winter's embrace, sending shivers cascading down her form. She realized that this place existed beyond the realms of mortal understanding, a twisted reality created from the foundation of dreams and nightmares.

Yet, amidst the ethereal dance of snow, a mysterious presence stirred, its approach heralded by a haunting hiss that cut through the silence with demanding force. The ground trembled beneath Katarina's feet as the forest groaned in protest, birthing forth her fate.

From the depths of the forest emerged the Lindwyrm, a serpentine behemoth cloaked in scales of deepest crimson. Each one gleamed with the dark beauty of a thousand lost souls. Its sinuous form undulated with a snakelike grace, leaving a trail of darkness in its wake as it slithered towards Katarina, a silent sentinel of doom.

With a gaze that pierced through the veil of reality itself, the Lindwyrm fixed its eyes upon Katarina, its eyes a tempest of swirling shadows and celestial light. Katarina felt the weight of eternity bear down upon her, the echoes of countless souls reverberating through the very core of her being.

Past, present, and future intertwined in a black hole of existence, blurring the boundaries between dimensions and lifetimes. In the core of the Lindwyrm, Katarina glimpsed the infinite expanse of the cosmos, a realm where mortal souls were but fleeting shadows adrift in the vast ocean of time.

Yet, amidst the chaos of the universe, Katarina remained grounded, her courage unyielding as she met the Lindwyrm with a quiet resolve. A voice within her whispered that she had no reason to fear. Though the abyss beckoned with its hymn of oblivion, she stood firm, a lone beacon of defiance against the unknown.

"I can see the source of life reflected within your being," Katarina uttered in reverent awe, her eyes locked onto the towering form of the Lindwyrm as it slithered gracefully before her, its scales glistening like shards of obsidian beneath the ethereal glow of the falling snow. "Hrafnildr". Katarina uttered.

"That is indeed my name." The Lindwyrm spoke in a contented tone. "You can hear me calling from within. I am a part of you, just like you are a part of me. I am connected to the lifeforce of all living beings, just as you are," the Lindwyrm responded, its voice a tranquil melody that resonated with the ancient wisdom of the cosmos. "Everyone is tethered to the same primordial essence, though many remain oblivious to its omnipresent embrace."

Katarina nodded slowly, her senses attuned to the mystical currents that ebbed and flowed around them, intertwining with the very essence of existence. "I have always felt a kinship with väsen," she confessed, her words carried away in the whispering winds of the winter night. The snow fell slowly upon her hair.

"It is because you perceive a reflection of your own soul mirrored in their quintessence," the Lindwyrm explained, its words suffused with a profound understanding of the interconnection of all things. "You recognize the fundamental unity that binds us together, transcending the boundaries of time and space."

"What is it that unites us?" Katarina inquired, her voice barely above a whisper as she felt the weight of countless lifetimes pressing down upon her, their collective memories swirling like snowflakes in the tempest of her mind.

"We are but echoes of the whispers of the universe," the Lindwyrm replied, its gaze fixed upon Katarina with an intensity that pierced the veil of mortal comprehension. "We are forever intertwined, woven into the spirit of creation itself, our destinies entwined in an eternal dance of light and shadow."

As the snow continued to fall, cloaking them in a veil of pristine white, Katarina felt a sense of serenity wash over her. The mysteries of the cosmos unfolded before her in all their wondrous complexity.

"What do you want with me?" Katarina's voice trembled as she confronted the enigmatic Lindwyrm, her eyes locked onto its mesmerizing form amidst the swirling mists of her nocturnal reverie.

"If you can perceive my words resonating within the depths of your being, then know that this is no mere dream," the Lindwyrm responded, its voice a haunting melody that seemed to echo from the furthest reaches of the cosmos. "It is a vision, a harbinger of truths yet untold, a message that beckons to you from the realm beyond."

"I do not understand," Katarina confessed, her senses awash with a potent mixture of fear and fascination.

"One day, you may," the Lindwyrm intoned cryptically, its serpentine form undulating gracefully against the backdrop of the ethereal landscape. "And when that time comes, the meaning shall reveal itself with utmost clarity."

"I will seek you out," Katarina vowed, her resolve unwavering despite the uncertainty that clouded her mind. "I will unravel the mysteries that shroud your existence."

"If you do," the Lindwyrm murmured, its voice laced with an otherworldly allure, "then know that I shall await your coming, a silent sentinel amidst the shifting sands of time. Remember my name, Hrafnildr."

With that, the Lindwyrm slithered away into the veils of mist, leaving behind a trail of shimmering gold that danced upon the surface of the snow like liquid fire. Katarina watched in awe as the spectral apparition vanished into the night, its presence lingering within the recesses of her soul like a haunting refrain.

"This must be a dream," Katarina whispered to herself, her heart heavy with the weight of the unknown. "But a dream with a message, a calling that beckons me toward the darkness that awaits."

CHAPTER 20

The night fell as Katarina heard a noise and ventured outside, where she spotted Ulrik departing the house, enveloped by the protective darkness of the seemingly endless night.

"Where are you going?" she asked, carefully examining his body language. Ulrik was clad in his crimson red, long coat, and black gloves. His black hair playfully danced with the touch of the mysterious wind. His blue eyes sparkled like sapphires in the moon's blissful light. The leaves had begun to fall from the trees in the nearby forest, and Ulrik wore a stern and troubled expression, years of suffering and hardship reflected in his spirit. The scent of moist rain still lingered in the air; one could almost taste the end of autumn.

"I will fulfil my promise to the priest," Ulrik said devotedly. "I always keep my promises, I will vanquish the demon." A coldness emanated from his words, revealing that although Ulrik was accustomed to violence, it brought him no satisfaction within the endless cycle of despair and pain.

"I am going with you," Katarina said stubbornly, ready to leave as she took determined steps forward. Ulrik stood still, not moving a muscle.

"What do you mean?" he asked, surprised, and impressed by her strong spirit. "The strandvaskare is a dreadful creature. They enjoy torturing people and haunting them. You just got freed from the mare. I do not wish for another creature to try to kill you," Ulrik expressed concern for Katarina's welfare, his only desire being to protect and shelter her from danger.

"How are you going to defeat the strandvaskare?" Katarina demanded, unwilling to let him leave alone. Ulrik paused, considering her question. "Are you planning to engage in eternal combat, relying solely on your powers? Both you and the strandvaskare are already dead. How can two undead creatures battle each other and emerge victorious?" Katarina sought an explanation with her firm tone.

"You mean the world to me. I don't want you to get hurt," Ulrik said sincerely, the truth echoing from his heart. "You are safe here, and as you said, I am already dead. I will heal from all wounds, and the strandvaskare cannot use fire. But you're just a human. How are you supposed to kill him?" Ulrik tried to convey his concern without sounding patronizing. The thought of losing Katarina haunted his reality, fear evident in his words.

"I want to help the strandvaskare, I do not believe that killing him is the answer." Katarina said as she walked up to Ulrik and took his hands in a comforting gesture.

"He is a demon. He doesn't deserve it," Ulrik responded with an unforgiving tone, ready to face yet another enemy.

"He died at sea, unable to find peace," Katarina continued gently. "He is not inherently evil, no one is. Everyone and everything simply are."

"I cannot protect you if I am fighting him," Ulrik admitted, his words tinged with the fear of losing Katarina.

"The solution is not always violence," Katarina said

convincingly, her words infused with hope. "That's how you've lived most of your life, and it hasn't been beneficial. I'm going with you," she declared in a stubborn voice. Ulrik looked at her, admiring her courage, unable to resist her determined spirit.

"You are very courageous for someone without immortal powers," he said, mesmerized by her strong heart.

"One does not need magical powers to be brave," Katarina responded and began to walk. Ulrik followed, joining her side. Together, they made their way to the stable and prepared a horse. Ulrik mounted first and assisted Katarina up behind him.

"Hold on tightly," he cautioned, his voice cutting through the dense shroud of the forest's eerie warnings. "The forest is filled with dangerous creatures at this hour. Many will try to harm you." Urging on the horse, they set off into the darkening night. Katarina strained her eyes against the abyss, but the only clarity came from the cacophony of nocturnal creatures. Their unseen forms lurked just beyond sight. The horse nervously stepped forward into the unknown territory, guided solely by Ulrik's command, placing complete trust in its handler. Darkness reigned supreme. The scent of pine trees filled the air. Elongated shadows murmured their inscrutable dialogue, whispering their incomprehensible words. The presence of väsen thickened in the environment, warning all who dared to enter. Katarina was aware of the dangers that lurked in the forest's dark protection. The horse snorted nervously, its nostrils flaring with trepidation.

Sitting resolutely, Ulrik attentively absorbed the darkness, seamlessly integrated yet distinct from its essence. Though the cold pressed tightly against Katarina, she felt safe in Ulrik's presence. The horse bravely continued toward their destination.

After a while, they arrived at the house where the priest had mentioned the strandvaskare dwelled. At the end of the lake, there stood a small, forsaken structure. Katarina could already discern the tortured creature's rasping cries, echoing ruthlessly within her body. Each wail was a symphony of agony that reverberated through her bones. The screams evoked unsettling memories of dying rabbits, their desperate pleas for life panicking in fear. Petrified, Katarina began to breathe rapidly, her heart racing. Ulrik, attuned to her escalating heartbeat and rising adrenaline, sought to comfort her.

"You need not fear," Ulrik reassured her, dismounting the horse to assist Katarina. "Do you wish to return home?" he asked, concern etched into his voice as the encompassing darkness of night surrounded them with its deep shadows. The light of the moon gleamed distantly in the sky.

"No," Katarina replied bravely, confronting her fears head-on. "I want to see this through." Ulrik nodded, taking her hand as they cautiously approached the pitch-black house. Nearby, the lake perfectly mirrored the ethereal glow of the moon, while the wind remained hushed and still. The air felt infected with an oppressive serenity, the silence punctuated only by the distant cry of the strandvaskare.

Drawing a deep breath, Katarina felt the dry air fill her lungs, infusing her with renewed vigour. Ulrik's presence offered stability in a tumultuous moment, urging her not to falter. Convinced she could handle the situation, Katarina prepared herself for what lay ahead. She wanted to help the strandvaskare find peace. As the strandvaskare screamed once more, its cries thundered through her bones. A crackling and creaking emanated from within the house, accompanied by dark smoke billowing forth. Through a window crack, a ghastly creature squeezed itself out, choking the air with its acrid stench. Bearing some semblance to a human, its swollen face possessed a sickly green-grey hue, while its body resembled the mud of a swamp, a twisted mockery of humanity. Towering in stature, its head appeared partially severed, reeds protruding from its hair, lips the colour of purple, and face marred by numerous bite marks. When noticing Katarina, the strandvaskare launched a violent assault. Reacting swiftly, Ulrik intercepted the demonic creature, engaging in combat while Katarina stumbled backward onto the ground.

As the skirmish ensued, water dripped from the strandvaskare's body with each movement, yet the creature proved sluggish compared to Ulrik, who easily gained the upper hand. With unwavering strength, Ulrik threw the strandvaskare to the ground, his grip firm and resolute.
"Stop!" Katarina urged compassionately, her voice a plea for mercy. Ulrik regarded her with surprise.

"He was about to attack you," Ulrik's words rang out, laced with a fierce protectiveness as he tightened his hold. Mercilessly, the strandvaskare struggled to break free. The creature exuded the stench of decaying fish and crayfish. Its agonized wails cascaded through the night. Katarina regarded the strandvaskare with pity, slowly advancing toward both of them. The creature appeared more akin to a wild animal than a man, consumed by its own rage. Locking eyes with the entity, Katarina discerned anguish and torment. An unheard injustice refused to release its hold and move forward, an unspoken plea for release from its eternal torment. As she drew nearer, the creature gradually calmed, its frenzied struggles ebbing.

"Release him," Katarina insisted emphatically, facing Ulrik.

"He will cause you harm," Ulrik warned, apprehensive of her potential injury.

"No, he will not, I can feel his lost spirit," Katarina countered confidently, placing her trust in her connection with the tormented soul. "I will help you find peace," she addressed the being. "I understand your pain, I know you've suffered unjustly. I'm here to guide you through letting go of the horrors that bind you, so you can find peace and move forward." Katarina spoke with a soothing voice, captivating the strandvaskare with her kindness. It ceased its frenzied movements, listening intently to the sound of her voice, its decayed teeth grinding slowly. Ulrik leaned in closer to the beast.

"If you lay a hand on her, I will destroy you!" he warned, releasing the strandvaskare forcefully, shadowing him closely to prevent any harm to Katarina. The strandvaskare rose to its feet and approached Katarina slowly, halting just a meter away, studying her intently. A glimmer of humanity flickered in its eyes upon hearing Katarina's words, its tumultuous existence momentarily stilled by her mellow presence. As the creature hesitated, a ray of soulfulness shimmered within its eyes, a shard of remorse among the darkness that had consumed its being.

"I understand your pain," Katarina continued in a compassionate tone. "Once, you were a man. Something dreadful occurred, leaving you to wander alone, unable to find peace. What happened to you?" she inquired genuinely. The creature extended its hands towards Katarina, she accepted its hand with empathy. At that moment, Katarina glimpsed the memories of the strandvaskare. She witnessed his joyful moments with his family, a life filled with love and harmony, before witnessing his brutal end, murdered at the lake, condemning him to a watery grave. He had been assaulted and battered. His assailants bound his limbs before casting him into the water from a small boat, leaving him to struggle for his life as he sank into the icy depths, destined for a cold, certain demise. Releasing Katarina's hand, the entity took a step back, meeting her gaze.

"They murdered you," she said, her voice heavy with sorrow. "I'm sorry for what you endured. Holding onto this form will only prolong your suffering. It's only when you let go that you can find peace." The strandvaskare growled in displeasure, a primal manifestation of its inner turmoil. "I understand you seek vengeance," Katarina acknowledged, hearing his pain and desire for retribution. "But that won't resolve anything," she explained. "This all happened many years ago. Your spirit has lingered at this lake for decades. It's only been a couple of weeks since you began haunting this place, but your death occurred long ago. The people who harmed you are likely deceased by now. By clinging to your anger and suffering, you're only punishing yourself. They've already moved on. Please, for your own sake, accept what happened and move on." The strandvaskare growled once more. "Yes, I know," Katarina said sympathetically. "Letting go of the past is not easy. But you don't belong here. This isn't life; you're trapped in between." Katarina reached out and touched the strandvaskare's hand. "It's okay. You can rest now," she assured him. "I know your story. Give me a token that belonged to you, and I'll bury it here on these shores so that something of yours is properly laid to rest." The strandvaskare handed Katarina a glove that had been embedded with his body. "I'll keep my promise," Katarina vowed. The strandvaskare slowly receded, turning into brown mud on the cold ground, leaving a sense of peace. Ulrik approached the spot where it had once stood. The earth beneath his feet stirred with unseen currents, bearing witness to the upheaval that had occurred in that hallowed place.

"Seems like he's gone," Ulrik said, relieved. "Impressive. You're indeed a very resourceful woman."

"Yes," Katarina replied, a mix of sadness and relief in her voice.

"How is it that you handle demonic creatures so well?" Ulrik inquired, his voice coloured with genuine curiosity and admiration.

"They're not demonic," Katarina clarified. "They're lost souls, wronged and unable to find their way back. All they want is peace. All any creature ever wants is peace." She glanced at Ulrik. "Isn't that what you want? To find peace?" She paused, studying his expression. "If I can help someone, then I will. Fighting fire with fire doesn't always work. I know many people and väsen believe that violence and death are the only solutions to winning a fight, and sometimes they are, but not always. Before resorting to arms, always try the more peaceful solution." Katarina wore a determined expression while uttering her hopeful words.

"Come," Ulrik said, putting his arm around her. "Let's go home."

CHAPTER 21

Ulrik lay ensconced in the darkness of their chamber, gazing at Katarina. Her deep, brown eyes exuded a friendly warmth, reflecting a kind soul always ready to offer compassion and see the best in others. Ulrik admired everything about her. In her arms he found peace, a sanctuary from the relentless horrors that plagued his restless mind, a place where his demons seemed far away. She brought out the goodness within him, anchoring him to this world. All that was beautiful in life seemed to emanate from her. Katarina was the beacon of light amidst his darkness; without her, hope would fade, and life would descend into a bleak nightmare. Affectionately, Ulrik ran his fingers through her hair, listening to the rhythm of her breathing, her heartbeat echoing his own desires. The warmth of her body beside him filled him with contentment; in her presence, the weight of past regrets and guilt seemed to dissipate, and the haunting memories retreated into the distance. The thought of a life without her was unfathomable, too agonizing to contemplate, impossible to endure. Katarina lifted her head and met Ulrik's gaze.

"What are you thinking?" she asked softly, her voice filled with admiration.

Ulrik's gaze softened as he beheld her, his lips tenderly touching hers in a gentle caress. "No one could ever compare to you. I would traverse the realms of hell itself to shield you from harm, confront every demon for you to safeguard your purity from the taint of darkness. I would sacrifice my life before anyone could lay a hand on you. In this world and the next, your essence will forever dwell within the depths of my soul. Your memory will resonate within my soul across lifetimes. I was destined to stand by your side for eternity," he whispered, his words carrying the weight of an unbreakable oath.

"I always sensed your love for me," Katarina said. "Initially, I hesitated when your father offered me the opportunity to work here again, but I'm glad I accepted. You were distant and cold for so many years. And now," she smiled, gently caressing his hair, "Now, all I desire is to be close to you."

"You ignite a flame in my darkness, bringing hope where none existed," Ulrik spoke romantically. "Your spirit dispels the shadows. With you, the night seems brighter. With you, all emptiness disappears. You draw me closer to my humanity. But I am damaged. As a draugr and returning warrior, I've sought to keep my distance from everyone, grappling with my own struggles," Ulrik confessed, turning away as haunting memories clouded his gaze. "Yet, I've always kept an eye on you, hoping one day you'd grant me the pleasure of your company. You are everything I ever wished for, everything I ever desired, and I will destroy anything that dares to harm you. Let me be your eternal guardian, your forever protector. I love you now, as I have loved you through the ages, and I shall love you until the stars themselves grow cold." Ulrik implored, his words filled with devotion and poetic longing. "Marry me, be mine for the rest of your life. I shall take no other; my heart will beat solely for you. I will always remain loyal, and my life will end the day you depart this world. I love you; I always have, and there will never be a day in the future when I do not. My heart beats for you and you alone, my devotion unwavering until the end of days." He declared. Katarina smiled upon hearing Ulrik's heartfelt words.

"Yes, I will," she agreed, "but you don't have to be so dramatic. I know you don't age, and you'll likely outlive me, and that's okay. I don't want you to perish just because I'm gone," she reassured him as an agonized expression flickered across Ulrik's features. The weight of eternity pressed down upon his weary heart.

"I cannot bear the thought of your death," he confessed, his tone filled with pain. "I dread the day when you won't be here." Rising from the bed, Ulrik returned with a small jewellery box and presented it to Katarina. As she opened the box, her breath got caught in her throat at the sight of the exquisite ring within.

"Do me the honour of being my wife," Ulrik declared faithfully. Katarina smiled and slid the ring onto her finger.

"You are my reason to exist," Ulrik declared.

"Yes," she agreed, admiring the ring.

"I will summon the priest tomorrow," Ulrik announced. "He has agreed to officiate our marriage, even though I am a draugr. The church may not recognize our union, but that matters little to me. I am determined to make this vow to you, to promise you forever. And if the Christian God denounces our union, then so be it. I will remain faithful and honour my commitment to you," Ulrik declared earnestly, offering Katarina all that he was. "I have no doubts in my mind that I will be a devoted husband to you. I will provide you with everything you need. I will always be by your side, for as long as you want me."

"And I will be your loyal wife," Katarina vowed, gently touching Ulrik's cheek. "I never envisioned falling in love with you, but now, I can't wait to spend my life with you," she expressed happily. "Your once cold exterior has transformed into that of a loving and loyal man," she observed, feeling Ulrik's sincerity resonating in her heart. Meeting his gaze, Katarina felt a surge of emotion as Ulrik leaned in to kiss her.

Ulrik's hands reached for the edges of her clothes, caressing the fabric as if in reverence to the beauty it cloaked. He assisted her in shedding the garment that shielded her from the chill of the world outside. His fingers traced the silhouette of her frame, lingering over the curve of her shoulder and the arc of her neck. Each movement reflected the depth of his affection.

As the weight of Katarina's clothes fell away, yielding to Ulrik's passionate touch, she felt a sense of erotic liberation wash over her being. Watching each other's naked bodies, the space between them seemed to shrink, collapsing into a singularity of shared intimacy and unspoken desire. Revelling in each other's presence, they stood suspended in time, two spirits bound together by an affection that defied the constraints of mere words.

Ulrik leaned in, his breath mingling with Katarina's in the intimate dance of romance. He cupped her face, his fingertips caressed the softness of her lips, a silent hymn to the beauty that enraptured his soul. As their gazes locked in a silent connection, the world around them faded into obscurity, leaving only the pulsating rhythm of their intertwined hearts. Ulrik's lips met Katarina's, closing the distance between them in a moment of longing and presence.

Ulrik's fingers danced upon Katarina's body with a fervour born of unspoken yearnings, coaxing forth moanings that painted the air with hues of longing and ecstasy. As Ulrik let his kisses descend towards Katarina's hips, he surrendered to the primal rhythm that pulsed within him. She moaned out and let herself be overwhelmed by passion as he put her down on the bed and parted her legs, beginning to lick her clitoris. Katarina's erotic calling became a vessel through which the very essence of her longing poured forth. She basked in the streams of desire that coursed through her veins as his tongue played vividly between her legs. Ulrik's tongue traversed the realms of tempo with the grace of a celestial waltz when wholeheartedly committed to pleasuring Katarina. His moist tongue spiralled in intricate patterns that mirrored the eternal rhythms of the universe as he indulged himself in her taste, savouring every moment. Like a cosmic ballet, his tongue pirouetted between moments of serenity and storms, paying close attention to Katarina's every reaction. Excitement and ecstasy exploded within her every cell; passion took over her essence as Ulrik put his entire tongue inside of her. Each shift in tempo was a journey unto itself, a voyage through the heated corridors of emotion and fire. His tongue was a blessing of contradictions, where tranquillity met turbulence, and harmony arose from discord. As Ulrik's tongue circled within and without Katarina's body, she started to move her hips, embracing the pleasure pulsating through her yearning body. She stood poised at the precipice of orgasmic completion; her entire body started to move in unison with the call of passion.

Suddenly, Katarina withdrew, her essence shimmering with the enigmatic allure of a celestial being. She cast a fleeting glance at Ulrik, filled with a myriad of meanings. She beckoned him to lie down, and in the unspoken language of lovers, he acquiesced without hesitation. Gently Katarina took Ulrik's penis in her mouth, her body consumed by desire. She cradled his erected penis within her mouth, moving to the cadence of his desires. While committing to pleasuring him, she let her hands move over Ulrik's body while his erection smoothly slipped in and out of her mouth. Katarina groaned in encouragement when feeling Ulrik's penis deep within her mouth and throat. Taken over by desire, Ulrik grabbed hold of Katarina's body, moving her hips towards his face. Katarina could feel his penis swell within her mouth and his moanings became louder as he started to lick her clitoris.

As Ulrik pulled Katarina's hips towards his mouth, his lips

meeting her clitoris, a harmony of sensations unfolded. The first delicate touch of sweetness against his tongue sent ripples of pleasure through his being, igniting a dance of senses within his body that transcended the mundane. With each languid lick, Ulrik rejoiced to the ecstasy of the moment, savouring the intricate interplay of flavours between Katarina's legs. Each swirl and whirl of his tongue painted a masterpiece upon her clitoris. Ulrik licked Katarina with a hunger that mirrored the primal yearning of a sailor adrift in the vast expanse of the sea. With each morsel, he delved deeper into the gastronomic mixture unfurling before him. His senses were attuned to the symphony of flavours that danced upon his tongue. Each lick was a pilgrimage, a journey into the heart of culinary alchemy, where tastes were transmuted into ambrosial treasures. In the hushed ambiance of passion, where the very air crackled with a sexual energy, his stride quickened when Katarina reached her orgasm. Ulrik felt her clitoris pulsating upon his yearning tongue as her climax reached its final. The sensation was enough to push him over his border, climaxing within Katarina's mouth. They yielded to the magnetic pull of their entwined souls, their bodies converging in a symphony of longing and belonging. They surrendered to the gravitational pull of their shared passion, falling into each other's arms, embracing the approaching night.

CHAPTER 22

Katarina walked to the nearby neighbour's house, situated not far from the estate where she worked. Elsie had asked for her help in gathering some items she lacked the time to retrieve herself. Katarina was happy to assist her friend and didn't hesitate to venture out into the beautiful autumn day. The sun was shining brightly, its golden rays danced upon the crimson leaves that adorned the branches of trees. Half of the leaves had already fallen from the trees, creating an endless loop of colours on the cold ground. The atmosphere was notably tranquil, a remarkable calmness that appeared somewhat unusual for the ongoing season, evoking a subtle sense of unease as if hinting at an underlying anomaly. The scent of inevitable winter hung delicately in the air.

As she walked, Katarina felt a sense of both tranquillity and unease. An ineffable essence lingered in the air, a shadowy presence unwilling to dissipate. The stroll allowed her to contemplate and organize her thoughts. She reflected on her impending marriage to Ulrik, a man she had initially approached with caution and hesitation. However, she had since fallen in love with him and was grateful that they now could begin planning their future.

Katarina had been married before. Her first marriage had been orchestrated by her family, and while she had adapted to the circumstances, it lacked the depth of personal connection she sought. Now, with Ulrik, she felt a profound desire to offer herself wholly. She yearned to share her life entirely with him, confident in his commitment to safeguard her and steadfastly support her throughout their days together. Her heart overflowed with love and passion when she thought of Ulrik. His protective nature and unwavering devotion made her feel secure.

Katarina was certain that Ulrik loved her more than she could comprehend, he had loved her his entire life, and now she welcomed their union with open arms. She felt fortunate for everything life had given her. Katarina didn't mind that he was a draugr, she held a longstanding appreciation and respect for supernatural beings. She did not perceive them as malevolent or tainted; rather, they represented diverse entities coexisting within the world. Contemplating the notion of a divine creator responsible for all life, she questioned how väsen could be deemed inherently wicked. Recognizing the societal classification of draugrs as demons, Katarina refrained from passing judgment on Ulrik. His gentle demeanour and attentive care overshadowed any past misdeeds. She cherished him for his present character. The actions from his past were not for her to judge, as long as he remained a changed man.

Suddenly, a sharp sound pierced the air, causing the surroundings to tremble with unease. Before Katarina could react, she found herself encircled by ominous creatures. A chilling sensation of impending doom and loss seized her very core, while the lingering scent of decay clung tenaciously to the air. Abruptly, darkness enveloped her, and she succumbed to unconsciousness. Dark shadows lurked around in broad daylight, searching for their victim. Their twisted, crippled hands seized Katarina and bore her away to an unknown destination, where shadows danced with malice and nightmares prowled in the realm of reality.

CHAPTER 23

As consciousness clawed its way back to Katarina, she found herself engulfed in a suffocating prison of darkness. Waking up in a state of distress, her heart almost beat out of her chest. Confusion enveloped her as she struggled to grasp her surroundings. Disoriented and lost, she battled to piece together the fragments of her fractured reality. It all seemed like a blurry, incomprehensible dream, a distant illusion. Each disjointed thought felt like a jagged shard slicing through the fog of her awareness. A faint scent of unfamiliar spices lingered in the air, a haunting aroma that dallied in the stagnant atmosphere, delicately teasing her senses. Her temples were throbbed with a dull ache as a relentless drumbeat echoed the discordance within her mind.

The surface beneath Katarina's body yielded to her touch with a softness reminiscent of fur from a formidable beast. Its texture gently caressed her fingers. Questions invaded her thoughts: Where was she? What had happened? For how long had she been unconscious? The room was warm, but darkness blurred her vision, allowing only vague shapes to emerge: some form of furniture on the opposite side, a window to her left, and a door directly ahead.

Rasping sounds emanated from behind the door, accompanied

by voices speaking in an unfamiliar language. Gathering her resolve, Katarina rose from the bed and approached the door cautiously. She made sure not to make a sound, pretending to still be asleep.

Suddenly, a light flickered on in the adjacent room, casting a faint glow from underneath the door. Katarina hesitated, stepping back to examine the window, but finding it securely locked with no means of escape. The door remained her only option.

With no recourse but to confront the mysteries that lay beyond, Katarina inhaled deeply, summoning her resilience, uncertain of the peril awaiting her on the other side. With a determined exhalation, she pushed the door open. The light attacked her eyes with an intense force, while the scent of unknown spices grew stronger. Blinking against the onslaught of light, Katarina's eyes struggled to adjust to their new surroundings. As her vision gradually cleared, the menacing tableau that awaited her emerged from the shadows with chilling clarity.

At the centre of the room sat a well-dressed man cloaked in an aura of malevolence, clad in a cobalt blue coat. Beside him lurked four grotesque creatures, their visages twisted and contorted by decay. Skin hung from their faces in tattered strips, their clothing nothing more than rags clinging desperately to their emaciated frames. Dirt and mud covered their bodies. Katarina stood frozen; her breath caught in her throat. The well-dressed man stared at her with a chilling, yet charming grin. His long, meticulously maintained blond hair framed intense grey eyes. His pale white complexion and strong, masculine features exuded a graceful allure mingled with lethal savagery.

Despite his captivating appearance, there was something terrifying about his predatory grin and gaze. His eyes bore an indifferent, bloodthirsty gleam, indicative of a creature inclined to violence and deriving pleasure from the suffering of the innocent. He seemed devoid of compassion and empathy, inherently cruel and vicious. And yet, he was a master of deceit.

Katarina's blood ran cold as she beheld the man. She felt paralyzed, unable to speak or breathe. Every instinct urged her to flee, but she knew it would be futile. The man possessed powers beyond the mortal realm; escape was useless. He would capture her effortlessly.

The other demonic creatures seemed to have caught her scent and turned towards Katarina, growling in an unbearable chorus. Their eyes were scarcely visible behind their twisted, decaying faces, dead flowers and leaves entwined within their flesh.

"I hope you enjoy the aroma of this exotic spice," the blond man remarked effortlessly, gracefully rising from his chair. He was tall and walked with a confident, arrogant stride, as if the world were his playground and he could bend it to his twisted desires. His movements exuded a calculated confidence that bespoke a dominion over the realms of darkness itself. "I have the courtesy to mask their scent while we have company," he added, attempting a polite smile that Katarina saw through, revealing the core of a monstrous and violent creature who would stop at nothing to fulfil his will. A being of boundless cruelty and unyielding desire stood before her. His smile, a grotesque parody of politeness, twisted upon his lips like a serpent preparing to strike. Katarina took a step backwards, unsure of what to do next.

"Where are my manners, allow me to introduce myself," the man continued, his voice a chilling whisper that echoed through the room like a ghostly lament. "My name is Vasilij," he bowed courteously. "I am certain you have heard of me." Vasilij locked eyes with Katarina, attempting to enslave her soul. A ruthless, ice-cold gaze seemed to pierce her very being as she met the stare of this draugr. "Do not be afraid," he crooned, his words dripping with honeyed deceit. "I will not harm you, not now at least." With a mocking laugh, Vasilij retreated to his seat, his eyes fixed upon one of the demonic creatures that served at his bidding. A silent command passed between them, and the draugr obediently fetched another chair before vanishing into the shadows at his master's command. "Leave us," Vasilij's voice carried the weight of ancient authority. With a collective shudder, the hideous beings slunk away, their forms melted into the darkness like wraiths fleeing the light. They left the room with haste, akin to smoke billowing from a fireplace. Katarina watched them with a mixture of dread and fascination. She was unsure whether they were corporeal beings or mere phantoms haunting the edges of her sanity. They seemed more like ghosts than physical demons like Vasilij and Ulrik. Their unearthly forms seemed to glide effortlessly above the ground, emitting spine-chilling, despicable wails that echoed through the room like the anguished cries of lost souls.

With an unsettling smile that failed to mask the sinister intent lurking beneath, Vasilij invited Katarina to sit beside him. Every fibre of her being screamed for her to flee, but she knew that defying him would only lead to her death. Katarina's only chance of survival was to comply with Vasilij's commands if she wanted to emerge from this situation unscathed. Slowly, Katarina settled into the chair next to Vasilij, her gaze fixed upon his hauntingly beautiful visage, attempting to maintain her distance and buy time.

"I apologize if they frightened you," his voice was as smooth as silk yet tinged with an undercurrent of malice. Vasilij poured a cup of wine and extended it to Katarina. "They are dreadful, unlike me and Ulrik," he added with a hint of contempt in his voice. "We are special, different, but I'm sure you already know that." The emphasis on the last syllable echoed in Katarina's ears with an insistent force.

"Ulrik is unique. I've encountered many draugrs, and turned quite a few, but most of them turn out to be very disappointing. Don't get me wrong, Ulrik has disappointed me too. After all, he left me in the middle of nowhere without a word of explanation," Vasilij remarked, his voice dripping with a blend of reverence and bitterness, disappointment haunted his words. A simmering undercurrent of anger and betrayal tainted his words. While speaking of his elusive protégé, Vasilij's eyes glinted with a mixture of admiration and resentment.

"But he is more refined, more sophisticated, and more graceful than those monsters you saw dining with me. They don't want to dine; they want to skulk around graveyards and lurk within tombs and graves, forever obsessing over dead men's belongings and occasionally killing by passers. But Ulrik..." Awe filled Vasilij's eyes as he spoke his disciple's name, a note of wonder creeping into his tone. "He can resist the urge that calls to us from within. You see, every draugr has this longing, this obsessive yearning that consumes us. We are drawn to corpses, to sleep in the ground and watch over the departed. But he would never let that weakness overtake him. I'm the same," Vasilij said with pride.

"Most draugrs aspire to live like this, but they lack the discipline and strength. Sometimes they succeed halfway and end up as some kind of half-breed. But Ulrik..." Vasilij's eyes reflected both obsession and admiration. "He doesn't even smell like a draugr anymore. From what I know, he doesn't even kill anymore." A flicker of disappointment passed over Vasilij's features, overshadowing his earlier admiration.

"It's such a shame," he lamented. "He was such a talent. I must admit, I was rather offended when he left me. How dare he leave me!" A violent darkness consumed Vasilij's voice; his eyes turned black, and his lips became purple. "But now I've finally found him again." The darkness that had momentarily clouded Vasilij's demeanour receded, replaced by a veneer of composure.

"What is it that you want?" Katarina asked, afraid to know the answer, stumbling over her words.

"What do I want?" Vasilij repeated. "I want him back," his tone dripping with possessiveness. "He belongs to me. I made him. I claimed dominion over him. I am his maker!" Vasilij hissed like a snake.

"Does a maker own their protégé?" Katarina questioned, her voice edged with rebellion, careful not to overstep the boundaries of the draugr master.

"No," Vasilij admitted, his demeanour eerily calm. "But he is mine, and I always get what I want," greed shone through his words. "I do not get what he sees in you," Vasilij continued, his gaze scrutinizing Karin with disdain. "You are just an ordinary human. I have seen so many extraordinary beauties, and you are just a sweet housemaid, nothing more." A sense of disappointment coloured his words. "I was hoping for a queen or a goddess," he drummed his fingers on the table. "Oh well," Vasilij continued.

"What do you want with me?" Katarina asked, her heartbeat betraying her confidence.

"With you?" Vasilij repeated, his words echoed ominously in the room, his voice dripped with sinister intent. "Nothing, really," he continued, his tone filled with a menacing edge. "It is Ulrik that I desire, and now that I have you, he will surely come. And when he does, we shall leave this tedious and mundane countryside. There is nothing of interest here," he scoffed. " Have you seen the world?" Vasilij paused, looking at Katarina. "No, of course you have not," he sneered, his voice laden with contempt. "You are but a penniless woman."

"How come you are not like other draugrs?" Katarina inquired, trying to stay calm. "How come you are different? I assume that Ulrik learned his way of living from you," Katarina continued, her words shaded with a feigned curiosity as she sought to stall for time. Vasilij fixed her with a penetrating gaze, his eyes gleaming with intrigue.

"Of course, you should be interested in my history," Vasilij mused, a sly smile tugging at the corners of his lips. "Maybe there is more to you than meets the eye," he remarked cryptically, a secretive look fell over his face.

"I would like to know your story," Katarina declared, meeting Vasilij's gaze with a mixture of trepidation and fascination. "Such a formidable draugr must have a mesmerizing past."

"You are trying to flatter me, and it is working!" Vasilij acknowledged, a smug grin spreading across his features. He seemed content, intrigued to share his story. "Very well, I will do you the honour of indulging you in my saga," Vasilij said theatrically, moving his hands. "It all began a very long time ago," Vasilij's voice resonated with passion and fervour. "It was about five hundred years ago in Rus. I was an ordinary man, no one special. I lived a calm, boring life with my family in my village. And then they came," he growled, his voice darkening with hatred, "the plunderers from the north, the pale shadows with long hair and beards. Brutal men without a conscience! These raiders invaded my village, slaughtered the people, raped the women, and enslaved the children. They tortured and massacred my people! I was left to slowly die from my wounds. I felt the chill biting my body and the enticement of vengeance fuel my resilient spirit. Suddenly a creature appeared. I was unable to move and could not clearly see its face. But I felt the stench. I knew that I was going to die, but I could not find peace with the thought of my enemies raiding freely in my country, destroying everything I held dear," he continued, his words dripping with poison.

"I felt a sharp bite in my neck and the creature started to feed on the remaining of my blood. Before I lost consciousness, the creature opened my mouth and pushed something down my throat, forcing me to swallow," Vasilij confessed, his spirit aflame with righteous fury. "A couple of hours later I woke up again, but something was different. I could not feel my heartbeats. The decaying creature was sitting right in front of me, this time I could see its face clearly. Once it had been a woman, now only a twisted memory of something resembling a woman remained. She stared at me, almost unable to speak. My maker had taken pity on me. She wanted to give me the opportunity to avenge my perpetrators. She too had been wronged, raped, and tortured, left for dead by the berserkers," he recalled, a shudder coursing through his frame.

"The berserkers had a draugr among them who viciously tortured my people. The draugr turned women into other draugrs for fun, to torment and taunt them. You see, not everyone can make the transition. To become a draugr, one needs a certain type of darkness within, a darkness that a lot of humans lack. My maker turned me to help her, to get me to fight alongside her against those despicable men. And I did, one after one I killed them in cold-blooded murder! Revenge has such a sweet taste! My maker was weak. She had her demonic strength, but she could not resist the urges of the draugr and slowly lost her connection to the outside world. That is what happens when a draugr spends too much time in a tomb or in a grave. They lose touch with who they were. They only remember that they are a draugr and that they desire blood and treasure." A ghostly undertone haunted Vasilij's words.

"But I did not. I kept away from that life, always focusing on my mission. I remembered my mission. And I noticed that I could consume all the blood I wanted without decaying. At first, I did it for fun, to get back at my enemies. There was something almost poetic about drinking my enemies' blood," vengeance echoed through Vasilij's words. "Revenge tasted so seductive. After killing every single one of the berserkers and burning the draugr, I was finally free. There is only so much vengeance can do for you, it tastes divine, but it will not keep you satisfied." There was both emptiness and pride in Vasilij's eyes, mirroring a complex character.

"But what was I supposed to do? I started to travel around and found new prey. For that is what we are, make no mistake. I know that you love him. I can smell it on your hormones and pheromones when mentioning his name. But he is just like me, a predator, dangerous to every human, regardless of what you may think," Vasilij warned. "And my journey continued. There was a whole world just waiting for me, blood, and violence everywhere! And I was the top predator, stronger than most demons." A greedy look appeared in Vasilij's eyes. "But after a while, one gets bored. I encountered many demons and creatures. I turned several into what I am, but they all disappointed me. You saw the creatures sitting at this table. They are ugly swamp trolls, unable to control their hunger and impulses!"

"But then I met him, Ulrik," the way Vasilij said Ulrik's name echoed in Katarina's ear with passion and awe, a mixture of dread and desire. She knew that she stood on the precipice of a nightmare from which there could be no awakening. "He is sublime, like no other. So violent and strong, yet in control of his desire. He was my favourite, my masterpiece, and I need him back," Vasilij paused.
"Perhaps I should turn you into a draugr," he suggested and smiled. Fear infected Katarina's veins, and her face turned pale. "I could make you my eternal supporter, my haven, but no one knows how someone will be affected by the transition. Besides, I do not think that anyone would be able to turn you. I cannot sense the darkness that is required. And I need you to make Ulrik follow me peacefully. I do not wish to battle him; he is very strong and capable. Even though I am older and more experienced, he has a certain way. We are more monstrous than those draugrs you just witnessed," Vasilij contemplated. "We are not bound to the ground; we walk freely in the world, free to slay whenever we want!" Vasilij's eyes darkened, the shadows within

them swirled like an untamed tempest.

"What if he does not want to go with you?" Katarina asked, afraid to hear the answer.

"He must," Vasilij said with darkness in his voice. "If not, then I will take your life in the most gruesome way. I have a very vivid imagination. As long as he is with me, you are safe. He loves you so much; I am certain that he will go with me."

"What if he will fight you?" Katarina pressed, her heart pounding in her chest, her words trembling.

"He will not be that foolish. I have four of my companions with me. I was impressed by how you vanquished the mare. Bravo, I did not expect that from such a fragile creature like yourself," there was both admiration and contempt in Vasilij's voice.

"How do you know that he will come for me?" Katarina asked, trying to mask the truth of their bond. Vasilij leaned in closer to her.

"Because, my dear, you are the reason he returned," Vasilij whispered, his words echoed with a chilling promise. "We need only wait."

CHAPTER 24

Ulrik felt a compelling tug within his veins, something pulled him from the inside. Whispers echoed in his ears; an internal voice that refused to be silenced. Its claws dug into his skin, demanding his undivided attention. The subtle murmurs of the night beckoned to him, their eerie voices freezing his marrow and causing his bones to shiver. They seemed to emanate from the shadows, swirling around him like phantoms in the night. With a heavy heart and a mind clouded by uncertainty, Ulrik succumbed to the call of the abyss. Each step he took felt heavier than the last, his path shrouded in darkness. Yet, a sense of inevitability drove him forward, propelling him towards a destiny he could not escape.

"Where are you going?" Else inquired, taken aback as she observed Ulrik. His gaze bore the depth of the darkest night.

"They are here," Ulrik's response was curt, his gaze fixed with determination as he left his home, striding purposefully toward the forest, drawn involuntarily towards the looming darkness of the woods. Emerging from the shadows of the trees, four haunting figures materialized. Their foul stench assaulted his senses, filling his nose with an unbearable odour. Their twisted forms cast macabre silhouettes against the moonlit backdrop.

Ulrik stood his ground, prepared to defend himself if necessary. Every muscle in his body tensed, ready to spring into action.

He remained silent, listening to the drooling, and whispering sounds of the draugrs that surrounded him. Their guttural growls and sibilant whispers filled the night air. Alone, he braced himself for yet another encounter with unknown adversaries. The gnarled figures, grotesque in their decay, gathered around him, their movements as unsettling as the howling of the night. Ulrik stood tall and resolute, undaunted by the odds arrayed against him. He had faced greater numbers and fought battles where hope seemed but a fleeting dream. Death and suffering held no fear for him. With a silent command, the draugrs commenced their ominous procession, their twisted forms contorted in an unsettling dance of shadows. Their growls echoed as they floated above the ground. Without hesitation, Ulrik followed, his senses attuned to the foreboding atmosphere that enveloped them, every muscle primed for combat. The gentle touch of the wind ruffled his hair as he traversed the forest, the hard, cold ground beneath his feet, accompanied by the rattling sounds of the draugrs in motion. The demons moved with a labored gait. Their movements betrayed the weight of centuries upon their withered frames. Yet, Ulrik knew that within a draugr lay formidable strength; even if they appeared weakened or sluggish, their capabilities and power remained undiminished. With each passing moment, the shadows grew deeper, obscuring the path ahead in an impenetrable veil of gloom.

As daylight faded, giving way to reigning darkness, the draugrs seemed to find solace in the diminishing sun. In silence, they continued their march, with Ulrik carefully assessing the situation. With each passing moment, the shadows grew deeper, obscuring the path ahead in an impenetrable ocean of misery. One of the draugrs halted, turning to gaze at Ulrik with eyes devoid of life, now mere empty husks. Such was the true nature of a draugr, a form Ulrik had sworn never to succumb to, striving to maintain his humanity for Katarina's sake. The draugr inspected him wordlessly. Time had eroded its consciousness, its awareness distant, its spirit lost within the unknown. Left behind were only the vestiges of a tortured existence, adrift in the void between worlds. Ulrik knew that many draugrs entered this state after years of confinement in graves, becoming mere shadows resembling ghosts. Those who lingered too long in the realm of the dead, gradually descended into madness.

The other draugrs emitted a dreadful cry, the chorus of the damned reverberating through the stillness of the forest. With a guttural growl, the draugr turned away, and continued walking. Together, they traversed the forest like soulless demons until, after hours of travel, they arrived at a house. Ulrik concentrated all his energy, channelling every ounce of his resolve, advancing toward the dwelling with determination. He knew what would await him.

It was a big house, its interior illuminated with light. Ulrik recognized the dwelling—a few years prior, a wealthy family resided there, until tragedy struck, and they succumbed to an unknown illness, leaving their home deserted. The heavy oak door creaked open under his touch. Behind him, the draugrs slunk into the darkness of the foyer, their forms melding seamlessly with the shadows. Sensing his maker's presence, Ulrik felt a pull from within, every fibre of his being responding to the call. He knew Vasilij was present; all he had to do was follow the internal whisper, an invisible tether drawing him irrevocably toward his fate. Every muscle in Ulrik's body tensed, prepared for whatever awaited him in the next room, knowing Vasilij to be a ruthless opponent.

As Ulrik entered the room, he met Katarina's fearful gaze, her eyes pleading for salvation from the dangerous creature seated beside her. Vasilij's smile, wide and disarming, seemed to stretch impossibly wide across his pale visage as he beheld Ulrik's arrival.

"Ulrik!" Vasilij's voice boomed with an unsettling cheerfulness as he rose from his seat, his movements oozing with an unnatural grace. "Ulrik, my dear protégé, you're finally here!" Vasilij enveloped him in an embrace, gently caressing Ulrik's face. "How I've missed you." Taking Ulrik's hand, Vasilij led him to the table, his grip firm and unyielding.

"Come, sit down," he instructed. Ulrik remained composed, assessing the situation as he settled into a chair directly across from Katarina, who appeared more at ease now that Ulrik had arrived.

"Now that we're all gathered here, let's enjoy some dinner!" the draugr master insisted playfully.

Vasilij's palms met with a sharp clap. From the depths of the kitchen, a raspy growl emerged, accompanied by the unmistakable shuffling of decaying footsteps. The draugrs appeared, carrying food with them. Katarina's expression turned to disgust as she watched their rotting limbs touching the food. Her stomach churned at the mere thought of consuming anything tainted by these grotesque creatures. With a loud clatter, the draugrs put the food on the table, spilling half of it. Ulrik remained poised, his gaze locked in a silent battle of wills with Vasilij.

"Please, eat!" Vasilij instructed with a hint of aggression in his tone. Katarina hesitated, fearing the potential consequences of consuming food that had been in contact with the bodies of these disintegrating creatures.

"Do not eat it," Ulrik commanded, his eyes fixed unwaveringly on Vasilij. Katarina sought reassurance from Ulrik as the draugrs ceased eating, beginning to hiss in a dreadful manner, their heads jerking back and forth in displeasure. Saliva dripped from their mouths, staining the floor and walls.

"You see, now you've upset my friends," Vasilij remarked with disappointment, his expression taking on a psychotic edge.

"Katarina will fall ill from consuming that," Ulrik warned, his gaze never leaving Vasilij's unnerving smile. "She will not eat it. Where did you find these inadequate draugrs? They've been in a grave for so long that they've nearly lost all semblance of humanity!" Ulrik expressed his disgust, his voice tinged with revulsion.

"Well, they are my protectors," Vasilij's smile widened, a macabre display of amusement danced in his eyes. "They may not possess your beauty and grace," he replied, his voice a sickening blend of mockery and menace, "but make no mistake, as you well know, a draugr retains its powers until the day it is vanquished. You are vastly outnumbered. Though I admit I am intrigued; I'd like to see you attempt to defeat us all. It would be quite spectacular. I am aware of the true extent of your abilities," Vasilij's tone darkened. "If it weren't for her, you might have attempted to fight us all. But you cannot defend her and fight us at the same time," he added, glancing at Katarina.

"Run! Get away from here, save yourself!" Katarina urged, looking at Ulrik.

Vasilij's laughter echoed through the room like the toll of a funeral bell, his gaze fixed upon Katarina with a chilling certainty. "He won't abandon you," he asserted confidently. "He is a man of steadfast convictions, incapable of betraying his morals. I'll make this simple for everyone: if you come with us, I will spare her life; if not, I'll end her myself while you watch," a cruel smirk twisted Vasilij's lips as he delivered his ultimatum, his words a toxic promise.

"It's alright, Katarina," Ulrik reassured her. "I will go with you," he stated, fixing his gaze on Vasilij, "but on one condition, you leave her unharmed. Neither you nor your companions will touch her." A surge of defiance coursed through Ulrik's veins as he met Vasilij's gaze head-on, his resolve unyielding. "I demand your word," he growled.

"I swear," Vasilij replied, his smile self-righteous, raising a hand in mock solemnity.

"I do not trust your words," Ulrik retorted, his tone harsh.

"So, you would doubt me?" Vasilij snarled, his tone laden with anger. "Well, good boy! You've seen enough to know my true nature." With deliberate movements, Vasilij walked over to a drawer, slowly opening it to heighten the suspense. From within, he retrieved a necklace adorned with sparkling sapphires. With a theatrical flourish, Vasilij revealed a treasure trove of glittering jewels. Its beauty was captivating, radiating like a beacon of opulence. The dazzling stones illuminated the room, commanding attention with their presence.

"Look, something I acquired from a European princess," Vasilij announced with a smile. Katarina's breath caught in her throat as Vasilij closed in on her, his presence a suffocating weight that pressed down upon her like a leaden incarceration. With practiced ease, he adorned her with the stolen finery, each piece a chain that bound her ever tighter to his will.

Returning to the drawer, Vasilij selected a ring, a bracelet, a set of earrings, and a tiara, adorning Katarina with each piece. "There, much better!" he declared, content with his handiwork. "A reward for your loyalty, my dear. She can have it, as a gift, a handsome compensation for losing you as her provider," Vasilij declared, his gaze fixed on Ulrik, his voice a thunderclap that shattered the oppressive silence like glass. "Sign over your estate in her name, we can wait a couple of days before departing. Make the arrangements. She will return home, escorted by my friends. You may accompany them if you wish, ensuring you witness my commitment to keeping my promise. Leave all your possessions to her. And she may keep the jewellery; I have no issue acquiring new ones. In fact, I rather enjoy it!" Vasilij grinned ruthlessly, his eyes gleaming with the hunger of a predator that had found its prey. "We will vanish, never to return, and we shall not harm her, as long as you remain with me. You may retrieve her now. After that, kindly escort my friends to the graveyard. They are becoming unnervingly restless in this house. They are not like us after all. They need to commune with the dead," Vasilij stated with sincerity in his eyes. Katarina sat in silence, careful not to provoke Vasilij.

"How much blood has been spilled over those jewels?" she inquired with horror, her gaze lingering on their undeniable beauty.

"More than you can imagine," Vasilij's response slithered forth like a serpent's whisper, his gaze pierced through the veil of shadows that cloaked his intentions. "But fear not, my dear. Their worth outweighs the sins that taint their past." The room seemed to darken as Vasilij spoke. "But you needn't concern yourself with that. You could sell them and live like a duchess for the rest of your days, in addition to inheriting Ulrik's estate. What more could Ulrik desire? His one true love will be provided for indefinitely," Vasilij attempted to sound romantic. "You see, I am displaying great generosity here. I could have killed you immediately," Vasilij turned towards Katarina, "but I've chosen to spare your life and bestow upon you these invaluable gifts. Show me some gratitude!" Vasilij's eyes darkened, and his lips took on a purple hue as he spoke.

"I will accompany her, bid farewell, and transfer my estate into her name," Ulrik declared, his heart filled with pain.

"Indeed, do so, and then return to me." A predatory gleam flickered in Vasilij's eyes as he uttered the words.

CHAPTER 25

"What are you doing?" Katarina's voice wavered as Ulrik pressed the weight of the paper into her trembling arms. The parchment whispered of a future she had not dared to envision. His frustration and pain were heart-breaking, evident in the way he moved. Despite his efforts to shut down and maintain a pragmatic demeanour, the emotions still managed to seep through, colouring his actions with a sense of inner turmoil.

"This is the deed to the house," Ulrik explained, pushing away his feelings from his words. Each syllable was heavy with the burden of his decision. "I have written you as my heir in my will. I have informed everyone here of my decision; they all agree and are happy to have you as their lady of the house," he continued, his tone devoid of emotion, as if he were but a vessel carrying out a predetermined fate, detaching himself from the situation.

"So, you are just leaving?" Katarina's disappointment seeped into the room like a noxious fog, her voice a lamentation tinged with sorrow and betrayal. "I thought that you would stay and fight for me!?" Her words hung in the air like a curse. Pain echoed within her words. Ulrik stopped, haunted by her words, afraid that she would misinterpret the situation.

"I am fighting for you," he said with a devotion that lingered within his heart. Slowly, he turned around to face Katarina. "I am ensuring that you can live comfortably for the rest of your life," his voice strained with the weight of his sacrifice. Ulrik looked at her with pain in his eyes. Letting go of her yet another time was excruciating. An unbearable feeling pounded within his chest, draining his life-force from the inside.

"Without you!" Katarina's anguish reverberated through the room; pain shone through her words. "That is not how I want to live!" Her words were a haunting echo of the love and loss that now defined their fate.

"I must go with Vasilij; if not, then he will kill you," Ulrik stated, tormented by his choice.

"We can find a way to defeat him!" Katarina sounded hopeful, eager to find a solution. "Please do not go with him, do not leave me!" She pleaded. "I need you," she whispered, her voice barely notable above the haunting whispers of the night. Ulrik smiled and touched her cheek, a lifetime of devotion within his touch.

"You do not need me," Ulrik's voice was a chilling murmur. "You killed a mare, you defeated the lyktgubbe and the strandvaskare," he said with admiration. "You will do just fine on your own."

"I did not defeat the lyktgubbe and strandvaskare," Katarina corrected. "I helped them find peace. And even if I can live alone, I do not want to. I want you to be by my side."

"There is nothing more I wish for in this world than to remain by your side. You helped me to find peace too," Ulrik said with a sincere tone, his smile genuine but tinged with sorrow. "You gave me hope, you are my reason to live, my light through the darkness of this world. I would sacrifice everything within this universe for you. My only reason for breathing is to protect you. And unfortunately, this is the only way of protecting you," Ulrik sighed, tormented, the depth of his devotion unfathomable.

"What do you mean?" Katarina asked. A cold sternness appeared in Ulrik's eyes.

"I cannot vanquish him, I cannot vanquish Vasilij," the painful truth echoed within his words. "A draugr cannot cause the death of its maker."

"I can do it for you," Katarina said courageously and loyally, wanting to do everything in her power to fight for their love.

"No!" his voice thundered, stopping her. "It is too dangerous. He is too powerful and has too many connections. There are few creatures in this world that would dare to go up against such a formidable draugr. Demons everywhere do his bidding. You would die; he is too strong," fear of losing Katarina haunted Ulrik's words, consuming his core.

"Fire would burn him!" Katarina insisted, trying to find a solution. "I could burn down his house while he was sleeping. He does sleep, does he not?" Katarina asked with the heart of a warrior ready for battle.

"Yes, my habit of not sleeping is rare among draugrs," Ulrik contemplated. "But he would hear you coming; he always has several other demons nearby. Not only the draugrs that escorted us here. It is too dangerous; I do not want to risk your life. Vasilij is a very cruel creature," fear briefly flickered in Ulrik's eyes, a fleeting but undeniable glimpse of vulnerability amidst his usual composure. "I have seen his true nature!"

"Then what creature could face him and win?" Katarina asked, unable to accept the situation. She wanted to fight for their love.

"I do not know," Ulrik replied with hopelessness in his voice, conveying the weight of his despair and the dimness of his outlook. "A fire-breathing dragon, perhaps," Ulrik attempted to smile through his joke, though the strain was evident, revealing the effort he exerted to maintain a sense of lightness despite inner struggles. He gently touched Katarina's hair. "The memory of your touch will always linger in my mind, your presence the only one that will ever occupy my heart. I have loved you from the first day I laid eyes on you, and I will love you until the very last day that the devil vanquishes me. Even as I suffer in hell, the memory of you will still give me comfort, even in the most dreadful moments. My life has not been a waste, for I have loved you. And if there is anything like a next life, then I will find you, and I will love you then. I would carry all your sins to hide them from God himself. Forever I am yours, not even eternity will rid me of your blissful influence. My soul will forever love your soul, my soul will forever yearn for yours."

"Please, do not leave!" Katarina pleaded, her arms enfolding Ulrik in a desperate embrace.

"I do not wish to part from you," eternal love hidden within his words, "you shall forever remain in my dreams, a beautiful shadow of the past." The draugrs growled from outside the house.

"I must leave now," Ulrik uttered with a heavy heart, his words carrying the burden of sorrow or concern that weighed heavily upon him. The agony of their separation was etched upon his features.

"Forever, you shall have my love," he declared, sealing his oath with a kiss that conveyed a lifetime of affection. Katarina accompanied Ulrik outside, her heart heavy with burden and ache, her mind overwhelmed with frustration. Ulrik pressed his lips to her hand. "Forever yours," he vowed before relinquishing her grasp and disappearing into the approaching dawn, his silhouette swallowed by the commanding shadows.

Sadness and grief exploded within every cell of Katarina's body; her heart teetered on the brink of despair. She could not bear the thought of losing him. The realization ate her from within, threatening to consume her. At first, hopelessness and fear took hold of her being, then she had an idea. A wistful thought galloped through her mind. Within the depths of her sorrow, a spark of defiance ignited. With determined strides, she hastened to the barn, her mind ablaze with a plan born of desperation.

"Tomte!" Katarina called out upon entering the stable, the smell of animals floated in the air. A rustling sound was heard from the hay, and a creature began to move underneath. The tomte appeared, sporting a confused look on her face. The creature frowned her eyebrows. Her long hair was filled with hay and leaves.

"Are the demons finally gone?" the tomte asked, glancing at Katarina. Her eyes were kind and friendly. "Dreadful creatures! Not at all like Ulrik."

"You heard what happened?" Katarina asked with a worried heart.

"No, I just noticed their presence. But I am just one tomte; if they attacked the animals, I would not be able to protect them from their fangs!" Hatred tinged her voice.

"Ulrik signed the deed of the estate over to me," Katarina elucidated. "Vasilij, Ulrik's maker, returned and threatened to kill me if Ulrik did not come with him."

"I see," the tomte said compassionately. "How sad. I like that draugr, and after all the two of you have already been through. I am sorry, but there is nothing I can do about that." The tomte sounded sincere, accepting the hopelessness of the situation.

"But I do think that you can help me," Katarina spoke, casting a mysterious and serious gaze upon the tomte. Her hair cascaded over her shoulder, adding an enigmatic allure to her demeanour.

"How so?" the tomte inquired, sensing the gravity of Katarina's words.

"Well, what can defeat a draugr?" Katarina inquired, her voice measured and inquisitive, betraying a keen curiosity.

"Fire," the tomte replied, her voice tinged with a weary resignation born from centuries of witnessing the horrors of the supernatural realm.

"But is there something more, something more powerful?" Katarina asked, building suspense within her question.

"Probably," the tomte responded cautiously, her gaze wary as he observed Katarina's unfolding plan with a mixture of apprehension and intrigue.

"Potentially, what would that be?" Katarina asked, intrigued by her plan.

"Another draugr," the tomte said, unimpressed, "but this Vasilij seems to surround himself with a lot of other dreadful demons, just look at the demons who just left. No draugr would challenge him. And how would you convince another draugr to take on that mission?" The tomte sounded confused. "It is better if you accept the inevitable."

"I was not talking about another draugr, nor demon. How about a stallo or a hrimturs?" Katarina asked.

"There is a chance that they could," the tomte pondered, "but they would not attack a draugr. They have nothing to gain from that, and you could not bribe them. There are few creatures that you could bribe into attacking a draugr. Few would dare to go up against their might."

"How about a Lindwyrm?" Katarina asked, putting emphasis on the last syllable. The tomte almost fell backward upon hearing the word Lindwyrm, recoiled at the mere mention of the word. Her eyes expanded in alarm. Sweat ran down her forehead.

"Are you demented?" the tomte asked, upset, while looking around, ensuring no one else heard. "The Lindwurms dwelling in these forests are not the good kind. They are savage, bloodthirsty beasts that would tear your limb from limb without a second thought!" The tomte warned harshly. "You should speak no more of this."

"But could a Lindwyrm kill a draugr as powerful as Vasilij? Would a Lindwyrm fear the other demons that travel in his company?" Katarina asked curiously, a glimmer of hope igniting within her as she sensed the potential of her idea.

"A Lindwyrm does not fear anyone or anything," the tomte said, almost hissing. "A Lindwyrm would vanquish any creature foolish enough to stand against them! Their magic is strong, their size enormous, and their strength unmatched. A Lindwyrm would swallow a draugr in one piece without hesitation, that is if it wanted to. And there would be no way for a draugr or demon to kill the Lindwyrm. You must remove their head with a silver-mixed sword, and silver is the only metal that a draugr cannot touch. But Lindwurms are capricious creatures. They do not answer to anyone but themselves. They hunt in the forest, or they sleep in their cave. How would you get a Lindwyrm to eat Vasilij?" The tomte's curiosity was piqued, a flicker of interest dancing in the depths of her ancient eyes.

"I have seen her in my dreams. Hrafnildr. She has been calling out for me," Katarina's gaze turned focused, remembering her recurrent dreams. "Is the Lindwyrm not a greedy creature? Does the Lindwyrm not value treasures and desire gold and jewellery?" Katarina's voice resonated with confidence.

"They do," the tomte said. Katarina showed the tomte the jewellery she acquired from Vasilij. Their sparkling facets cast fractured rainbows of light upon the walls of the room.

"I will buy its service with this," Katarina explained. "And I will ask why she has summoned me. She has been calling out to me, there is something she wants me to do."

"Summoned you?" The tomte sounded confused.

"Yes, I hear her at night, whispering to me in my dreams. I shall go find her; there is something she wants from me," Katarina's mind seemed to travel to another dimension while uttering the words.

"And how would you stop the Lindwyrm from simply just eating you and taking your jewellery?" the tomte asked unimpressed. "How do you know that the Lindwyrm has not summoned you just to eat you?" there were grave warnings in her voice, her eyes narrowing in scepticism. "Or maybe it is just a dream, maybe she is not calling out for you, maybe it is just your imagination playing tricks!"

"It is not," Katarina said, convinced. "I can feel her presence, I can feel our connection. I cannot explain it, I just sense it. I do not know what will happen, but I must try," Katarina asserted determinedly. "I have nothing to lose."

"How about your life?" the tomte pressed, her voice a low, rumbling growl of concern. "Do you not have children that are still alive? Do you not own the deed to this house now? Is your draugr worth that?"

"Yes," Katarina replied with steely determination. "My daughter lives in another country with her husband and family. She is safe and has a good life. I do not have to worry about her. As for my life, I cannot just stand aside and do nothing. I must try. I must save Ulrik and free him from the dreadful grip of his maker. It is the right thing to do," Katarina replied, each syllable carrying the weight of her adoration.

"Do you not fear the Lindwyrm?" the tomte asked with a quizzical tone.

"No," Katarina said with an accepting voice. "I have glimpsed her in my dreams, I have heard her calling out to me. I do not yet understand why, but I believe she is looking for me for a reason"

"Why do you not fear the Lindwyrm?" the tomte asked curiously, her voice carried a weight of ominous concern. "It is a dangerous creature."

"I have a different perception of the Lindwyrm than most people do," Katarina answered mysteriously. Her eyes gleamed with an enigmatic resolve as she met the tomte's gaze.

"I cannot go with you," the tomte declared without being asked. "I am bound to this place, and I am sane enough to fear the Lindwyrm."

"I know. Just tell me where to go," Katarina said softly. "I will find her and find out what she wants and make my offer."

"The forest is a very dangerous place; you already know that. Even if you find the way, there are still many creatures dwelling in the dark, waiting to attack!" the tomte cautioned, her voice heavy with warning. "I beg you, rethink your decision. Ulrik does not want you to jeopardize your life."

"I have made my decision. It is mine, and it does not belong to anyone else but me," Katarina declared, meeting her gaze with compassion and gratitude.

The tomte regarded Katarina with a mixture of admiration and concern, her features softened by a flicker of sympathy. "I know that he loves you beyond life and reason. Do you harbour the same feelings for him?" the tomte inquired. A mild smile graced Katarina's lips as she nodded.

"Yes, I do love him, and I am willing to risk my life to save him."

"Very well," the tomte conceded with a heavy sigh. "The Lindwyrm dwells in the cave close to the green mountain. Few people dare to go there; they all know about the beast who guards those lands. If you ride now, then you will make it by nightfall. However, I would not recommend riding back home during nightfall, and I would even less recommend staying in the forest near the green mountain after dark! You will be trapped there until daylight returns," the tomte cautioned.

"Thank you," Katarina replied. "Can you help me with the horse?"

nodding solemnly, the tomte moved to help Katarina prepare for her perilous quest. As she mounted the horse and rode off into the mythical shadows of the forest to face the divine beast, the tomte watched in silence, her heart heavy with worry for Katarina's fate.

CHAPTER 26

Ulrik halted at the threshold of the desolate churchyard, careful not to pass the border, patiently respecting its front line. Daylight broke over the horizon, its intensity met his eyes. The other draugrs screamed out in agony when the rays touched their bodies, their wretched forms writhed in torment. Each beam of sunlight cast a spooky glow upon the scene, illuminating the grotesque tableau before him. The stench of death and decay filled Ulrik's nose, mingling with the metallic tang of blood that permeated the atmosphere. The draugrs' grey skin turned almost blue when the sun was near, and their stonelike complexion cracked even more beneath the sun's unforgiving gaze. The demon's dreadful screams were a torment for the ears, twisting the intestines within. Ulrik looked around; no humans seemed to be in sight yet. The leaves had almost fallen off the trees, filling the ground with an ocean of red, orange, and yellow. With a steely resolve, Ulrik turned his attention back to the tortured figures of his undead companions, his jaw set in determination.

"We are here," Ulrik announced, his voice a sombre echo in the stillness of the churchyard. "This is the church graveyard. You can go in now and find graves to rest in. Return to Vasilij in a couple of days, and we will travel onwards away from this land," his words dripped with disdain, a silent condemnation of the unholy existence he and his companions endured. Ulrik had always thought that their way of life was despicable. The draugrs moved with ephemeral motions, they hovered above the ground as they swirled in an ungraceful dance of whispers and murmurs. With a sense of urgency, they dispersed among the graves, seeking refuge from the impending daylight. The draugrs disappeared quickly into different graves, like ghosts walking between worlds, eager to hide from daylight, leaving the world behind. Ulrik stood still, watching their unworldly forms vanish into the earth. The demon's translucent figures melded seamlessly with the gloom. As the pale light of dawn began to seep across the horizon, casting long, sinister shadows over the graveyard, Ulrik remained waiting, his gaze fixed upon the church before him. Though the daylight posed no physical threat to him, its presence was an unwelcome intrusion upon his nocturnal domain. Unlike his undead brethren, Ulrik met the light with a stoic indifference.

"Ulrik?" A voice cut through the stillness of the graveyard. Ulrik turned around to greet the priest, who was dressed in formal clothes. "What are you doing here?" the priest asked, surprised. "There are four draugrs hiding in the graveyard," Ulrik said with an unbothered tone, letting his eyes fall across the tombs.

"Draugrs?" The word escaped the priest's lips like a curse, his face paling at the mention of the abominable creatures. "Not like... you?"

"Exactly, not like me," Ulrik affirmed.

"But they take the lives of anyone that passes through the graveyard!" the priest exclaimed in fear, dreadful of the gravity of the situation.

"No, they will not," Ulrik said with a gathered look. "You have another beast, more powerful than all of those draugrs, guarding your church," Ulrik stared out into the air, tension spreading within his core. "And those draugrs have no idea that such a powerful beast guards these borders. The senses of a draugr are highly elevated, and yet, we cannot smell its presence; it lays perfectly masked within the church."

"What do you mean?" the priest asked, trying to hide the truth echoing within his lie.

"Do not try to hide it from me, father," Ulrik's voice took on a steely edge, turning towards the priest. "Do not try to mislead me!"

"Hide what?" the priest continued, insisting on his unawareness.

"The kyrkogrim that haunts this cemetery," Ulrik said, his eyes bore into the priest with a frightening intensity.

"Oh," the priest fell into a heavy silence, his expression clouded with unease. "That was a very long time ago, it was back when the church was built. I had nothing to do with that, it was long before I was born," he excused hastily.

"The grim awakens at nightfall. The draugrs are exhausted. I do not think that they will leave their graves tonight, they need more rest."

The priest's face blanched at the mention of the kyrkogrim's wrath. "Is that not a good thing?" the priest asked hesitantly, his voice betraying his mounting dread.

"The grim will kill them right away; the grim knows the nature of us draugrs. If you are unlucky, the grim will burn down half your churchyard just to get to the draugrs. It will stop at nothing when destroying its enemies!" Ulrik said with a serious look. The priest recoiled at the bleak prospect; his eyes wide with terror.

"What can we do to stop it and still get rid of the draugrs?" He implored, turning to Ulrik for guidance.

"I cannot vanquish these draugrs for you," Ulrik's tone brooked no argument, his resolve unyielding.

"Why can you just not go over there now and burn them inside the graves? I will put out the fire afterward," the priest pressed, desperation creeping into his voice.

"They will hear me coming and awake to defend themselves," Ulrik's voice carried a weight of inevitability. "I cannot defeat all of them. But the kyrkogrim can. It is an impressive enemy. We must wait until nightfall. Just be sure to leave the torches up when the night arrives. You can worry about the fire afterward. Come, let us wait until nightfall," Ulrik instructed.

Throughout the day, Ulrik stood vigil, his presence a demonic sentinel among the graves. The priest, unsettled by the looming night, continued his tasks with a wary eye cast towards the horizon. As twilight descended, Ulrik issued a reminder:

"Do not forget the torches!" his voice echoed through the stillness. The priest nodded, still not happy about the idea. Reluctantly, the priest obeyed, planting the torches around the cemetery. As the night fell, the wind almost entirely vanished; there was a disturbing silence hanging in the air. Anticipation grew strong. For the first time, the churchyard seemed haunted. The priest joined Ulrik outside of the church border when everything was done for the day.

"Why are you standing here outside? You have been standing here all day, you could have gotten inside. Can you not enter a church?" The priest asked.

"It is not the power of your God and church that I fear," Ulrik's gaze remained fixed upon the graveyard, his voice coloured with reverence. "It is the wrath of the kyrkogrim. I have not set foot here since I was turned into a draugr. The kyrkogrim has no reason to hunt me. But if I tread its land, it may want to take vengeance and hunt after me. I am yet to meet a creature that can face a kyrkogrim and live. It would be unwise to upset it." Ulrik had respect in his voice, unwilling to engage in a fruitless battle.

"I see," the priest replied, his voice a tremor in the stillness of the night. "Would it harm a human?" He asked nervously. After all, the priest was a gentle man, unused to violence.

"I do not know," Ulrik said with a grave tone. "Perhaps one can never be too careful when it comes to the kyrkogrim."

As the night fell, a dark shadow pushed itself up from underneath the church, rising like a primordial terror from the depths. From the darkness emerged a colossal beast, its form an abomination of nature. Its growling spread across the churchyard, shattering the night. With twin heads, one resembling a rooster's fierce appearance and the other a hound's ferocious countenance, it stood tall like a brave titan. Its size was rivaled only by its malevolence. The monster's hind legs bore the claws of a hound, while its forelimbs ended in taloned rooster's feet. Upon its back were the wings of a monstrous eagle, casting a menacing silhouette against the moonlit sky. The kyrkogrim emitted a guttural, otherworldly cry as it prowled the churchyard. Quickly, the creature prepared to defend its domain. Its gaze pierced the darkness with fiery intensity.

"What is that?" Ulrik turned to the priest with an appalled tone, his voice laced with horror. "I was told that you only buried a rooster when building the church. That is blasphemy! No one should bury two kinds of animals, they could emerge into one, leaving an unspeakable beast like this!" The eyes of the kyrkogrim shone in a dark orange colour. The beast started to move across the churchyard, hunting like a monstrous predator. Its every step echoed like a drumbeat of doom.

"I did not know," the priest said, frightened. He was almost unable to move, laying eyes on the dreadful monstrosity. "Will it attack us?" The priest asked, frightened.
"Maybe," Ulrik said. "If it deems it necessary. Have you done anything to harm the church?" he inquired, his gaze piercing into the priest's soul.

"No," the priest replied honestly with a loyal tone.

"Then you should be safe," Ulrik said, though his words offered little solace.

The kyrkogrim presence appeared an ominous shadow against the night. Its body ambled past a flickering torch. With a swift movement, it seized the torch in its gnarled fangs. As the entity carried the flame towards a nearby grave, its eyes glinted with a predatory gleam. With a hoarse growl, the kyrkogrim hurled the torch at the burial mound, igniting the dry ground with a malevolent fury. A bloodcurdling scream tore through the air as one of the draugrs clawed its way back to the surface, its ashen form wreathed in flames.

The kyrkogrim wasted no time. It descended upon the wretched draugr with a brutality born of ancient enmity. It pinned the writhing creature to the ground, its monstrous form unharmed by the searing heat. The draugr's anguished cries echoed through the night as the flames consumed it. Futile struggles proved no match for the kyrkogrim's relentless grip. The kyrkogrim was too strong.

"I did not know that a draugr would catch fire that quickly," the priest remarked, sounding surprised. He watched the unrealistic spectacle unfold before him, with horror and awe.

The other draugrs, roused by the commotion, hissed in defiance at their attacking enemy. Yet their defiance proved pointless against the relentless advance of the kyrkogrim. With supernatural grace, the mighty creature seized another torch in its monstrous jaws. Its movements mixed in a morbid dance of death as it pursued its quarry with implacable determination.

One by one, the draugrs fell to the kyrkogrim's wrath, their wails of agony drowned out by the beast's triumphant howls. In its wake, nothing but ash remained.

Proudly displaying its gruesome victory, the kyrkogrim turned to face Ulrik with a gaze as cold and merciless as death itself. The priest, overcome by terror, stumbled to the ground. He lost his ability to breathe as he struggled to comprehend the abhorrence that had unfolded before him.

Ulrik remained stoic, his gaze unwavering as he met the gaze of the powerful entity that now ruled the churchyard. He knew there was no escape from the kyrkogrim's wrath, no sanctuary to be found in this haunted place. Should it decide to attack, this would be his final moment. The kyrkogrim's gaze pierced into Ulrik's very core with an intensity that threatened to crush him, silently pondering whether to extinguish his life or spare him. Time stood still, bowing to the creature's might. With a final, chilling glance, the kyrkogrim turned away, vanishing into the darkness as quickly as it had come.

As the echoes of its departure faded into the night, Ulrik turned to the half-conscious priest.

"Is it gone?" The priest asked, his eyes darting nervously around the dimly lit churchyard.

"No," Ulrik replied, his eyes resting upon the church, "but it is finished with its mission. Go home now, return tomorrow as usual."

"I do not know if I can return, knowing that such a beast lives under the church!" The priest was petrified, his blood boiling with fear.

"It is not a beast," Ulrik's tone was firm, his words weighted with an otherworldly wisdom, "it is a guardian. It will not attack you; if it wanted to harm you, you would have already been dead. This is just a reminder to respect the church and your work here." Ulrik gazed out into the night, the wind returned to grasp his dark hair, nature seemed to mirror his inner contemplation. "I will leave you now; I have signed over the deed of the estate to Katarina," he explained with tormented words.

"What?" confusion clouded the priest's features.

"My maker has returned; I must go with him. If not, then he and his minions will kill Katarina and everyone in this county. The kyrkogrim cannot help you, it only protects the church, and I am alone, just one. This is the only thing I can do to save you all," Ulrik said with sadness in his voice.

Silence hung heavy in the air, broken only by the distant hoot of an owl and the rustle of leaves in the night breeze. The priest, overcome with emotion, offered a nod of understanding. "I understand, thank you. I have always liked you, even when you were a draugr." He whispered; his voice choked with emotion. A solemn nod was Ulrik's only reply, a silent acknowledgment of their shared bond in the face of darkness.

"Good luck, my friend," Ulrik turned and vanished into the night, his form swallowed by the shadows.

CHAPTER 27

Katarina had ridden all day, a heart filled with determination and love, spurring her onward. As the crimson hues of sunset bled into the deepening shadows of the forest, Katarina's long journey led her to the mouth of the cave. The wind embraced the leaves, guiding them in a harmonious dance. The quiet murmur of animals traversing the forest teased the senses, while the aroma of nature lingered in the air. Katarina had been here before; she could feel it in her soul. She knew the tales surrounding this place. Legends cloaked this dark enclave, tales of terror that echoed through the centuries, chilling the marrow of even the bravest souls. Everyone kept their distance from this cursed part of the forest, home to hellish beasts and lost to endless shadows.

Here, beneath the canopy of ancient trees and twisted roots, the Lindwyrm dwelled. It was a creature of nightmares, feared by stallo and hrimtursar alike, shunned by all who knew its name.

All attempts to kill the Lindwyrm had been in vain. Some tried smoking it out, others attempted to shoot or burn it. But all efforts only angered the Lindwyrm further, provoking the merciless monster.

Dismounting her horse, Katarina let it roam freely, prepared to flee if she failed her mission and faced her demise. The night air was chilly, and Katarina wrapped herself in her long coat. Around her neck, she wore the necklace Vasilij had given her. Slowly, Katarina approached the cave as darkness took over the forest. Breathing sounds emanated from within the abyss, as if the earth pulsed to the Lindwyrm's heartbeat. The very earth seemed to thrum with a powerful rhythm. It was a macabre sound conducted by the presence of the Lindwyrm. Otherworldly echoes reverberated in her soul, creating ripples between worlds. Katarina halted at the entrance, uncertain of what creature awaited. Her heart hammered in her chest as she braced herself for the unknown. Shadows of the future drowned the air, promising both mystery and danger. A cacophony of deep sounds reiterated from within the cave. Katarina stepped forward, her dedication tempered by the desperate need to fulfill her mission, no matter the cost.

"Hello!" Katarina called out into the yawning abyss of the cave, her words hanging in the stagnant air like a delicate offering to unseen forces. She was unsure of what to expect. All Katarina knew was that she intended to be respectful yet true to her mission. "I am here to meet the great Lindwyrm," she called, her voice echoing off the damp stone walls, reverberating through the suffocating darkness that overpowered her.

For a heartbeat, the cave fell silent, the only sound the steady drip of water echoing like an unnatural pulse. The scent of damp earth and decaying vegetation ruled the air. It mingled with the faintest hint of something primal and untamed, a smell that spoke of ancient secrets buried within the very marrow of the earth.

Within the pitch-black cave, Katarina stood in silence, awaiting the response of the creature that reigned over these lands. Her senses were attuned to the slightest shift in the oppressive stillness that surrounded her.

A blend of trepidation and excitement floated in the air in an uneasy harmony. Suddenly, the ground began to shake violently, accompanied by a deafening roar that sent fear coursing through the heart of the forest. As the earth itself trembled beneath her feet, the forest seemed to flinch in fear, the very trees swaying and groaning in protest at the impending arrival of an ancient and undeniable force.

Katarina instinctively retreated from the cave, realizing it was too late to attempt escape now. Though her heart raced with insecurity, she maintained a calm exterior, knowing that panic would not aid her. From the void within, the great Lindwyrm emerged, the ground trembling in deference to its enthralling presence. As the creature's divine form surged forth from the stygian depths, a deafening roar split the air.

The creature's yellow eyes glinted in the fading light as it leaped from the cave. The Lindwyrm unleashed a torrent of searing flame that licked hungrily at the darkness, casting long, twisting shadows that danced like wild phantoms. Despite the damp ground, the flames ignited fiercely, showcasing the creature's magical strength. Katarina remained still, understanding that her only chance of survival lay in maintaining her composure. Her heart remained courageous, her gaze fixed upon the serpentine beast that coiled and writhed in a deadly dance of death and destruction. The Lindwyrm roared once more, circling her just beyond the blaze it had ignited.

Its colossal form loomed large against the backdrop of the forest, stretching impossibly long, like a serpent of olden tales woven into flesh and bone. The Lindwyrm's eyes were blazed with an otherworldly intensity. The world bowed to its greatness.

Its form was a beautiful amalgamation of serpentine grace and draconic ferocity. Two hind legs supported its massive frame. Its head was adorned with massive horns that arched protectively over its scaled brow, floating like jagged spires down its formidable spine. The creature's body, encased in an armor of crimson scales, gleamed with a divine luminescence in the mysterious forest.

Even though it had no wings, the Lindwyrm exuded an aura of primal power that seemed to drench the very air around it. As it brooded over Katarina, the creature's massive jaws parted to reveal rows of lethal fangs, each one as sharp as a razor and twice as deadly.

Trapped within the grip of the Lindwyrm's gaze, Katarina found herself paralyzed by a potent mixture of awe and terror. Her every instinct screamed for flight even as her resolve held firm against its magical might. With every fiber of her being, she steeled herself against the mythical entity, drawing strength from the knowledge that her cause was just and her determination unyielding.

"Who dares disturb my slumber?" The Lindwyrm's voice resounded in Katarina's mind, commanding a storm of respect. Though spoken without moving its mouth, the words echoed hauntingly within Katarina's head, evoking a mixture of fear and courage.

"I come in peace, oh great one," Katarina replied, bowing respectfully to the Lindwyrm. A sense of familiarity washed over her. Katarina knew that she had encountered this creature before. The Lindwyrm regarded her with a mixture of curiosity and intrigue, its piercing gaze penetrating to the very depths of her soul.

"Few dare to tread upon these lands, and fewer still possess the courage to approach my cave. You are the first to summon me," the Lindwyrm stated, its gaze fixed upon Katarina, who could discern her own reflection in the creature's powerful, ancient eyes. Its snakelike tongue hissed near Katarina's ears, yet she remained dedicated in the face of fear, regarding the Lindwyrm with reverence. She knew this was the same creature that had been calling out to her. She knew that the two of them were connected.

"Never have I beheld such a formidable creature," Katarina remarked sincerely, admiring the Lindwyrm.

"You attempt to flatter me," the Lindwyrm responded with a softened tone. "Most flee in terror, while those who dare to approach me often seek to plunder my treasures. None have survived," the creature warned, its voice resonating with authority, causing the ground to tremble.

"I have not come to steal from you," Katarina assured. "I approach with respect, recognizing you as the most powerful creature in these lands. I seek your aid and offer compensation for your trouble," she continued, maintaining her composure. The Lindwyrm chuckled, a sound that echoed like distant thunder rolling across the sky.

"Why should I involve myself in the affairs of humans?" the Lindwyrm hissed, its voice tinged with scepticism.

"I offer you treasures," Katarina replied, revealing her necklace, as a token of her sincerity. "I possess an entire chest of jewellery. It is yours if you assist me," she promised, willing to trade everything for Ulrik's safety. The Lindwyrm began to coil around Katarina, hissing, seemingly preparing to strike. Its scales gleamed in the light of the fire.

"Do you believe you can buy my favour?" the Lindwyrm asked, sounding offended, its voice laced with offense at the implication.

"Please," Katarina pleaded. "I sought you out, knowing you are the mightiest of all creatures. I implore you," she continued, desperation evident in her voice. "You have called out to me. There is something you need from me. I believe I can help you, but I also need your assistance."

"Why should I aid you?" the Lindwyrm inquired, curiosity evident in its tone. Its gaze pierced through Katarina's facade to search for the truth hidden beneath her words. "I do not know you. I did not summon you."

"I need your help," Katarina persisted. "I have seen you in my dreams and heard your calling. There is a connection between us."

"We are not connected," the Lindwyrm replied, regarding Katarina with eyes reflecting eons of wisdom. "Do you not understand my nature?" the Lindwyrm questioned, its voice carrying the weight of centuries of solitude and despair. "Do you not know that I am dangerous and malevolent, a symbol of war and destruction?" Lowering its head to meet Katarina's gaze, the Lindwyrm continued, "Yet you do not fear me. Why? All creatures tremble before me! I am the scourge of the forests, the terror of the lands!" it proclaimed with a powerful voice. Katarina held its gaze, her heart racing with nerves but devoid of fear.

"No, I do not fear you," Katarina replied, her voice steady despite the tremors of uncertainty that threatened to betray her resolve. "However, I do respect you, for what you say is true. You are the most formidable creature in these lands, which is precisely why I have sought you out. I am seeking your counsel," she declared sincerely. "I know you are not merely the beast or monster many perceive you to be. I have heard your voice in my dreams, sensed the boundless wisdom within you."

"I have slain men, laid waste to territories. How can you not consider me a monster?" the Lindwyrm inquired, its words hissing with curiosity.

"Are you not the Lindwyrm?" Katarina countered. "The Lindwyrm can bestow great fortune and treasures, bring happiness and joy to those fortunate enough to encounter its majesty," she stated, offering a hopeful smile.

"I am not that kind of Lindwyrm," the creature declared. "I am not one to grant wishes."

"Does the capacity for both destruction and hope not reside within you?" Katarina continued, her words imbued with a sense of hope and optimism. "With powers like yours, I believe you can choose which path to take. It is two sides of the same coin," she asserted confidently.

"A clever observation," the Lindwyrm acknowledged. "Yes, I can alter my appearance and bring about either destruction or bliss upon those I choose," the creature warned. "But you see me in this form now. Why do you not fear me, knowing I am the embodiment of war?" the being's tone softened, less aggressive.

"If you desired my demise, you could easily kill me," Katarina replied. "Taking my life would be effortless for you. Yet, I do not believe you will."

"Is that so?" the Lindwyrm inquired curiously.

"Yes, if you truly wished me harm, you would have acted already," Katarina answered truthfully. "There must be something else you seek from me. There must be a reason why you have been calling out to me."

"I am an ancient creature; I can wait for your demise. I do not have to kill you; in time you will wither and die," the Lindwyrm countered.

"I see not a beast, but a creature like any other, striving to survive in this world," Katarina responded. "Few of your kind remain, most slumbering deep within their mountains. I know you possess the ability to take my life or aid me. I hope you will consider my proposition, and I am eager to learn what you seek from me. Your voice within my dreams has been as clear as it is today."

"You intrigue me, little human," the Lindwyrm conceded, its voice a rumbling echo of centuries past. "Very well, present your suggestion before I decide whether or not to consume you," it threatened, moving its enormous body in circles.

"I want you to eat a draugr," Katarina began.

"Devour a draugr!" the Lindwyrm sounded surprised. "They certainly do not taste good! I would prefer to burn it! Not all Lindwurms possess my power, the power to breathe fire, I am very powerful among my kinsmen. Why do you need me to eat a draugr?" the Lindwyrm asked, both appalled and intrigued.

"I cannot do it myself," Katarina answered. "I am in love with a man who is a draugr. His maker returned to claim him, and he threatened to take my life if he did not go along."

"And a draugr cannot take the life of its maker," the Lindwyrm acknowledged, its voice rumbling with understanding.

"Exactly," Katarina affirmed. "If his maker is gone, then he will be free."

"You love him enough to take a life for him?" the Lindwyrm asked, intrigued by the little person standing in front of her.

"Yes, I would sacrifice my life for him," Katarina declared, love burning intensely in her heart.

"Dying for someone and killing for someone is not the same," the Lindwyrm retorted, its voice a rumble of contemplation. "Although I do smell demonic blood on your hands."

"A mare tried to possess me," Katarina explained, studying the Lindwyrm's impressive size. "I had to vanquish it to survive and get rid of its presence. I do not wish to harm anyone; I will always choose a peaceful way first, but I do not wish to die."

"And yet, here you are, asking me to commit a heinous act," the Lindwyrm hissed, its massive form slithering sinuously around the flickering flames on the ground. The cavernous chamber seemed to shrink in the presence of the ancient beast. Its scales shimmered a deep crimson hue in the fiery glow, as the light of the fire danced.

"I regret to say that sometimes there is no other way. I wish that the world was different, but sometimes the peaceful solution fails. Please help me," Katarina pleaded. "I would forever be in your debt, and I will help you with whatever you ask of me. I will give you all the jewellery I have."

"Why does everyone assume that us Lindwurms covet treasure above all?" the Lindwyrm retorted wearily, its voice heavy with the weight of centuries of misunderstanding.

"I need your help," Katarina persisted, her voice filled with fervour. "I know that you are a creature of great powers, a creature that decides whether or not she wants to help a human or bring destruction upon them. And I am here to ask you to bring fortune upon me. Please help me, you are my only hope."

The Lindwyrm studied Katarina closely. "It is a curious thing," she began, "monsters who come here deem me to be a monster."

"We all have a monster inside of us," Katarina replied solemnly. "Some let the monster rule and lead the direction, others do not feed the monster inside. But no one is truly a monster, there is always a shade of light within."

"Not even a demon?" the Lindwyrm queried, its voice laced with scepticism.

"Most demons were humans once; they were capable of good. Even if they are lost now, there has always been light within them, even if it was just a little," Katarina said with a hopeful heart.

"Some men are truly cruel," the Lindwyrm acknowledged.

"Indeed," Katarina answered, "some men commit the most gruesome acts. Maybe all hope has gone lost for now, but no one is born good or bad. Life and other circumstances affect us, some are stronger, and some are weaker by nature."

"You are indeed an interesting creature," the Lindwyrm remarked, impressed. "I have lived for thousands of years; I do not get impressed very easily. I will agree to help you. I will agree to eat the draugr if it is indeed true what you have heard my calling."

"You will? Thank you," Katarina burst out in joy. "I am so grateful. Yes, it is true, I swear."

"However, there is a condition," the Lindwyrm interjected, its tone grave. "You claim to have heard my summons, seen me in your dreams. Is this true?"

"Yes, I have had recurring dreams of Lindwurms, calling for me, asking me to come look for them, that they are part of my destiny."

"How do you know that it is me calling and not just a dream?" The Lindwyrm asked.

"Your name is Hrafnildr," Katarina said with a gentle voice, remembering her dreams. "You told me in my dream." The Lindwyrm laughed contentedly when hearing Katarina's words. "What is it you want from me?" Katarina asked, curiosity colouring her tone.

"Indeed, that is my name. Unknown to anyone who is not a Lindwyrm! You did not lie; that is my voice you have been hearing. I have been calling for you. Do you know how to write and read?" The Lindwyrm asked, its eyes fixed intently on Katarina.

"Yes." Katarina replied without hesitation.

"Then I want you to come here and listen to my stories. I want you to write them down and spread them across the world. There are few of us left. One day our existence will be forgotten, but I want my story to be immortal!" The Lindwyrm said with an intrigued tone.

"Agreed," Katarina said affirmatively. "I promise that I will return and write down your story. Your memory will not be forgotten."

"And I want you to safeguard my egg," the Lindwyrm continued.

"That is the true reason for my calling."

"Your egg?" Katarina sounded confused. The forest echoed with sounds of the dark night.

"Yes, others, men with great strength and power are coming for me, they wish to vanquish me. They want to take my egg and my life! You must keep my child with you, you must protect it until it hatches," the Lindwyrm explained, a note of fear creeping into its voice. "If I return victorious, I will come back to retrieve it. If not, it will be your task to protect it."

"Would you entrust me with such an important task?" Katarina asked, honoured by the inquiry. "We have just met."

"I have been calling out for you in your dreams. Just like you said, we are connected. My powers go beyond this world. I have been summoning a creature with a heart worthy of looking after my egg, a creature connected to me. Only one with a trustworthy nature and a loyal mind would be able to hear the calling." The Lindwyrm leaned in and let its tongue touch Katarina's hair. "Yes, I can feel it in our essence! Our fates intertwined. My words etched upon your life; your destiny is bound to mine! Besides, my enemies are coming here," The Lindwyrm proclaimed. "I must fight for my survival. I might not make it out alive," a sadness echoed in the Lindwyrm's voice. "There are no other Lindwurms nearby. All who have come have tried to steal my treasure and egg. An egg like that is worth more than a fortune! Do you swear to protect the egg, and to release it to this cave when hatched?" the Lindwyrm demanded answers.

"Will it not need someone to take care of it, will it not need a mother?" Katarina asked. "Will it not be defenceless after hatching?" her maternal instinct echoed within the inquiry.

"No," the Lindwyrm replied. "When we hatch, we are able to hunt on our own. We are quite defenceless at first, but that is just life. Those who are not strong enough will perish; only the strong will make it."

"Sometimes we all need a little help, we need to protect those who are more fragile than us. I could not release a defenceless creature out into the wild, knowing it would be too small to defend itself," Katarina said compassionately. Chuckling softly, the Lindwyrm acknowledged Katarina's compassion.

"That is why I would entrust you with my egg, your heart is different. No wonder a draugr loves you. But you must swear it, you must swear that you will protect the egg until it is hatched!" the Lindwyrm hissed with a firm tone.

"I swear," Katarina promised.

"A promise to a Lindwyrm is eternal, it is written in the annals of time. A promise to me is unbreakable, etched in magic, forever imprinted upon your soul. If you break it, misery will haunt you forever!" the Lindwyrm warned solemnly. "The consequences will be devastating. Your blood would freeze, and worms would eat you alive from within!" the Lindwyrm's warning echoed like a chilling prophecy. "We possess great magic, and we do not look kindly upon disloyalty! The magic floating between us Lindwurms would avenge me. You must understand that breaking a promise to a Lindwyrm will lead to a painful and merciless death. Your betrayal would haunt you in lifetimes to come!"

"I promise," Katarina pledged honestly, her vow etched in the darkness like an unbreakable bond.

"Very well," the Lindwyrm hissed, its eyes piercing the shadows of the night. "Where is the draugr you want me to eat?" I will keep my part of the agreement. You have sworn loyalty to me, to fulfil your vow, and you know the consequences should you fail to honour it. And I, in return, will help you."

"He resides in an estate near Ekslingan," Katarina explained. "But they will leave soon, to travel to another country."

"Do you have something that belongs to him?" the Lindwyrm

asked. Katarina pointed at her necklace.

"He gave this to me. Along with a bunch of other treasures," Katarina revealed.

"You can keep your treasures," the Lindwyrm dismissed. "Wait here," she commanded, slithering back into the depths of the cavern. When she emerged, cradled gently in her jaws was an egg, large as a hound. "Come, show me your home. I will leave the egg with you, after that I will go out and search for your draugr. I will kill him for you, according to our agreement. But the hunters will come soon, I do not know how much time I have left," she warned ominously.

"Why do you not flee after vanquishing the draugr?" Katarina asked.

"I will not flee!" the Lindwyrm said determinedly. "I fight, I defend my forest, even if it is for a lost cause! A Lindwyrm does not flee! There used to be many of us, we used to rule the forests. And they all feared us, but now few remain, the enemies grow stronger every day; soon we will all be gone, defeated as humans increase their numbers."

"I am sorry to hear that," Katarina offered sympathetically. "What can I do to help you?"

"Simply uphold your promise," the Lindwyrm replied. "Let us go now; the forest is a very dangerous place at night for a lonely human. I will accompany you on your journey back."

CHAPTER 28

The sun was shining, casting its golden rays upon the horse rider who sat gracefully in the saddle. His chestnut-coloured hair shimmered in the sunlight, accentuating his features with a rich hue. Rider and horse moved with a captivating grace, exuding strength and endurance, a sight to behold.

The young man was adorned in majestic attire, befitting a king. Yet, it was not just his clothing that commanded attention. An undeniable charm and charisma radiated from him, akin to that of a celestial being.

From a distance, Vasilij observed the man closely, careful not to startle his prey. This man was flawless, possessing an exquisite beauty that precisely matched Vasilij's desires.

Though Vasilij loathed the sun's rays, he couldn't deny the captivating aura that enveloped this handsome man, as if the elements themselves were enchanted by his mystical allure. Vasilij typically did not care for his victims, but there was something extraordinary about this man. His essence seemed to embody both feminine grace and masculine strength. His beauty transcended the ordinary with an ethereal quality that hinted at undiscovered talents and hidden depths. No, this man was different, he was not mere prey to be devoured.

As the horse came to a calm halt and the man dismounted, he surveyed the landscape with a gaze that carried a poetic and romantic essence. There was a serene beauty in his demeanour as he beheld the scenery. The man's presence captivated Vasilij's attention from afar. Vasilij, always drawn to beauty and accustomed to obtaining what he desired, approached slowly, careful not to disturb the enchanting tranquillity that surrounded the man and his steed. Vasilij wanted to savour this moment, recognizing the allure of the fleeting tranquillity that preceded the inevitable fate awaiting those touched by the curse of a draugr.

There was a certain allure within pain, a beauty found in the fleeting moments before one's soul succumbed to darkness. And in this young, remarkably beautiful man, Vasilij discerned the potential for such darkness. It lurked just beneath the surface, patiently awaiting its chance to emerge. It merely required the right kind of encouragement, and Vasilij was adept at nurturing such darkness. Would this man possess the strength to resist the ominous call of the draugr? Could he stand alongside Vasilij and Ulrik, or would he get lost between the graves? The relentless beckoning from within was unforgiving. Few could withstand the allure of death. There was a certain thrill in the uncertainty. Would this man become an eternal blood angel, or would he degrade into a decaying disappointment? It would be a tragedy to see such a magnificent creature go to waste. Yet, conversely, the prospect of such beauty embracing eternity was undeniably alluring.

Intrigued by the impending choice, Vasilij advanced slowly across the autumn meadow. The man remained oblivious to his presence. Vasilij fixed his gaze upon the young man with the intensity of a lynx stalking its prey. The man, lost in reverie, gazed into the distance, seemingly absorbing the landscape into his very soul. The horse stood serenely just a few meters away. Suddenly, the man turned toward Vasilij, the sun cast a perfect light upon his features. A harmonious blend of delicate femininity and robust masculinity danced across his being. Vasilij was more than convinced that this man would soon fall under his sway, subject to his control and command.

"Can I help you?" The man's voice was soft, yet harboured a dormant mystery, poised to be unleashed. Vasilij advanced another step, exuding the calculated strength of a predator closing in on its unsuspecting prey, preparing to strike. The light caught perfectly in the man's amber eyes, gleaming like precious gold.

"I couldn't help but notice you," Vasilij replied, stopping just a few meters from the man. His smile was laced with both malicious intent and captivating charm.

"Are you lost?" The man's question held a hint of confusion. His fair skin seemed almost tantalizing. Vasilij eagerly longed for the sensation of the man's skin between his teeth. He yearned for the rush of fear pulsing through the man's veins, the taste of despair as his soul slipped away.

"I've found exactly what I was seeking," Vasilij responded mysteriously, his gaze fixed on the man with a satisfied gaze. "What is your name?" Vasilij asked. The man hesitated, sensing the unsettling presence emanating from Vasilij.

"Erik," he replied, feeling compelled to answer. Anxiety coursed through every fibre of Erik's being as he realized he stood before something more than an ordinary man, a fearsome beast from another realm. The gentle breeze tousled Vasilij's blond hair, accentuating his features as he continued to regard Erik with a gaze that spoke of both brutality and longing. An unholy obsession gleamed evident in his eyes.

"What are you?" Erik asked, contemplating the potential lethal danger this creature posed to him. A sense of unease reverberated within his core, warning him of the sinister presence now confronting him.

"You know what I am," Vasilij replied with unwavering certainty, his smile both captivating and repugnant.

"I do not," Erik insisted, attempting to summon courage while anxiety strangled him from within. He had heard the stories of demons and other ungodly creatures hunting and kidnapping noble men and women. The blood within his veins almost froze when realising the potential threat. Erik yearned to escape, to flee, but this demon refused to release him, its devilish eyes narrating tales of unspeakable atrocities and profound violence. But how could he outrun such a monster? How could he survive this encounter?

"I am here to offer you an opportunity," Vasilij declared, his eyes ablaze with desire for dominion and the subjugation of souls.

"You should leave! Return to where you came from!" Erik urged, bravely voicing his concern, determined not to reveal weakness. Despite his fear, he remained a nobleman, resolved not to succumb to disgrace. If this was the end, surely, he must meet it with dignity. Vasilij took another step forward, relishing the thrill of the hunt coursing through his bloodstream. The satisfaction of tormenting humans filled his mind.

"I will not depart," Vasilij proclaimed. "In fact, I intend to make you my eternal apprentice. You will be mine for all eternity."

Erik's heart froze at these words. Fear took dominion over his soul. What manner of monster stood before him, threatening him with a fate worse than death?

"And if I refuse?" Erik asked, attempting to discern the fate that might await him. What sort of demon could transform him into its likeness?

"Then there is only death," Vasilij replied, the word 'death' resonating with cruelty as it left his lips. Erik sensed the malevolence of the creature before him, feeling its insidious whispers in his soul, tempting him to yield to the darkness. "I know there is darkness within you," Vasilij continued. "I can smell it on you and sense it pulsating through your heart. Submit to me or meet your demise. I am very hungry."

"What are you?" Erik inquired once more, unable to recall ever encountering a demon that could walk in daylight. Moreover, this demon appeared human.

"Do I need to spell it out for you?" Vasilij grew impatient, finding the man's presence increasingly irksome despite his extraordinary beauty. "I thought you would be smarter, already piecing it together," Vasilij paused, awaiting Erik's reaction. "I am a draugr," he declared to hasten the matter.

"That is impossible," Erik replied. His pulse racing. "In the stories I have heard..."

"Well, you heard wrong," Vasilij interjected brusquely.

"So, my choice is death or to become a bloodthirsty murderer?" Erik queried, both frightened and enticed by the darkness standing before him. He harboured no desire to transform into a hideous, decaying draugr, yet the man before him bore no resemblance to the creatures he had read about. This man was beautiful and refined. Erik felt the darkness tugging at him from within, fearing the consequences of becoming a draugr. But he also feared the darkness lurking within his own heart. Would he be strong enough to resist the allure of evil, or would he succumb to temptation and lose his soul entirely? Yet, Erik also feared death, panic coursing through his body as he realized these might be his final moments alive, and he was determined to do everything in his power to avoid death. A draugr lived forever, after all.

"I am offering you the world and all the possibilities within it!" Vasilij's words dripped with greed, his tone both frightening and seductive. "Come with me! Join me!" Vasilij urged.

Erik felt the conflicting forces waging war within him. He knew there was no way to kill a draugr; his only options now were either to die or to become a monstrosity. And death was Erik's one and only true fear. "Will I become like you, or like those repulsive creatures haunting graves?" Erik asked, his tone filled with concern. Though the prospect of eternal life seemed tempting, he couldn't bear the thought of spending eternity as an ugly, hideous creature. After all, he valued beauty and took great pride in his appearance.

"That is entirely up to you," Vasilij replied. "Whether or not you can resist is out of my hands."

"Will you help me?" Erik asked, his stomach turned inside out at the thought of drinking human blood and consuming flesh. He felt dizzy, nauseous, and on the verge of vomiting. The idea of becoming such an unholy creature made him sick to his core. But despite his dread of living as a notorious monster, he feared death even more. The inevitable end of life haunted him, leaving only anxiety.

"And if I run?" Erik contemplated the possibility of escape, though he knew deep down it would be futile.

"You know I would catch you," Vasilij replied, a smirk creeping across his face. "Although I must say, I would very much enjoy hunting you down! I love to play games!"

"Why would you choose me?" Erik asked, his emotions a mixture of flattery and fear. "You don't know me. I would be missed. People would come looking for me."

"Yes, I can see that you are a man of great value," Vasilij replied, his gaze lingering on Erik's features. "That makes it so much more fun!" Vasilij's tone almost hissed with anticipation.

"What will become of me if you turn me into what you are?" the question continued to haunt Erik's mind.

"You will become everything you have ever desired. The world is yours to claim!" Vasilij emphasized, extending his hand towards Erik. "Take my hand. Come with me, and I will give you everything in this world!"

Erik hesitated, his mind consumed by questions and fears. He knew he now faced a choice that would shape the rest of his days. He could either choose to die at that very moment or take his chance and try to live a life like Vasilij. No, the fear of death was too strong. Carefully, Erik examined the man before him. Maybe it wouldn't be so bad. Maybe he could make it. Anything would be better than dying. He must do whatever it takes to survive. Slowly, Erik extended his hand, ready to face whatever peril awaited him.

CHAPTER 29

"It's nearly light outside," Vasilij pointed out, his gaze fixed on the window, eyes filled with mystery and a longing to unleash havoc upon the world. "I do love these countries during fall and winter. There's everlasting darkness, we demons thrive under those conditions," Vasilij smirked, reminiscing about parts of his eventful life. "Perhaps it wouldn't be a bad idea to linger, just for the season. There are plenty of prey nearby," a malevolent look appeared on his face as he carefully observed Ulrik's reaction. They sat across from each other at the dining table.

"Oh, do not worry, my precious," Vasilij continued. "I am sure that I will convince you to return to your old self. You will once again be the warrior I once knew." Vasilij looked pleased as he scrutinized every ounce of Ulrik's body. As daytime grew closer, he gazed out of the window once more.

"It has been two days," Vasilij continued suspiciously, all the playfulness that had danced in his face now gone, vanquished in the blink of an eye. "They have not returned yet. Ulrik, where are they?" Vasilij turned towards Ulrik with a displeased look. "I am your maker," Vasilij said neurotically as he walked over to Ulrik and leaned closer, his presence filled with anger. "You cannot lie to me! Our bond compels you to tell the truth." Aggression permeated his voice. "Where are they?!" Violence echoed within his words.

"At the graveyard," Ulrik responded calmly. Vasilij let his fingers slide down Ulrik's neck. His gaze fixed on the reluctant fireplace, filled with struggling flames.

"Why do you insist on keeping a fireplace? We only keep a fireplace when humans live with us," Ulrik asked, trying to distract himself from the claws of evil. "The flames detest us, they want to devour us, they long to consume our bodies," he added, glancing at the flames.

"I like to taunt the enemy," Vasilij responded, running his hands through Ulrik's hair. "The flames keep reaching for us, wanting to kill us, wanting to take our life, just like the enemies we faced on the battlefields. But they are trapped, they cannot get to us. So, I keep them there as a reminder that they cannot claim my life and as a reminder that the enemy is always near, eager to end you, and you never know who they are!" Vasilij tightened his grip on Ulrik's hair. "What did you do to them?" he whispered in Ulrik's ear.

"I did nothing to your minions, I simply delivered them to the churchyard to sleep, just as you instructed. And then I came back here," Ulrik explained calmly. Vasilij looked at Ulrik with distrustful eyes.

"What happened to them?" Vasilij's voice took on a threatening tone. His blue eyes shimmered in the light from the fire.

"The kyrkogrim took them," Ulrik replied, turning towards Vasilij, meeting his gaze. Vasilij's eyes darkened with anger, but slowly he forced himself to smile, his mind filled with aggression.

"Well, I will not punish you. After all, I have longed for you for so many years. And now that we finally unite, who can blame you for wanting me all to yourself?" Vasilij touched Ulrik's face with a possessive gesture. "But make no mistake," he warned with a hissing voice, "I will not accept that kind of behaviour. Do you understand me?" Vasilij scratched Ulrik's cheek with his fingernail. Drops of purple blood started to drip down Ulrik's face onto his clothes.

"Do not ever forget, you belong to me!" Vasilij let his hands slide over Ulrik's face in a possessive movement. "It is nearly light outside," Vasilij walked over to the window. His eyes examined the forest outside. "Come, it is time to sleep."

"You know very well that I do not sleep," Ulrik said with a cold voice, looking at Vasilij with indifferent eyes.

"Right, you're still tormenting yourself like that?" Vasilij seemed annoyed. "You've got to relax! It's easy, just sleep," Vasilij smiled a vicious smile. "Nothing bad will happen. You cling too much to the past. Don't let those kinds of things bother you," Vasilij studied Ulrik as he sat, still staring into the flames. "Suit yourself," Vasilij continued. "Just remember, the mind starts to play strange tricks when one doesn't sleep. Even for a draugr, rest is needed." Vasilij left the room while Ulrik remained staring at the fighting flames.

Ulrik held onto the memory of Katarina. His memories, always present beneath the surface, unable to deny their existence. She had been the light of his life. In her presence, everything else faded away, all darkness vanished, and the traumas lost their significance. When Ulrik was with Katarina, he could focus on her presence and immerse himself in her beauty. The past did not exist, all that he knew and felt was Katarina's love and support. Forever he would be bound to her memory. Even if his entire life was cursed with darkness and torment, the memory of Katarina would forever give him hope, igniting peace into his troubled core. As long as Katarina was safe, Ulrik would endure all the pain and horrors the world could curse him with. She would forever be his reason to fight; she would forever be his reason to face any peril. The flames continued moving more aggressively, taunted by the presence of a draugr, while Ulrik kept pondering on how to defeat the enemy.

CHAPTER 30

"Now, let us leave this boring place," Vasilij said while opening the door, inviting Ulrik to step outside. The night descended with an ominous weight; the air was thick with portent. The heart of the forest pulsated in synchrony with an encroaching peril, its presence manifested clearly. A mysterious energy seemed to permeate the air. The sensation tugged at one's senses with an unseen force, deceiving the mind. A murder of crows circled above. Their piercing cries echoed across the sky, evoking a sense of looming death.

There was a carriage with horses waiting for them, along with several men and their horses awaiting instructions to gather everything Vasilij wanted to bring with them on their journey. "Empty the house, pack all our belongings," Vasilij instructed the men, "we can't leave anything in this filthy palace!" he looked around with a condescending gaze. "Come now, my dear," he linked his arm with Ulrik's and guided him toward the awaiting carriage. The chill wind gently touched Vasilij's impeccably groomed locks. "I can't wait for us to return to a more civilized place," Vasilij added with contempt, his lip curling in disgust as he surveyed their surroundings with disdain. "This country is so poor, so dull and rustic. It has no charm whatsoever; I don't know what you were thinking when you wanted to return here."

After assisting Ulrik into the carriage, Vasilij followed and took a seat facing him. A content smirk grew on his lips. The carriage exuded an old-world, rustic charm, yet intricate details adorned its interior.

"Oh, don't pout!" his gaze locking onto Ulrik's with a mix of amusement and cruelty. "We will be going somewhere much more fun, so you can forget this awful place. We will have so much fun," he smiled viciously. The beautiful evening light started to spread over the landscape. Ulrik adorned himself in a crimson coat, while Vasilij was garbed in the finest attire.

"Where exactly are we going?" Ulrik asked, feeling a certain hopelessness. He didn't really care for the answer. The only thing that would bring light into his world was being at the same place as Katarina.

"Oh, do I have a surprise for you," Vasilij exclaimed excitedly, clapping his hands. "On our way, I thought that we should recruit some more demons; after all, we are going to need new minions!" Vasilij's voice grew cold as he stared at Ulrik for a second. "But I understand, they were utterly ugly creatures! However, it's not easy to find potential draugrs like us."

"I do not find the same pleasure in consorting with demons as you do," Ulrik remarked with an indifferent tone, revealing his longstanding aversion to the presence of other heartless demonic beings.

"No, you are not a very social character," Vasilij remarked, his eyes cold and lacking sympathy, showing an inability to empathize with others. "Quite hard to understand, very mysterious," Vasilij added, a smile adorning his features. "But I do favour you," his voice softened as he looked at Ulrik, "that's why I have a surprise in store for you." The door of the carriage opened, a young man entered, taking a seat beside Vasilij. The man appeared to be no more than twenty years of age. His complexion boasted a pallor unmarred by the sun, indicative of careful upkeep. With brown hair framing amber eyes, soft features, and a slender countenance, he bore the unmistakable mark of noble lineage. The young man wore fancy attire and opulent shoes. His beauty was striking, coupled with a gentle, fragile air about him, characteristics that aligned with Vasilij's preferences. The young man seemed petrified, the scent of humans still lingering on his features. Ulrik assumed that Vasilij had turned this man just recently. A cruel game designed to torture them both.

"Who is that?" Ulrik asked, watching the man closely. Vasilij revelled in the sinister allure of intricate mind games, relishing the twisted depths of psychological manipulation. Despite Ulrik's fervent efforts to distance himself from Vasilij's machinations, the fangs of darkness inevitably caught him, binding his fate to the whims of a maleficent force beyond comprehension. Their lives became inexorably intertwined in a dance of deceit and despair, as Vasilij's twisted games plunged them deeper into the abyss of terror from which there could be no escape.

"This?" Vasilij touched the cheek of the man, who remained frozen in fear. With a possessive gesture, he continued stroking the man's face. "This is Erik. I found him a couple of days ago," Vasilij's voice held a content tone. His enthusiasm for the twisted was evident in every word. Erik's breath came in anxious whispers, as if each exhale bore the weight of a thousand unspoken fears.

"No," Ulrik said with concern. "People will miss him. He looks like someone important, and his absence will be noticed," Ulrik warned, cautious of drawing attention to themselves.

"I know, it's marvellous!" Vasilij exclaimed happily, his eyes gleaming with twisted delight. In the recesses of Vasilij's mind lay memories of an era when they ruled like ruthless monarchs. They wielded power with impunity, their dominion unchallenged by the mortal coil or the ethereal realm. It was a time when fear bowed before them as a loyal subject. Even the shadows dared not cast their gaze upon the draugrs' sovereign presence.

"I'm surprised he survived the transformation," Ulrik remarked, looking at Erik, who seemed distant, lost in his own horrific nightmare.

"It's splendid, isn't it?" Vasilij said excitedly. In the gloomy recesses of Vasilij's consciousness, a wild curiosity stirred as they found themselves once more reunited. A chilling sense of intrigue gripped them tightly, like the cold fingers of a phantom reaching from the depths of the unknown.

"Why did you turn him?" Ulrik asked, casting a sympathetic glance at Erik. "He won't survive as a draugr. He'll likely perish, finding solace in a grave, remaining underground for the rest of his existence." Erik winced in fear at Ulrik's words. Ulrik empathized with Erik, recognizing the dim prospects ahead of him. He knew all too well the cruel faith that could await the new blood.

"Yes, he may be fragile, which is why he needs you," Vasilij looked at Ulrik. "You could use a new project, and since I know you'd never create one of your own, I made the decision for you. Now it's up to you to take care of him so he doesn't die."

"Why did you choose him?" Ulrik's question hung in the air, his voice heavy with sorrow.

"Because he is fragile," Vasilij's voice slithered through the air like a viper's hiss. "And you have a soft spot for the fragile, don't you? You want to mend them, protect the weak, and care for those in need. He has just enough darkness within him to endure the transformation, but not enough to navigate a single day without guidance. So, the choice is yours. Will you let him perish, or will you take him under your wing and mentor him?" Vasilij paused for emphasis. "It would be a tragedy to let such a beautiful creature perish." A predatory grin danced across Vasilij's lips as he leaned in closer to Erik. "He still retains the fresh scent of a frightened human." Erik shivered in fear, unable to utter a sound when Vasilij was nearby. He was paralyzed with terror. "You harbour guilt for the deeds of your past, so you seek redemption by saving the weak. I would prefer you fully embrace the darkness; we could have quite the adventure," Vasilij murmured, his words like venom dripping from fangs. Vasilij let his nails graze Erik's neck. "But I can be patient. For now, he's yours." With a flick of his wrist, Vasilij pushed Erik toward Ulrik, an ill-intended gift bestowed upon his reluctant apprentice. "Consider him my gift to you until you fully embrace your darkness." With a manipulative undertone infusing his voice, Vasilij's words came forth. Beside him, Ulrik extended his assistance to Erik, guiding him to settle into the darkness that enveloped their encounter. In the eerie stillness that reigned in the air, each movement carried a portentous weight.

"I don't want to babysit another draugr," Ulrik growled, his voice a low rumble that echoed with the weight of his burden. He had no desire to assume the mantle of a creator.

"You don't have to," Vasilij replied indifferently, his tone devoid of empathy. "Let him be. We can leave him here." Vasilij grinned. Erik looked at Ulrik with fear in his eyes, silently pleading for guidance and salvation.

"No, he can stay," Ulrik sighed, feeling burdened by the situation. His relentless conscience tussled with the unbearable notion of forsaking this newly transformed soul to navigate the world in solitude.

"Excellent," Vasilij smiled, a cruel glimmer danced in his eyes. "I believe the three of us will have quite the adventure. Once we arrive, I'll enlist the help of some lesser demonic creatures to assist us in establishing our new life."

Erik, trembling with uncertainty, dared to speak. "Where...

where are we headed?" his voice quivered like a leaf in the wind, seeking shelter in Ulrik's stoic gaze.

"There," Vasilij replied contentedly. "If you're going to survive your first few months as a draugr, you need to abandon the victim mentality."

"Yes, but where exactly are we going?" Ulrik pressed Vasilij for clarity.

"Oh, it's a surprise, but you're going to love it, I promise," Vasilij exclaimed. "I've arranged everything. For now, it is a secret I shall keep," he teased. Ulrik knew that Vasilij had connections worldwide; he was adept at manipulating both humans and demonic beings to fulfil his desires and obtain what he wanted. The draugr lord wielded influence that spanned continents, his network of allies and minions infiltrated at the core of the supernatural world. Suddenly, the carriage came to a halt, jolting its occupants from their reverie. Vasilij's expression darkened with annoyance, a tempest brewing beneath his cool facade. "Why have we stopped?" he demanded, his voice rising. No one dared to respond. Vasilij couldn't tolerate disobedience or being ignored. With anger etched across his face, he stormed out of the carriage. An insidious compulsion seized control from within, driving him onward with an irresistible force.

"Where is he going?" Erik asked, glancing at Ulrik, a tremor of fear coursing through his veins.

"To cause trouble," Ulrik muttered as he rose from his seat. "Stay here," he instructed Erik firmly. "If anything happens, you must do exactly as I say. Understand?" His words bore the weight of command as he fixed Erik with a steely gaze. Erik nodded obediently, his eyes wide with trepidation.

Once outside the carriage, Ulrik found the hired help frozen in fear, their faces drained of colour.
Time halted its relentless march, ensnared by the captivating power of the moment. Vasilij stood a few steps ahead, gazing at

the horizon. A subtle shift in his energy betrayed the creeping tendrils of insecurity seeping through the very corners of his essence. A massive Lindwyrm emerged in the distance, swiftly approaching. Its enormous form overshadowed the forest as it hurtled toward them with relentless speed. Covered in horns and adorned with blood-red scales that shimmered in the moonlight, the Lindwyrm was a sight to behold. Its great might stirred a profound sense of divine presence within, evoking reverence and amazement. Ulrik stared at the creature with astonishment. His breath was caught in his throat as he beheld the creature. A mixture of awe and fear coursed through his veins.

The feeble attempts at describing the entity's divinity paled in comparison to the creature now standing before him. It was as if life and death had merged into an unfathomable expanse where the constraints of time and space ceased to hold sway. Though tales of Lindwurms' strength and prowess were many, he had never encountered one in the flesh. Once common, their numbers had dwindled over the ages, relegated to the realm of myth and legend.

With a sense of purpose that brooked no delay, the Lindwyrm surged forward, racing towards them. The earth shivered and the ground bent to its might. The forest bowed in submission to the ferocity of the Lindwyrm, its ancient trees trembling under the weight of the creature's power. The Lindwyrm's thunderous approach sent the hired help scattering in panic. Some fled on horseback, their mounts galloping wildly in their haste to escape the impending demise.

"Come back here!" Vasilij's scream pierced the air with rage, his eyes flashing with an unholy fervour as he lunged forward, seizing one of the men in a cruel grip. With a swift, brutal motion, Vasilij extinguished the man's life, breaking his neck. His untamed anger fuelled the violent and vindictive act. But the rest of the hired hands, their hearts pounding with terror, fled into the darkness. They were desperate to escape the imminent threat, terrified for their lives.

Meanwhile, the Lindwyrm continued its unrelenting advance. Its draconic form sliced through the evening with deadly purpose. No one could deny its might. The creature's eyes gleamed with a sublime luminescence. Its gaze locked onto Vasilij with chilling intensity, as if peering into the depths of his ancient core. Ulrik, despite the mounting danger, couldn't help but marvel at the creature's sheer magnitude and power. Lindwurms were renowned for their breath-taking presence, capable of bestowing either great fortune or swift death upon those they encountered. It was abundantly clear that this specimen harboured no benevolent intentions. It seemed like the creature was heading for Vasilij.

As the Lindwyrm came closer, its aura suffused with ancient wisdom and primordial hostility. Ulrik couldn't shake the realization that even Vasilij's cunning paled in comparison to the enigmatic intelligence of the Lindwyrm. As the antediluvian creature hissed, its overwhelming voice echoed in the forest. The leaves quivered in terror; their delicate forms trembled beneath the oppressive presence of the unknown destiny.

Ulrik sensed an unusual tremor in the air. A fleeting moment of uncertainty seemed to emanate from Vasilij, even though his back was turned. It was a rare occurrence, an uncommon deviation from the tenacious confidence that typically defined Vasilij's demeanor. His maker was scarred. Never had Ulrik witnessed Vasilij falter; never had Vasilij been the prey. He was always the one instilling fear and trepidation in his adversaries. The Lindwyrm's sleek form sinuously advanced through the approaching darkness. It surged forward with alarming speed, its massive frame eclipsing the light as it bore down upon the carriage. It bared its fangs with a menacing sound.

Vasilij, caught off guard by the sudden onslaught, attempted to evade the creature's lethal grip. In the heart of the dense woodland, under the cloak of the newly fallen night, an eerie game of cat and mouse unfolded between two legendary beings. The Lindwyrm slithered through the undergrowth with deadly grace, its eyes glinting with hunger. Across from it, Vasilij moved through the darkness with a wraith like agility born of necessity. He had always been a survivor and did everything he could to stay alive. This time would be no different, even when faced with a superior opponent.

The Lindwyrm's presence was a tangible menace. Its elegant form moved through the twisted roots and tangled vines with lethal accuracy. Vasilij, sensing the imminent peril, rushed between the gnarled branches and shadowed hollows, his ghostly figure barely discernible in the approaching moonlight. With each stride, he felt the deadly breath of the Lindwyrm on his heels. Its relentless pursuit was closing in.

Evading the creature's tenacious advances, Vasilij's mind raced with strategies for survival. He was a survivor at heart. To flee and survive was better than to fight and die. Devoid of weaponry, he relied solely on his cunning and instincts, sharpened over centuries of existence.

Without warning, the Lindwyrm struck, lunging forward with blinding speed, its mouth snapping shut just shy of Vasilij's form. The draugr stumbled, as he narrowly avoided the deadly jaws of the creature.

With renewed determination, Vasilij pressed on, his movements fueled by an instinctual drive to survive. This was not the way he wanted it all to end. The forest blurred around him as he ran through the labyrinth of trees.

Yet, the Lindwyrm remained undeterred, its savage pursuit matched only by its ferocious hunger. Time and again, it surged forward, its venomous gaze fixed on its elusive quarry. Miraculously, Vasilij managed to stay one step ahead. His evasion tactics kept him just out of reach.

In a daring gambit, Vasilij spotted an opportunity among the chaos. With a surge of adrenaline, he leaped onto the Lindwyrm's coiling body. His demonic form clung desperately to the creature's undulating scales. He scrambled upwards, his fingers finding strength on the creature's sleek neck.

For a moment, it seemed as though Vasilij's audacious maneuver might succeed. With a nimble twist of his body, he attempted to trick the Lindwyrm's twisting form into tying itself into a knot, hoping to ensnare the beast in its own coils.

But the Lindwyrm was no mere foe, it was a creature of cunning and ferocity. With a furious sound, it thrashed beneath Vasilij's grip. Its body contorted and writhed in defiance. The draugr's efforts proved futile. His plan unraveled before his eyes as the Lindwyrm's strength proved too great to overcome.

In a burst of rage, the Lindwyrm reared its head. Its eyes were blazing with fury as it attempted to dislodge its unwanted passenger. Vasilij clung to the creature's neck with all his might, but it was all in vain. With a violent shake of its massive form, the Lindwyrm sent Vasilij tumbling through the air. His unholy form crashed to the forest ground below.

As Vasilij staggered to his feet, he could feel the weight of the Lindwyrm's wrath bearing down upon him. With a deafening roar, the ethereal creature launched itself at him once more. The Lindwyrm's hunger now laced with a seething anger born of betrayal. As Vasilij stared into the creature's wrathful gaze, he knew that his attempt of survival had only served to stoke the flames of the Lindwyrm's fury. A chilling knowledge settled within. There was no way for him to end victorious. He was going to die. His efforts proved futile against the Lindwyrm's ruthless assault. The draugr had no time to react, no time to think or comprehend that the end was near.

With horrifying swiftness, the Lindwyrm ensnared Vasilij in its wide jaws. Its cavernous mouth descended upon him like the gaping maw of some prehistoric abyss. In a petrifying spectacle of annihilation, Vasilij was consumed in a single, agonizing chug. His anguished cries were silenced by the insatiable hunger of the Lindwyrm's ravenous appetite.

A content smile spread across Ulrik's lips, a grim acceptance of the inevitable fate that now stood before him. The ghost of the reaper, long awaited yet now imminent, cast its shadow over him. He too was going to die. But within the inevitable end, there was a glimmer of liberation, a fleeting reprieve from the torment that had haunted him since the moment of his creation.

With a sense of tenebrous satisfaction, Ulrik beheld the demise of his maker, a tyrant whose wicked reign had brought untold suffering upon the world. Though his own life hung in the balance, Ulrik found acceptance in the knowledge that Vasilij's reign of terror had finally ended, if only for a fleeting moment. Now he was finally free, peace settled within his core. The wind seemed to still itself and the night suddenly seemed brighter. The birds fell silent, their melodious songs silenced by fear.

Inhaling deeply, he gazed at the Lindwyrm, allowing his hands to fall to his sides in a relaxed manner, welcoming death. With a steady breath, he relinquished himself to the inevitability of his fate. A sense of calm washed over Ulrik like a tide of darkness. There would be no more suffering, there would be no more pain. It all would be over.

The Lindwyrm, a creature of primordial dread, regarded Ulrik with a soul cutting intensity. Its zigzagging form coiled sinuously around him like a serpent preparing to strike. With each languid movement, it seemed to convey a silent message of unfathomable power and unyielding purpose, a messenger of the final demise that awaited its prey.

Ulrik looked into the mesmerising eyes of the transcendent creature. The Lindwyrm returned his stare, its sharp teeth gleaming as it emitted an incomprehensible hiss. Slowly, the monstrous form crept closer, enveloping him in its menacing presence. It observed him with caution. Ulrik remained still, accepting his fate. His resolve unbroken even as the jaws of oblivion yawned wide before him.

"I have devoured your companion. Are you not afraid of me?" The Lindwyrm's voice reverberated, imbued with centuries of memories.

Ulrik regarded the monstrous creature before him with a mixture of solemn acceptance and quiet defiance. "What's the point of fearing the inevitable?" Ulrik responded sincerely, his voice carrying the weight of a lifetime spent on the precipice of darkness. "I've faced countless battles without surrender, but when confronted by an enraged Lindwyrm, surely the end is near. I accept my faith, finding peace at the end."

The Lindwyrm regarded Ulrik with a measured gaze, its ancient wisdom echoing through the cavernous depths of its voice. "Do not seek death so eagerly," the Lindwyrm replied. "Death will come to us all, sooner or later. I have not come to claim your life."

"Then why have you come?" Ulrik's brow furrowed in confusion. A glimmer of hope flickered with hope.

"I have kept my promise. Go home now. It is not your life that I wish to extinguish," the Lindwyrm declared, its voice echoing with a strange mixture of menace and benevolence. "Go now, before I change my mind!" With a warning, it slowly slithered back into the forest, leaving behind a trail of unanswered questions. Ulrik continued to stare after the Lindwyrm, feeling both relieved and confused. A murmuring chorus arose among the crows. Their mysterious voices conversing in hushed tones as if sharing secrets of the impending doom. The wind surged with newfound vigour, lifting the wings of the crows with an irresistible force. Its strength compelled the birds to take flight into the starlit heavens above.

Once again, Ulrik had evaded true death and escaped his fate. A sense of peace settled within his heart. The forest echoed in calmness; the leaves rustled softly upon the ground. Freedom began to spread across his body. The moon shone brighter than before. Its beauty was undeniable. The sound of small animals making their way into the night reclaimed its presence.

Vasilij was no more, his dark reign ended by the jaws of the ancient creature. Ulrik was free. With a relieved smile, Ulrik turned away from the forest, feeling the weight of centuries of torment finally lifted from his battle-scarred shoulders.

Returning to the carriage, Ulrik found Erik still seated inside, his eyes wide with fear and confusion. The newly turned draugr's eyes glimmered with an intense look. Ulrik regarded him with compassion. He possessed intimate knowledge of the myriad challenges that accompanied the transformation into a demon. The young man had no easy path ahead.

"Vasilij, the man who turned you, is gone. You are free now. You do not have to fear him anymore. Your life is yours; you can do whatever you want with it," Ulrik spoke calmly, his voice carrying through the eerie silence of the forest. Erik lifted his head in confusion, seemingly lost in his own inability to comprehend the meaning of the words. A disorienting fog of confusion descended upon his mind, clouding his thoughts and casting shadows over his senses. Ulrik began to walk away, his footstep left a cold trail of uncertainty.

"Wait!" Erik called out, fear evident in his eyes, lost amidst the merciless void. He was now alone, lost in a world unfamiliar to him. "I do not know how to survive like this!" his voice trembled with hopelessness. Vasilij had been a cruel maker, yet he had been there, offering a guiding hand in this new reality. "The hunger calls from every cell of my body. I do not know how to control it. I do not know how to survive like this. I cannot go back to my family. I am afraid I will harm them, eat their flesh, and drink their blood," Erik pleaded in agony, terrified of the darkness now dwelling within him. Panic exploding within every cell of his body. Anxiety took over his heart. Erik's lips turned purple, and his breathing quickened. The fear of death still haunted his mind. His thoughts wandered aimlessly. Ulrik paused, a heavy sigh escaping his lips. He had no desire to take on a new responsibility, all he wanted was to return home to Katarina. Yet, he knew this man would wreak havoc, causing harm to innocent victims without guidance. Leaving a newly turned draugr alone would indeed be a cruel faith. Alone in a world of chaos and ambivalence. The two conflicting sides battled within Ulrik. He did not want to be a maker, and yet he took piety on the fragile and lost man next to him. And Katarina, what would she say if he left Erik here all alone fending for himself, imposing threats upon all who passed by? It would be impossible to look Katarina in her eyes and tell her that he had abandoned someone who needed him.

"Very well, you can come with me," Ulrik relented, his resolve firm despite his reluctance. Ulrik forged ahead into the depths of the forest, Erik following closely behind, their fates intertwined in the shadowy embrace of the night.

CHAPTER 31

Relief surged through Ulrik's veins as he descended the hill and caught sight of his home. Peace slowly began to find its way back into his heart. The silhouette of his abode against the dawn sky stirred a sense of longing within him, driving him forward with renewed purpose. Finally, he would be reunited with Katarina, her presence a sanctuary in a world plagued by uncertainty. Now he was finally free from the shadow of his master. Now Ulrik could devote his entire life to Katarina.

"Wait!" Erik's plea pierced the air, halting Ulrik in his tracks.

Turning to face the troubled soul behind him, Ulrik's gaze held an implacable resolve. "This is my home," he declared, his words laced with warning. "There are many people here whom I deeply care for. You must not harm any of them. In fact, you must not harm any human. If you want me to take care of you, then you must abide by my way of life. I will treat you with respect and never force you to do anything against your will. But if you hurt or harm anyone in my home," Ulrik's gaze darkened. A weighty silence hung in the air, broken only by the rustle of leaves stirred by the morning breeze. Ulrik's eyes bore into Erik's, a silent challenge laid bare in their depths. "Then I will use every means at my disposal to stop you. If you follow my rules, I will help you survive and thrive. I live among humans, and you could lead an almost ordinary life with newfound abilities."

"Do I not have to feed on humans and live in graveyards?" Erik asked, his voice tinged with fear as he recalled his time with Vasilij. Fear of death and pain was still evident in his tone.

"No, if you can resist the urge, you can maintain your current form and live like a human," Ulrik replied solemnly, his footsteps echoing against the desolate landscape. The brisk autumn wind carried promises of the impending winter. With determined strides, Ulrik pressed forward, his destination clear in his mind's eye.

As he stepped inside, Katarina greeted him with a warm smile. Her eyes glimmered with an intense and unbridled joy, radiating a luminous warmth that seemed to light up the very depths of her soul. She enveloped him in a tender embrace, her touch gentle and affectionate. Ulrik held Katarina close, his embrace conveying a love that would never waver. Finally, she was back in his arms, nothing could tear them apart. An unbreakable bond forged between them that defied the forces of separation.

"I'm so glad you're safe!" Katarina exclaimed, her eyes alight with joy. Happiness took over her body, captivating her mind. "You are finally home." She smiled and touched Ulrik's cheek with a relieved look on her face. He tenderly took Katarina's hand, pressing his lips against her skin in a solemn pledge, vowing never to release her from his grasp again. With each caress, Ulrik pledged his unwavering commitment to safeguarding their love.

"I have returned to you, nothing could keep me away from you now," Ulrik murmured as he gently stroked her hair and kissed her. Their kiss, a sacred communion of souls, told tales that mere words could never encapsulate. Katarina noticed Erik behind Ulrik and regarded the man with curious eyes. She had not anticipated Ulrik's return accompanied by another individual. This man wore a lost expression on his face, as if adrift in an ocean of confusion. His eyes betrayed a soul searching for answers among the tumult of his new existence.

"Hello?" Katarina's voice faltered, hesitant as she addressed the unfamiliar figure. She consistently endeavoured to maintain a demeanour of warmth and respectfulness when encountering new acquaintances. The man appeared visibly shaken and in dire need of compassion.

"This is Erik," Ulrik reluctantly introduced his new companion. "Vasilij turned him just before he was killed. I will teach him how to survive as a draugr without harming anyone." Ulrik glanced at Erik. Scepticism lingered within him like a persistent shadow, casting doubt upon the legitimacy of the new situation.

"I am glad that Vasilij is dead and that you are safe," Katarina said calmly. Her words emanated a warmth and sincerity that cut through the lingering scepticism, offering a beacon of authenticity. "Welcome, Erik." Katarina spoke with genuine warmth, extending a welcoming hand to Erik.

"You do not seem surprised that I have returned, and you assume that Vasilij is dead," Ulrik observed, his gaze penetrating as he sought to unravel the mystery shrouding Katarina's words. Drawing her close, he inhaled the fragrance of her hair, a familiar scent that once brought stillness in times of turmoil. Finally, she was safe. Peace seemed close as he inhaled her scent.

"It worked," Katarina revealed with a secretive smile, her eyes alight with a clandestine understanding.

"What worked?" Ulrik inquired.

"The Lindwyrm," Katarina disclosed, her words laden with an unsettling gravity. "She killed Vasilij." Ulrik took a step back, surprise evident in his expression. For a moment his blood froze.

"What did you do?" he asked, his tone tainted with concern.

"I went to her lair and made her an offering. She had been

calling out to me in my dreams," Katarina confessed. Her gaze was unyielding as she unveiled the depths of her pact with the ancient creature.

"What did you offer?" Ulrik asked, his expression troubled as he recalled the old legends. An agreement with a Lindwyrm was unbreakable. An agreement forged with a Lindwyrm was a pact etched in blood, bound within one's soul until eternity ceased to exist.

"At first, I tried to bargain with the jewellery I got from Vasilij," Katarina revealed, her words echoing with a tinge of regret as she recounted her daring gambit.

"That was very brave but not very well thought out," Ulrik admonished, his expression twisted with horror at the thought of Katarina's dangerous negotiations.

"The Lindwyrm seemed a little offended, but she did not kill me. Instead, we agreed on another matter," Katarina continued, her tone veiled in mystery as she unravelled the enigmatic encounter.

"And what was that?" Ulrik pressed, his heart heavy with apprehension.

"If she killed Vasilij, then I would take care of her egg until it hatches," Katarina said devotedly. Ulrik's gaze softened as he drew Katarina closer, their foreheads touching in an affectionate gesture of solidarity. Her compassion stirred something deep within him, evoking a profound emotional response that resonated with the tender chords of his soul.

"It is a difficult task, but I am here for you. I will stand by your side. I will help you fulfil your promise," Ulrik vowed, his unwavering commitment mirrored in the depths of his eyes. He knew that they had to keep the promise to the Lindwyrm at all costs. If not, then all hell would break loose, condemning Katarina to eternal suffering. He had to protect her, no matter the cost. No matter what, she must keep her promise to the Lindwyrm.

"Thank you, thank you for saving my life and freeing me from the grip of my maker. I look forward to spending eternity by your side." A radiant smile graced Ulrik's lips, illuminating the darkness that once consumed their lives with the promise of a future bathed in newfound freedom and boundless love.

EPILOGUE

As the years passed, Ulrik remained true to his promise. He stood faithfully by Katarina's side as her days dwindled and death came closer, dreading the inevitable moment. To him, she never lost her beauty, even as time marched on. She remained an ethereal beacon that illuminated the shadowed corners of Ulrik's soul.

She would forever be his sole love. Katarina found joy and peace in each passing day, gracefully accepting the mortality of life. Together, they lived a tranquil and contented life. Each passing day was a blessing of shared moments, a manifestation of the enduring bond that tethered their hearts together in an unbreakable connection.

Then came the day when Katarina grew old and frail, her health failing. Her once-luminous spirit dimmed beneath the weight of mortality's poetic march. Despite her pain, her smile endured. She faced her impending fate with a grace and dignity that mirrored her peaceful spirit. Ulrik held her hand, kissing it gently as she lay in bed, awaiting the embrace of eternity, accepting her fate. The touch of her skin became a bittersweet reminder of the ephemeral nature of existence. Ulrik struggled to reconcile himself with the harsh reality of death's relentless pursuit. For Ulrik, the prospect of a world without Katarina was an abyss from which he could not escape. She was mortal, and he was eternal, yet without her, life held no meaning. The mere thought of facing each day without her was unbearable. As the final moments drew near, he struggled with the agony of eternal loss. The weight of grief pressed down upon him with its suffocating grip. With each labored breath she took, Ulrik felt his own spirit unraveling, torn apart by the cruel hand of fate.

Katarina smiled once more, seeking to alleviate Ulrik's anguish. She had long accepted her fate and was prepared to bid farewell after a lifetime of happiness.

"Please send a note to my daughter informing her of my passing. Let her know that I lived a peaceful life and that my love for her will endure forever. I trust you to handle all the necessary arrangements once I am gone, as I have already prepared. She will inherit everything I have," Katarina said with a calm voice, finding peace in her fate. The thought of her beloved daughter filled her spirit with joy and tranquillity. She knew that everything was going to be alright and that her daughter was safe. The time to let go was getting close.

"You can trust me. I will make sure that your daughter gets everything." Ulrik promised with a bleeding heart. He was wracked with agony; losing the light of his life felt like his very soul was being torn from his body. As Katarina's life ebbed away, Ulrik feared he would be left with nothing but emptiness. A solitary tear traced a path down his cheek, a heartfelt tribute to the profound depths of his love and the unbearable anguish of farewell.

"I cannot bear to lose you," Ulrik trembled with the weight of impending sorrow, each word heavy with the burden of his despair.

As Katarina spoke, her countenance radiated a serene acceptance, her eyes alight with the wisdom of one who has glimpsed the mysteries that lie beyond the realm of mortality.

"You will never lose me. I am forever yours, always by your side. I am not afraid of letting go; I am ready to embrace death. I accept it as a natural part of life. It's okay. I have lived an extraordinary life, filled with love. We will meet again," she asserted confidently.

"I have committed deeds beyond forgiveness," Ulrik's heart clenched at the thought of their inevitable parting. The horrors of his past deeds cast a shadow over their final exchange. "Where I am bound, there is no peace or redemption. We will be forever separated in life after this," he confessed, his voice heavy with indescribable sadness. "I cannot bear the thought of never seeing you again. I cannot part from you!" he cried out, drowning in sorrow and despair.

"I will find you," Katarina promised solemnly. "Death is not as cruel as you fear. Wherever you go, I will seek you out, using every means to bring your soul back to mine."

"I do not wish for you to join me where I am condemned to end up," a flicker of anguish passed over Ulrik's features. His heart felt heavy with the weight of Katarina's pledge.

"You are only condemned if you believe it to be so. You must forgive yourself, let go of mistakes and regrets. Allow yourself to find peace. There is no hell, there is only peace in death." Katarina's gaze softened; her eyes filled with an endless love.

"You were my reason for seeking peace," he confessed, his voice a fervent prayer. All hope would be lost without her. "Everything good in my life stems from you."

"Then come find me," Katarina entreated, her eyes shining with unwavering faith. "Do not let darkness weigh you down. Break free from the chains of guilt and seek me out. Fight your way back to me. Some souls are destined to find each other, even if they are separated in the next life," Katarina declared. Ulrik met Katarina's gaze with a solemn promise, his voice filled with eternal determination.

"I swear, I will find you, even if it takes me an eternity, even if I must atone for all my mistakes. No matter where I am or how far apart we may be, I will always find my way back to you. Across the boundless expanse of time and space, my soul will forever be bound to yours." Ulrik vowed, his words filled with undying devotion.

"And I will forever await your return," Katarina whispered as she felt the serene grip of death approaching. Ulrik held her tightly as death claimed his beloved, overwhelmed and tortured by grief, unable to fully grasp reality. In that moment, the world seemed to shatter around him, reality fragmented into a million pieces as grief consumed him whole. Ulrik's heart, once brimming with the warmth of Katarina's love, now lay wrecked and broken. Nothing more than a hollow shell of its former self.

As night descended and the household held a wake for Katarina, Ulrik started a bonfire near the forest. The flames danced with an aggressive fervour, sensing the presence of a condemned draugr, a reminder of the darkness that now consumed his world. Tenderly, Ulrik touched Katarina's cheek, reminiscing about all she had bestowed upon him in this life. The memory of her softness lingered on his fingertips.

As the flames cast their ethereal glow upon his face, Ulrik whispered words of love and gratitude to the night, offering silent prayers for Katarina's eternal rest. For though she had departed this world, her spirit lived on in the flickering embers of his heart.

With a heavy heart, Ulrik lifted Katarina's lifeless body into his arms and stepped forward into the roaring fire. The pain was unfathomable, but Ulrik remained composed, gazing at Katarina's peaceful face.

As the flames consumed their bodies, transforming them, Ulrik kept his gaze fixed on Katarina. As the flames enveloped them both, reducing their mortal bodies to ash, Ulrik's eyes never wavered from her tranquil face. Without her, there was no life; wherever she went, he would find his way back to her.

The flames crackled angrily as they devoured their forms, yet Ulrik remained true to his mission. He would be forever bound to find her again, transcending distance, time, and place. Across the chasm of life and death, he pledged to follow Katarina, to traverse the realms of existence until they were reunited once more. No force of nature, no barrier of time or space, could sever the bond that bound their souls together.